I trust that you will read many of these short stories to each other. Some of your family and friends are among unique Californians who are producing more intense and complex novels, but the ones in this anthology are quick, mostly fun, light efforts.

Pages 66, 72, 172, 178, 252, and 290 may be of particular interest to you. However, the genres presented here run the gamut: children, animals, family and comedy, as well as war and ghost stories.

Check out the Table of Contents and enjoy.

Most importantly, encourage the children to write. You may want to contribute to next year's anthology produced by our High Desert Branch of the California Writers Club. We also plan to publish four novels under the Writers' Lair label.

916-213-5467, bvlee2011@yahoo.com

Desert Gold

An Anthology
High Desert Branch
California Writers Club

Edited by Freddi Gold and Roberta L. Smith

2012 – 2013 HDCWC Board Members
Freddi Gold, President
Roberta L. Smith, Vice President
Jenny Margotta, Treasurer
Anita Holmes, Secretary and State Representative
Michael Raff, Member at Large
Amanda Smith, Membership
Rusty LaGrange, Newsletter Editor
Marilyn Ramirez, Historian

This book is a work of fiction. The events and characters described herein are imaginary and are not intended to refer to specific places or living persons. The authors have represented and warranted full ownership and/or the legal right to publish all the materials in this book.

Desert Gold
An Anthology
Copyright © 2013 California Writers Club, High Desert Branch.
All right reserved

Cover Photos: Gail M. Salinas
Back Cover Poem: A. J. Scott

http://www.hdcwc.com

ISBN-13: 978-1481029438
ISBN-10: 1481029436

Table of Contents

Introduction

Following the outstanding success of members' contributions for our previous anthology, the club Board of Directors decided to do it again and offer our writers an opportunity for publication and readers a sampling of some remarkable talent to be discovered on the pages within.

Our writers include members who are just learning, journalists, fiction writers, non-fiction writers, poets and published authors. An amazing milieu of different genres is represented. We have come to know one another, establish friendships, partake in critique groups and attend monthly meetings where we participate in interactive programs or listen to a wide variety of speakers who have given us incredible presentations.

This year we invited individuals in the Federal Correctional Complex in Victorville who participate in our Outreach Writers Program to enter submissions for inclusion in the anthology as well. Our outreach program is conducted by chair person, Bob Isbill, one of four core CWC members who meet monthly with intelligent, eager-to-learn, appreciative writers. These twenty participants have chosen to name themselves the Incarcerated Author's Group (IAG). They continue to perfect their own writing skills and talents with the mentoring efforts of our club members and other speakers. We received some wonderful work from them and their entries are found here as well.

Over ninety entries were submitted and it was a long and fruitful endeavor for us to read each one, and also to pass them on to our volunteer proofreaders and then our volunteer editors. After a system of evaluation and organization of the material, the results were sent to the authors for approval and then returned to us for publication.

At this point my co-editor Roberta Smith took over the process of coordinating fonts, sizes and further scrutinized each work and prepared the entries, title pages, this introduction, table of contents and general layout of each page and the order they would be in. Roberta also designed the beautiful cover of the book, front, back pages and spine.

To insure that we had not missed potential errors we submitted the entire work to Tammy Sparks (her blog is called Books, Bones & Buffy) who professionally proofread all of the pages in the anthology. After the return of the work, Roberta prepared the pages for submission to CreateSpace for publication.

We want to thank our amazing team of volunteers and editors who first evaluated and proofed the entries. We could not have done all this without your time, energy and effort. Thank you, Tom Kier, Naomi Ward, Jim Elstad, Bob Isbill, Virginia Hall, Dwight Norris, George Gracyk, Inge Stoltz, and Fran Savage.

Doing double duty by evaluating entries and then perusing each page for editing were Denny Stanz, Hazel Stearns, Linda Bowden and Amanda Smith. Thank you so much for staying the course and helping us to be fair to everyone in order to produce this exciting book.

It has been my honor and pleasure to help in the process of creating *Desert Gold*. I have been able to learn about our members and their interests through their writing and I have thoroughly enjoyed working with my co-editor as a team on this project. I know we both hope you will enjoy and find pleasure in the work within.

Freddi Gold
President

Desert Gold

DESERT GOLD

Naomi Ward

The visitor steps from the car armed with a camera, or maybe a sketch pad, awed by the sight of a golden carpet spreading from the pavement to the distant hills. The hard horizon of brown sand versus blue sky softens with the ruffle of swaying flowers intervening along the usually stern desert landscape. An orange flow streams from the hills to the desert flat, cascading into shallow ravines and dips, flying over small humps and rises. The heart sings; the spirit lifts as the desert shimmers and dances in the soft spring breeze and the beauty of a transformed landscape makes its sweet assault upon one's senses. There will be no harsh summer sun searing these golden offerings, for their short time atop the desert sand will be past and their seeds deposited for next year's display while spring-time's cool breath still moves across the softened vista. This, a golden gift to the viewer, is one of the desert's loveliest miracles.

THE COURT OF THE COBRA

Dwight Norris

$\mathcal{I}$n ancient times, in the land of the tiger, even farther north than the fortress of Agra, was a little village called Ghazni. It sat perched on the banks of the river Yamuna, and its people scratched their living out of the land and out of the river. And sometimes the people of Ghazni laughed, and sometimes they cried.

A court assembled in a humble building near the center of the village to judge one of their own, a working man named Sonjay Singh. Singh had made trouble for a local family by harassing their eldest son and assaulting his father when he came to his defense. He injured the man by punching him repeatedly in the face and head with his fists. Singh would have to answer for his crimes.

The magistrate of the court was Akbar, one of the wisest elders in the land.

"Let the court come to order," beckoned the sahib of the court.

The room was silent as Akbar took his seat in the chair of judgment.

"Sonjay Singh, you will please rise to your feet," said the magistrate.

"Mr. Singh, the charges against you are serious. It is said that you chased a twelve-year-old boy and when you caught him, you put your hands on him and shook him and struck him in the face. When his father intervened, you knocked him unconscious. Mr.

2

Singh, in front of this court and your peers, what say you about these charges?"

Singh stood timidly before the magistrate and hung his head. He was dirty and sweaty. His pants were soiled, his shirt torn and his hair messy because he was taken straight to the court from the very act of which he was accused.

"Lift your head and look at me!" commanded the magistrate.

Singh's hands trembled as his eyes met the magistrate's.

"Y . . .Your honor, I cannot deny the charges against me. I thought the boy had been disrespectful of me, and I ran after him. W-When his father jumped in and pushed me, I did not realize who he was. I just reacted as though I was being attacked."

"Mr. Singh, it is you who are the aggressor here. A man was bloodied and knocked unconscious because of your temper and your impulsive actions."

"But I thought . . ."

"Your thinking is not clear, Mr. Singh. A month ago you stood before me for a similar incident, and the month before that! If everyone in the village behaved like you there would be no peace in our homes. You need to change your thinking."

"But . . ."

"Enough!" demanded the magistrate. "I am sentencing you to twenty-four hours in the Court of the Cobra. Your fate is in your own hands."

"Aahhh," Singh wailed. Court officials gripped his arms and walked him out of the courtroom.

"Naja, naja," Singh screamed the Indian word for *deadly serpent.* He began to pull away but resistance was futile. Singh knew that no one had ever survived twenty-four hours with the cobra. The officials escorted him to a little hut outside the perimeter of the village built of the stout branches of the champa tree. The wood had been stripped of its bark and then plastered at the bottom of the hut with mud from the banks of the river. The process sealed air pockets between the timbers, leaving the air inside the house heavy and suffocating. The only light to enter the interior of the abode was from the opening in the top of the roof, a hole large enough for a man to slip through, but ten feet high in the middle of the structure.

Singh was stripped of all his garments and led to the only entrance, a narrow door on the side of the little structure. The court officials lifted the crossbar from its supports and pulled the door open. Light streamed into the darkened chamber and disturbed its lone occupant, a twelve foot king cobra. "SSSSSS!!" Four feet of the monster was erect in the air, its hood flattened in defiance and its menacing hiss penetrating the ears of all the people standing outside the hut.

Singh was thrust into the dim enclosure and the door was slammed behind him. He crawled to the opposite side from where the snake sat coiled and ready to strike. He sat in a closed squat, his legs guarding his privates. Sweat beaded through all the pores of his body, from his face and neck, to his arms, to his chest and back, to his legs and buttocks. He was slippery and glistening, a magnet for the dirt of the floor and the insects of the jungle. Singh's hands trembled and his legs shook. Salty drops of sweat fell into Singh's open eyes and burned and blurred his vision.

Despite blinking and squinting, he kept his gaze on the serpent in the dim light. "SSSSSS!!" The hiss was deafening inside the closed hut. Singh could not take his eyes off his angry adversary, and in a few minutes, as light continued to trickle through the opening in the roof, his eyes adjusted and he could see more clearly the form of the magnificent serpent.

Singh had heard of the regal king cobra, and had even seen one a few times in his life, but never so close. And never so real. The coloration of this king was a deep burnt mahogany that could have been considered quite beautiful if not housed in such terror. Its scales were laid in unison, forming a flexible and seemingly impenetrable shiny armor wrapping the serpent's entire tubular body. Though each scale was singular, together they were seamless, glowing from the sunbeams streaming through the opening in the roof, creating an almost hypnotic iridescence that Singh wanted to resist. Its body was thick and graceful as it swayed rhythmically back and forth. The hood of the cobra was spread wide in a brilliant display of color and strength meant to warn all enemies. Two piercing, bronze eyes dotted its strong head and complemented the color scheme in vivid presentation.

Singh observed that the cobra sat in a depressed area in the dirt, almost like the earth had been scooped out to provide a place for resting or a billet for nesting. It seemed to be its territory. So far, the snake had shown no interest in venturing out of that little zone. Singh also observed a sickle hanging on the wall above and behind the head of the erect cobra. Singh knew that the sickle was offered as the fighting chance, the one opportunity to prevail against the serpent. But how to get it, and would he have the skills to behead the serpent before it could sink its deadly fangs into his flesh?

The late afternoon sun began to dip in the sky, and the already dim atmosphere inside the cobra house became dark and dusky. The form of the cobra was less distinct, but its presence was undeniable. And the voice of the cobra, the fear-inducing, cell-penetrating hissing spoke of the cobra's ferocity, its intensity, its resolve. Yes, the hiss was the cobra's voice, but what was it communicating? Was it saying, "Fear me and flee for I am about to kill you?" Or was it saying, "Respect me and keep your distance?"

Dusk led to dark, and the only light were the moonbeams pouring down through the opening in the roof. The silhouette of the cobra was unmistakable against the wall of the little house— its posture dignified, vigilant, and focused.

Many thoughts raced through Singh's head. What if he fell asleep and the cobra advanced on him and injected its venom in the night? What if he stayed awake all night and the cobra still attacked? Unarmed, he would have no chance, and a serpent is nocturnal, is it not? The sickle was there for the taking. Yes, the taking. A nice thought, but how? One well-placed swipe of the sickle would sever the serpent's head and render it harmless on the dirt floor. And Singh would go free.

The sickle—his only chance to kill the snake. Could the snake be distracted so he could snatch it from the wall? But what could be of more interest to the giant serpent than Singh himself? And should he pluck the weapon from its hook, could he be quick enough to prevail? The sickle was his only chance to kill the snake, he knew, but was it his only chance to survive?

Black rhinoceros beetles, half the size of a man's hand, emerged from under the walls of the little house, three, four, five, crawling in his direction. Their antennae smelled his dried sweat and their pincers positioned themselves to sample his tender flesh. He flicked one of them off his forearm and it landed near the cobra's bed. "SSSSSSS!!" The hissing intensified. If the plop of a beetle had such an effect, how could he risk grabbing the sickle?

Singh's dried sweat and the night air brought a chill over his entire body. He did not know if he now shook from fear, or from the cold of the night, or both. The cobra stayed erect and did not remove his gaze from the naked man in the dirt. The cobra's fierce eyes made it look angry, but still it did not advance. Singh stayed as still as he could.

The night wore on and the moon reached its zenith in the sky. Just then a scampering and scratching outside the hut, and up the wall. Then another, and another. Now on the roof. A large rodent could be seen sniffing and poking its nose into the opening at the top of the house. Another joined him. Half a dozen rats circled around the opening. Scratch, scratch, scratch. Squeak, squeak, squeak. Singh did not want the cobra agitated by any kind of intrusion. But then more dread entered his mind as he realized the rats were there for *him*, in spite of the cobra. They would eat him alive if they could. *How ironic,* he thought. Just then a good-sized rodent dropped from the opening in the roof and landed on the dirt floor midway between the cobra and the naked man. It looked in the direction of the man and advanced quickly, its nose moving to the sensations of his pungent odor. Singh had the presence of mind to offer a juicy finger to the intruder, leading it in one direction, while grabbing it by the tail and swinging it around through the air. He flung his attacker against the wall in the corner where it dropped to the floor dead. "SSSSSSS!!" The snake responded, clearly agitated, but Singh had no choice.

No more rats dropped through the opening that night and Singh was grateful. He was drained in every way a human can be drained, but he dared not let his eyelids close, lest he fall asleep and topple over in the dirt. Singh adjusted his posture with the back of his thighs resting on his calves, lifting his buttocks off the ground so a beetle could not attempt to tunnel into his anus.

The next three hours were three years in the life of Sonjay Singh. He would fidget to fend off the beetles, but was careful not to create palpable contact with the dirt floor. He wanted no vibration to draw the serpent's attention to himself. No matter how the beetles crept upon him, Singh kept one eye trained on the menacing serpent.

Finally, the dimness inside the hut lifted as the luster of a new day began to fill the earth. The shimmer of fresh sunbeams washed over the wall, and the sickle, and even the great serpent itself. Singh could see the majesty of the creature and the masterful command it held of its territory, confident and established in its domain. The steel of the sickle gleamed in the new light, but faded from the mind of the naked man. And the beetles and the rats had retreated to their holes.

Singh was now stiff and cramped from crouching through the night, and knew he needed to move about. He slowly stood up, straightening his knees and stretching up from the waist and reaching his arms into the air. Singh knew that he still had eight or nine hours to spend with the cobra, but he began to entertain the thought for the first time that he just might live to walk freely in his life once again. As the hours moved forward, he began to feel thoughts of gratitude. He was thankful that he had gotten through the night unharmed, that the rats had given up their pursuit, that the beetles had become no more than a nuisance. And he was thankful to see the light of a new day.

High noon had passed. Singh knew this from the vertical lines of sunlight that had streaked the walls of the cobra's abode, and then retreated like a fading mist. The giant serpent stayed on its side of the hut, and Singh stayed on his. How much longer? An hour? Less? When would the crossbar be lifted and the door opened?

People began to assemble outside. Singh could hear them walking and talking. They wondered if he was alive. Until the door was opened, there was no way to know. No sounds would tell them, and he dared not call out. He heard men placing bets on his fate. Coins clanked to the ground and voices were raised as men gathered on the other side of the wall that belonged to the cobra. Now agitated voices rang out and two men were heard to be yelling at each other in a dispute over the wagers. There was a sound of scuffling as the two crashed against the wall of the little house. The cobra lengthened its body and began moving rapidly back and forth.

Suddenly, the snake broke from its territory in the direction of the side wall to the right side of Singh. Before it traversed the length of the wall, it changed directions and in the flicker of an eyelash oscillated directly toward Singh. Its body was graceful and fluid as it positioned itself no more than twelve inches from his flesh. Singh was standing, but not erect. He was stooped over in a position that called for calmness and reserve, arms outstretched. He was trying to show the serpent that he meant it no harm.

Eyeball to eyeball. Was it time to run for the sickle? Singh knew any such movement would be lethal. He must live or die in the presence of the cobra, but he must not run. He decided to move ever so slowly to the corner to his left, against the wall that housed the little door. He hoped the serpent would not follow. He moved his left foot in that direction, slowly, deliberately, silently, upper torso and head to follow, all the while riveted on the ominous vessel of death inches from his face.

On the interminable pathway Singh reached the corner, and once there, remained still as a stone. The cobra held its ground, but did not advance on the exhausted, naked man. Singh prayed for peace, and he prayed for life. In moments, the cobra retreated to the other side of the hut, to the recessed area that Singh had come to think of as the cobra's nest. Singh remained impassive in the corner of his prison.

Seconds later, the crossbar on the little door was lifted and the mouth of the pit was wrestled open, allowing sunlight to stream in as the day before. "SSSSSSS!!" The serpent signaled a final warning. An official of the court poked his head inside and saw Singh standing in the corner, and extended his hand toward him. Singh stumbled through the opening and collapsed on the ground outside.

Partisans of the captive raised cheers for his victory that day, while others who had lost money walked away, kicking the dirt. Neither the winners nor the losers understood what had occurred in the mind of Sonjay Singh. He was permitted to bathe, dress, and eat, and was taken before the magistrate.

"Mr. Sonjay Singh," the magistrate said, "you are the first prisoner to survive twenty-four hours in the Court of the Cobra. To what do you attribute your success?"

"Your honor, I could see that aggression on my part would be futile. And I could see after a short time that the cobra was not interested in being aggressive towards me. So I just respected its territory and gave it space, as much as I could."

"You have made a wise decision, Mr. Singh. You were correct to observe that the great cobra meant you no harm. It was interested only in being secure and protecting its territory. Most people are the same. If you leave them alone, they will leave you alone. If you do good to them, they will do good to you. Had you reached for the sickle, it would have meant certain death.

"Mr. Singh, I believe you will remember your twenty-four hours in the Court of the Cobra for the rest of your life. If you are wise, you will remember its lessons, to respect the space, property, and person of others. You are now free to go and live a new life."

So Sonjay Singh went into the community of Ghazni with a new view of his purpose, his presence, and his fellow citizens. And the people still work hard to scratch their living out of the land and out of the river. And the people still laugh, and the people still cry.

But now, when the people think of Sonjay Singh, they smile and think of courage and kindness. The way of the cobra has made it so.

THE WALL

J. P. Newcomer

"*D*are you. Double dare you." Suzie Viafora grins her usual taunting '*I know I'm better than you are*' grin and I know I'm in trouble. With Suzie, I'm always in trouble, but I can't help liking her. It's not until later—years later—that I begin to figure out why. It has to do with her fire. It's as though Suzie has a furnace inside and someone is always shoveling in the coal.

"Stay away from that wild one," my mother used to say while puffing on her Chesterfield and making the sign of the cross on her breast. "Stay away. You know how Italian girls are, Shelia. They're only good for having babies and getting fat. Stick with your own kind." I suppose it was to her credit that she didn't say "Wop," but she was always thinking it, and I could read the word in her pious smile.

Suzie shakes her head and one of her thick, coal-black pigtails with the triple-wrapped rubber bands at the tips flies toward my cheek. I back away and quickly duck. Those braids are like a whip! Suzie was doing the polka with one of her cousins at her brother Jimmy's wedding last summer when one of those braids hit her dancing partner—thud—across the face and the poor kid ended up with a nosebleed which ruined his new white shirt. Suzie's braids are dangerous. "Triple dare you," she says, glaring at us.

Maureen looks up at me with her blue-marble eyes and I know she doesn't want to do it, but she will if I say so. Maureen will do it because she's my best friend and she knows it will kill me to be labeled 'Chicken Mick' by Suzie Viafora. But I *am*

11

chicken. Besides, Suzie is eleven, a whole year older than us, and the wall is so high—higher than the Empire State Building, it seems. Or that new hotel in Copley Square which just goes up and up until it seems to disappear. The freckles dance across Maureen's sunburned nose and I begin to realize that there is no shameless way out of a triple dare.

Maureen, who seems to have already figured that out, is staring at me and I'm staring at the wall. It's an ordinary wall in most respects: cement blocks topped by chain link fencing—posts every ten feet or so, between which the chain link has been tightly stretched and securely fastened. *How securely?*

"OK," I say at last, refusing to give in to terror, "but dares go first." This is a thing I've heard my brother say and I hope it makes my OK sound a little less frightened. Suzie nods and it's hard to tell whether or not she can sense my fear.

The wall is built above a steep ravine which leads down to our neighborhood playground. Sort of like one of those Malibu beach houses, where you walk in the front door at street level and discover that the glassed–in living room is hanging on stilts a hundred feet over a rocky beach and pounding surf. Not that I'd ever seen a house like that back then. Back then, the only Malibu I'd ever heard of was a narrow strip of sandy shoreline just off the Southeast Expressway where dead jellyfish lined the beach at low tide.

The chain-link rises a uniform eight feet above the block wall, but the height of the wall differs greatly from front to back. On the street side it is a mere three feet high and easy to traverse. Anyone can stroll the wall on that side, stepping easily, even skipping at times and clutching the chain-link only if one fears losing their balance. But on the park side everything is different. The terrain drops off steeply and there's only a narrow passage as you cling to the chain-link and walk the concrete blocks, two—maybe three stories high at the end. The further you progress, the more the chain-link becomes your life-link. The wall stretches before me—and the park—an ordinary park with swings and slides and a baseball diamond/ice skating pond (depending on the season) winks up at me from far below. On this late spring day, I can see the baselines drawn from what seems like miles away.

Suzie leaps to the wall on the high side above the park and grips the chain-link. She intends to go to the very end. I can tell by the smug look on her face and her deliberate movements. Maureen and I are standing at the edge of the wall where the street side and the park-side merge, staring at each other.

"I think I hear your mother calling you," I say.

"Oh, yeah?" Maureen frowns and cocks her head. "I don't hear nothin'." By now, it's clear she knows what I'm up to. "I'm going," she mutters, "you can't stop me."

"But you don't have to."

"Shut up." Maureen is glaring at me. Her parents, like mine, don't approve of Suzie. Neither does Maureen, I sometimes think. Worst of all, she knows of my terror. Maureen knows everything about me. She smiles and nudges me with her elbow. "Let's go." She's even more afraid than I am, I begin to realize.

Maureen jumps to the wall. I follow, shameful, bringing up the rear. Suzie is laughing like a lunatic. I think that's when it strikes me. *Suzie will never be fat. Suzie will never have babies. Suzie will never be the person my mother expects her to become.*

This was maybe the first important insight I ever had in my life. And it was born of terror. Most real revelations come from pain, I later came to realize. At least, that's how it's been for me.

Maureen is breathing heavily and Suzie is a good ten feet ahead of us on the wall, skipping along fearlessly like some Amazon right out of the Sunday comics. I feel my leather-soled, Catholic school oxfords slip and slide atop the cinder-block, and I cling to the chain-link, trying to catch my breath. Pray, I tell myself, but I can't seem to pull it off. I never was much good at praying, to be honest.

We edge forward. Maureen's knees are shaking. I can see this clearly through her thin cotton leggings. Like me and Suzie, she's wearing her blue-green plaid pleated skirt, white starched shirt and plaid suspenders which crisscross in the back and are attached to her skirt in giant crab clasps. The outfit is supposed to be topped off by a large plaid bow-tie designed to dangle at the throat, but that was always the first thing to vanish when the school day ended. Ties are for boys, we told each other. Funny how we never complained about the suspenders!

Today, suspenders are in vogue. All it takes is waiting, I often think. If you wait long enough anything you ever wore, or ever did, or ever thought about doing will come back around. Even chain-link—as in metal—heavy metal—Chain Link Blues! I never suspected the song would hit the charts. Better if it hadn't, I sometimes think.

The song was a tribute to Maureen. I knew that the moment I heard Suzie sing it for the first time in that dingy recording studio in South Boston and I knew it was her best. But I never dreamed it would make her famous. I never dreamed it would make us rich.

Whenever Suzie belts out the melody I can't help but shiver. The song always takes me back to the wall. Maureen— struggling—me trying to say something funny, anything to change that glazed look in her eyes. I see her wobbling white-coated knees and hear the tremor in her voice. Even now, I get headaches.

"It's high," Maureen breathes, "way high." Her fingers, narrow lengths of newly sprouted vine, seem to be clutching every bit as desperately as mine to the chain-link. And her feet shuffle…shuffle, shuffle, like those of an old woman. We are above the steepest slope now with what seems like a million miles of rocky hillside with swings and see-saws and jungle-gyms spread out below. The chain-link is cutting into my fingers.

I have to make a game of this. "My mother's got a thing she says," I tell Maureen with a little smile, aiming for humor. I'm pretty dense when it comes to dealing with terror—mine or someone else's. Slog. That's the only way.

"What's that?"

"Wherever you be, let your wind go free."

"Like in farting? Are you serious?" Maureen blushes and looks embarrassed and I find myself shocked by my own words and the steep terrain beneath us and the trembling links to which I greedily cling. "That's so gross," Maureen mumbles, trying to look offended, but not quite pulling it off. Her eyes are still glassy. "Let's go back," she whispers.

"You go back. Just step around me." I remember my tone. Even now I can hear the dry-mouth quiver. I keep trying to swallow. Suzie is ahead of us and laughing. "Chicken Mick," she shouts. "You're a chicken Mick! Your father's a drunk and the cops have to bring him home every night. It's a good thing they know where he lives."

My father has nothing to do with this. Nothing at all.

"She's a jerk," Maureen is saying. We didn't say nasty words like bitch or asshole back then because our kid brothers owned that vocabulary. We were supposed to be better than that. Maureen is shaking so hard the chain-link begins to chatter.

"Never mind," I say. "Just stay where you are. I can't go back now. I'll scoot around you." *It's wide enough here. I can't let Suzie get away with this. I can't!* Maureen pushes back, frozen against the chain link, and somehow I manage to get around her. She stares after me with this puppy-sad expression on her face and that's when the world changes for all three of us.

I can see it yet. I continue to dream it—Maureen falling—falling toward the playground—falling into dreamland see-saws and jungle gyms and steep slides anchored into sandy plains and kids from last winter ice skating on frozen ponds of memories. Maureen plummets into all of that, her scream echoing in my ears and Suzie races toward me, shouting. I cling like a leach to the chain-link until the sirens begin to wail. Only then does Suzie succeed in prying me free.

Funny how things work out, I sometimes think. Who, on Malibu Beach, (the Boston one where we swam as kids) would have imagined that Suzie Viafora would someday be inclined toward fried hair, leather body suits and non-acoustical guitars? Or that I might end up becoming her manager, promoter and Girl Friday?

The last time we saw Maureen was at last year's AIDS Concert at Boston Garden. Suzie (Spirit is her stage name) did some fine warm-up licks for the headliners and the crowd seemed to be off on a laid-back, feel-good vibe and the whole world felt clean and new and free of boundaries to me that day. So much so, that I was thinking I might have rediscovered the sixties until I spotted Maureen.

She arrived in her nun's habit, walking with a slight limp— the legacy of the wall. After the fall she put her faith in a higher order—maybe that's how she finally made it out of the wheelchair. I'd been expecting her, knowing she wouldn't pass up free tickets and backstage passes to a world-class concert. (Even Roger Waters, renowned for his song of another Wall, is on the bill.) Somehow, I can see the old Maureen in her placid smile. *She should have gotten married and had children. We all should have gotten married and had children.* My mother didn't live long enough to realize the fallacy of her predictions.

"Hi, Shelia," Maureen says, her eyes sparkling with laughter. "Kind of a skimpy outfit you're wearing, don't you think?"

"It's supposed to be. This is show biz."

"So it is." She smiles. "The convent roof is leaking,"

16

"Oh." The convent roof is always leaking. Or the plumbing isn't working. Always, something expensive. Always, something.

"I'll handle it," I say softly.

"I know you will. I hope you're happy, Shelia. Are you?"

"Sure." That's more or less the truth,

"Bless you, Shelia." Maureen smiles and nods and squeezes my hand. I try to feel blessed.

FOR MY BOOKMATE

Mary Langer Thompson

We usually read side by side,
but tonight I feel your absence.
To ease my mind, I peruse alone
but have trouble following the twisted story.

This morning my romance
lies on the floor, closed.
I find my bookmark
on top of the sheet
under your down pillow,
saving your place.

TOMORROW'S DREAM

Denny Stanz

Little boy
Not sure who he is or where he's going
Mom is here, dad is gone
Searching for love he's not showing

Grab your football
Bat and glove
Shoot those hoops
Slop thru the mud

Sometimes he drifts into loneliness
Sometimes he's soaked with rain
Sometimes he's lost in friendship
Sometimes he's filled with pain

If today makes him unhappy
The fun not what it seems
He'll stay on the road less traveled
It leads to tomorrow's dreams

LEATHA IN THE RAIN

Diane Neil

I came to tell you goodbye, Leatha, behind this shopping center where I used to work. You aren't here, of course, but I had to come back to the place I first saw you. I'm getting married next week. A man shouldn't start a marriage remembering another girl.

You wouldn't understand any of this, Leatha, but it helps me to tell you. I'm leaning against the high board fence at the back entrance to the center, where my memories brought me.

I'd been at M'Lord's for a couple of months and I was already in solid with Mr. Javitts. Partly because I was a good salesman—it didn't take much to top poor Varney with his ulcers and fallen arches—but mainly because of Nadine. She had her hooks in me—nice, soft hooks with orange polish—and I liked it. I liked her blonde, magazine-cover looks and the queenly way she walked. I knew she was spoiled, being the Javitts' only child, but I figured a guy could do worse than marry the boss's daughter.

It was the first time I'd used this shortcut. Mr. Javitts had called me 'son' that day. I was wearing the Italian flannel sport coat he'd let me have at cost, and I was on top of the world as I hurried across the parking lot, despite the gray drizzle. I'd noticed this narrow entrance before; that day as I got in my car I wondered where it went.

Let's find out, I thought. *What the hell.* I had a dinner date with Nadine. The works at a Chinese place, maybe, or a pepperoni pizza.

I drove out into a narrow alley without sidewalks, bordered by weeds, like a vacant lot with a blind street down the middle.

And saw you. You knelt in the weeds searching for something.

Stopping the car, I rolled down the window. "Did you lose something?"

You went on digging as if you hadn't heard me. Eighteen, I guessed.

"Are you looking for something?" I called again.

"*Here* pretty!" You grabbed something in the grass and looked up.

"Oh," I said. Your lovely face. A wreath of straight, dark hair. Eyes like chips of blue china. Like a cloudless sky on certain April afternoons. Vacant.

You stood, surprisingly tall, and began to sing. "Pret-ty, pret-ty," just on the edge of breath. You cradled whatever you'd found, a button or a bottle cap, and rocked back and forth, oblivious to me, the rain, everything.

She's kidding, I thought. *She's putting on some kind of act.* But I saw your eyes again and knew you weren't acting. I sat in the car staring at you in fascination.

"Leatha!" a woman called from a nearby house. "Leatha!"

"Lea-tha," you said. The third time she called, you ran off in the direction of her voice. I watched you run down the street, your hair and jacket flying, and disappear into a house with yellow shutters.

I turned the key in the ignition and found my way home.

***

As it turned out, Nadine and I had dinner at Andre's, her parents' favorite restaurant. We didn't have pepperoni pizza. Watching Nadine across the linen-covered table, I knew she

21

belonged here with the silver and crystal. She had an elegance that demanded the best. Candlelight shone on her sleek blonde hair. *I remembered yours straggling in the rain.*

"You're quiet tonight, Rick" she said.

"I was thinking of a girl I saw today."

"Was she pretty?"

"Yes."

"Well!"

"It's not that. This girl was—she had the mind of a child." I started to tell Nadine about the way you sang to your bottle cap.

"Please," she said. "I'd rather not hear about it." She flashed her cover girl smile. "This is such a lovely dinner. Let's not discuss anything unpleasant. Are you enjoying your prime rib?"

Nadine's right, I thought. I decided to forget you.

But that wasn't easy to do. I discovered that the back entrance to the shopping center shaved a couple of miles off my route plus a lot of traffic and stop lights, so I began using it regularly.

The first morning I used the short cut I glanced at the weeds where I'd seen you, half hoping that I'd imagined you. But on my way home, there you were in a raincoat and galoshes, laughing and splashing in a puddle. The next day you had on jeans—you usually wore jeans—and you were in mud up to your ears. You had it on your face and in your hair.

Every time I drove through the alley I looked for you. I never stopped again but drove at a crawl until I reached the corner. Sometimes you were playing in the grass; sometimes you paced back and forth singing to something—once a dead bird—in your hand.

Often you sat beside the road staring straight ahead. Or you'd be in your yard. One day a woman was with you, trimming the tree roses. Your mother? I wondered. She seemed small and frail next to you. Old. Who would take care of you when she died?

Did you have a father? Were there other children? I used to lie awake at night asking questions I couldn't answer.

***

Things were going great at the store. Mr. Javitts would come in late or knock off early for golf, leaving me in charge. Varney never said a word, just looked like his ulcer was acting up.

At my suggestion, we switched out some stodgy old styles for classier, younger lines, and our clientele grew. I ran a local ad campaign, and it upped our sales. I was practically running the business, but I could never be sure whether it was because of my ability or because of Nadine.

Nadine started dropping by the store to see me. I didn't like mixing business with pleasure, but I figured as long as Mr. Javitts didn't mind, I shouldn't either. Hell, I told myself, when the business was mine, I could run it any way I wanted. But there were times when I wondered if it was the other way around, especially where Nadine was concerned.

Like on that late spring afternoon.

I was busy with a customer when Nadine came in, so she waited in the back room as usual. When my customer left, I joined her and we kissed. She was wearing some pink thing, and she looked all pastel and gold, more than ever as if she'd stepped off a magazine cover. Too pretty to be hanging around the shop keeping a guy's mind off his job. I told her to run along home and I'd see her after work.

"Oh, pooh!" she said. "Varney's out there. Let him earn his keep."

"He's due for a break. He likes to come back here and put his feet up."

"Alright. If you think more of Old Sourpuss than you do of me—" She jabbed a manicured finger at me. "If *I* was in charge around here, I'd fire him."

"Nadine, he's been with your dad for twelve years. He's a good, steady man, and most of the regulars are his customers. Look," I said, kissing her again, "I'll see you tonight."

Suddenly, it sounded like a commotion out in the store. "I'd better give Varney a hand." I hurried out.

And saw you. Poor, dear, funny Leatha. You clutched a green mohair sweater which Varney, looking more pained than usual, was trying to take away from you. Politely, for the benefit of two women gaping from the underwear counter.

"Mine, mine!" you kept saying.

"Miss, you must put that back. You need mon-ey." Varney gestured and enunciated. "She was headed outside with it," he muttered as I came up.

"Okay, I'll handle it. You wait on the other customers."

Sighing in relief, Varney limped to Underwear.

I turned to you, oblivious of Nadine at my elbow.

You cradled the sweater, lashes fringing your cheeks, tumbled dark hair wreathing your face. You straightened, and my heart nearly cracked as I looked into your china blue eyes.

And then, oh God, you started to sing. "Pret-ty, pret-ty," on the edge of breath as you rocked the sweater back and forth.

I wanted to hold you in my arms and tell you to keep the sweater, anything, only to please stop breaking my heart.

"How horrible!" Nadine shuddered. "Where did she come from?"

"This is the girl I told you about. She lives behind the center."

"Well, get her out of here!"

I couldn't believe the venom in her voice. I looked at her, the magazine cover crumpling. "Will you help me?" I asked, trying

24

to smooth it out. "I think we can lead her home if we're careful not to frighten her."

"I'm not getting involved with any retard. I'll call the police. They have places for people like that." Her heels clicked toward the telephone. "She should be locked up."

"Don't, Nadine!" I didn't even look at her. "I'll take her home."

I held out my hand to you. "Come, Leatha."

You were rocking the sweater and singing. You looked at me and clutched the sweater more tightly to your chest. "My pretty!"

"All right, Leatha. You can keep the pretty, but let's go home."

"Rick," Nadine whined. "That cardigan is over fifty dollars."

"Okay, take it out of my severance pay." It didn't hurt. I felt nothing. Except maybe contempt for a guy who'd marry a spoiled brat for her father's store.

I guided you across the parking lot and into your street, your hand warm and trusting in mine.

A pregnant woman ran toward us. "Leatha!" she cried. "You naughty girl! I told you to stay in the yard." She looked at me. "Where was she?"

"In the men's store. I knew where she lived, and I —"

"Oh, no! She took this?" She touched the sweater, which you jerked away.

"Please, let her keep it. I—wanted to do something for her."

"We all do." The woman's shoulders sagged. "I'm the neighbor. Her poor mother had a stroke last night and I'm trying to keep an eye on Leatha until her father can get her into a home. The phone rang, and I—She never went past the fence before."

"They're putting Leatha in a home?"

"Yes, it's the only thing. She'll be with her own kind. Trainable, they say. Should have done it years ago."

The woman talked on, and I stood looking at you, Leatha, crooning to the sweater in your arms.

"Pret-ty, pret-ty," you sang.

I stood in that alley and looked into your eyes and let my heart crack wide open.

Leatha, how those eyes have haunted me since. Sleepless nights I'd hatch wild schemes to take you out of that 'home' and keep you with me always. But mornings I knew that the neighbor and even Nadine in her cruel way were right. You are with your own kind, with people who know how to take care of you. Maybe it's true, and maybe I want to think so because I was never fool enough—or man enough—to do anything else.

I hope you still have the sweater, Leatha. It's small exchange for a life without liens.

***

If you knew her, you'd like my Sue. I told her about you once; she cried. I think that's when I began to love her. She's small and bright with warm brown eyes, and she laughs a lot. A pepperoni pizza sort of girl.

Shopping downtown on our lunch hour once, we were caught in the rain. We ran for cover, Sue's jacket flying, her hair a tangled wreath around her face.

I caught my breath and held the image of you.

Sue turned to me, laughing, her face fresh and alive and wet with rain, and—please understand, Leatha—I had to let yours blur away.

How do you say goodbye to a memory? I look at a patch of weeds, at puddles drying in the sun, turn my back on a street without sidewalks and walk away under a china-blue sky.

Goodbye, Leatha.

SOMETHING REALLY SCARY

Michael Raff

WARNING! Read at your own risk! Please be advised, if you have a heart, stomach, or any other medical condition, you should bypass this story and go on to the next. The author, editors, and the entire membership of the California Writers Club will not be held responsible for adverse medical or psychological effects associated from the reading of the following material.

*I*t all started when we were kids. My cousin Scott and I were the best of friends, and no wonder, we lived on the same block, were the same age, and even attended the same school in beautiful Buena Park, California. I guess you could say we were inseparable, until his parents divorced and Scott and his mom moved to San Diego. But we still kept in touch through the years and even managed to see each other every now and then.

We were a rowdy pair and into playing pranks on each other. My father had this plastic doggie poop, and you can probably imagine what we did with that. But the real fun began when we played "Do you want to see something really scary?" I would like to say that Scott started it, but as I recall, I'm the one who initiated the insanity around Halloween, 1980. My parents bought this little, two-foot-long rubber skeleton. Since I've always been cursed with a questionable imagination, I asked Scott, "Do you want to see something really scary?" His eyes grew wide and he answered, "Yeah, sure I do!" So I led him into my clothes closet, and pointed to the bony little guy that hung amongst my belongings. "You get it?" I hollered. "There's a skeleton in my closet!" I know that sounds lame, but we were only ten years old at the time.

Well, this rather moronic gag went on for years. Scott would frequently ask me, "Do you want to see something *really* scary?" On several occasions, he handed me a cardboard box. One time there was a mirror packed inside. Another time a live rat jumped out at me when I opened the flaps.

When Scott moved to San Diego, our little game went on hiatus for years until we both discovered the Internet. One day I received an email from him entitled "Do you want to see something *really* scary?" Feeling a sense of déjà vu pulsating through my veins, I anxiously opened it. Inside there was a picture of a four-hundred-pound, naked sumo wrestler. Scott was right. That guy was really scary.

So as two grown men with families, jobs, and all kinds of responsibilities, we embarked on our childish and sometimes deranged adventure. I would send him a really terrible photo of himself when he was a kid, and he would return a picture of some poor guy that was hit by a train. It was mostly Scott who got carried away, sending photos of mutilated accident victims and such. I tended to send superimposed creations like a dancing chimpanzee with my cousin's face pasted on it.

This new phase also went on for years. Then one day while we were on the telephone, Scott told me that he didn't want to participate in our silly game anymore. When I asked him why, he only answered, "It's getting old and I'm sick of it." Basically, I ignored him and mailed him clever little gems, like his face superimposed on an elite member of the Taliban, and zingers like that. But my cousin never reciprocated. He even fired off an irate email telling me how infantile I was. I didn't let that stop me. If he didn't want to play, too bad. I was having a great time and was finally kicking his butt to the curb.

About a month ago, I received a phone call from Scott's wife, Linda. My cousin had died in his sleep the night before. I was shocked and devastated. He was my age, only forty-two years old. It turned out that he had a rare form of cancer and didn't want anyone to know about it. I planned on attending his funeral, but with my job and all, the trip never materialized. I ended up sending Linda an expensive wreath of flowers instead.

Now here comes the really scary part. A week ago, I received an email from Scott's address entitled "Do you want to see something *really* scary?" I was completely stunned and appalled. I thought it was extremely tacky for a member of Scott's family to send me something like that so soon after his funeral. When I opened it, inside there was a picture of my cousin next to a creature that was both unbelievable and repulsive. The very sight of it made me want to rip my eyes out. Whatever that thing was, it wasn't human. It was deformed, incredibly hideous, and had horns, fangs, and the most fiendish eyes imaginable. In the background there was a wall of flames and naked people being tortured by several of those horrifying creatures. *What the hell?* I wondered. Was it possible that one of Scott's family created this monstrosity just to get even with me? And here I thought some of my cousin's former emails were in poor taste!

When I finally composed myself, I phoned Linda. After talking about Scott, the weather, and her job, I asked her if anyone she knew had access to my cousin's old email address. She answered that she had discontinued all of his computer accounts, including his email. Then she happened to mention that although it was extremely unusual, in accordance with his wishes, Scott was buried with both his laptop and his smart phone. I nearly fell over. Of course, I had always known that my cousin was a tad strange, but I had no idea that he was certifiable. So the highly creative but deeply disturbed perpetrator of Scott's mysterious email remained unaccounted for. Well, at least that was the end of it, or so I thought.

When I checked my computer a few days later, there were at least fourteen more "Do you want to see something *really* scary?" emails waiting for me. I didn't want to open any of them, and I tried to resist, but eventually I broke down. Otherwise, if I just deleted them, I would be lying awake at nights, speculating about their contents.

The first of the emails contained a photo of Scott sitting next to a man who resembled Adolph Hitler. The guy was naked, burnt to a crisp, and looked like he'd been dragged through a mountain range of razor wire. I've been into photography for thirty years, and have done my share of photo manipulations, and I can recognize even the most professional effort. So I knew every one of Scott's emails were legitimate, right down to the minutest detail.

The Hitler picture was gross enough, but the following ones were worse by far. There were photos of New York City, Los Angeles, Paris, and London, with every building and landmark scorched and lying in ruins. Rubble was everywhere, along with charred and broken skeletons. Underneath the last photo appeared the single phrase, "Armageddon, September, 2016." The whole thing made me sick, and I deleted every one of those emails without opening the rest.

The next day when I checked my computer, there was only one email from Scott. Of course, it was entitled "Do you want to see something *really* scary?" It took me awhile to decide if I should open it or not. I was feeling feverish and my hands were shaking. My battered sanity seemed to be hanging off Mount Everest. I sat there for what seemed like forever, agonizing over my situation. I could hear our antique clock ticking from the living room. I began sweating and my stomach dripped acid. Yet

I found myself growing unbearably curious. As impossible as it seemed, Scott had sent me fourteen emails the day before, and now today there was only one? Why would he do that? Regrettably, there was just one way to find out. I opened the damn thing, and so help me God, I wished I hadn't.

This time there were just two photos. The first one was that of a man lying on a morgue table. His chest had been surgically opened and his severed heart was sitting in a pan. The next picture was the guy's death certificate and it appeared frighteningly authentic. The recorded date on it was July 15, 2013, about a year from now. The cause of death was listed as a heart attack. But the really scary part was the identity of the man. To my absolute, undying terror, that poor dissected guy was me.

I don't surf the Internet anymore. In fact, I gave my computer away. I'm doing a lot of exercises that are supposed to be good for my heart, plus I'm eating right. I hope it helps, but I still get this pressure in my chest and then I become scared, *really* scared. I don't think highly of Scott these days, but I have to admit, he really kicked my butt to the curb this time.

THE CARDS

Linda Bowden

The cards,
The letters,
The smiles, the sentiment,
Cannot erase the pain,
That springs forth from the shattered heart.
Time, they say the healer,
Does not heal,
But sits on pain like a rock,
Smothering the pieces,
Forging and weighing the cracks,
Into a new heart, a little less broken than today.
Keep the cards,
The letters,
The smiles and the sentiment.
Give me back the stone which pierced this heart
In one quick blow,
Give me back the time that was once not lost,
Give me back the less pain that I feel on this day.
Give me back yesterday.

Prologue from the novel
THE ACCORDO

Roberta L. Smith

1637 – Country Villa Outside Florence Italy

When they had finished making love, Lavinia Rossi Zanetti held the coverlet to her breast, rose on one arm, and stared at her beloved. He lay on his back, gulping the air, sweat upon his brow. She watched and waited for his breathing to grow calm. Then she leaned down and kissed him softly on the mouth.

Keeping his eyes closed, he grinned.

"You have a pleased-with-yourself smile," Lavinia said, her voice low, almost a whisper. She still wasn't smiling, but she added, "You should see mine."

Agostino reached for her with one hand and stroked her long unruly hair. "I am pleased. Always pleased when I am with you."

She took his hand, held it to her cheek, and gazed upon his face. *Such a beautiful man. I love your fine features. Your strong chiseled bones. Thick eyebrows. Short black beard. You are perfection.*

Perspiration caused his dark hair to cling to his forehead in ringlets. She drew a finger through the sweat then lightly traced his nose from bridge to tip. She drew her finger along the crevice where his lips met and he kissed it. Her finger went under his chin, traced his throat and stopped in the middle of his naked chest. She extended her fingers and pressed her hand to his body as her mind indulged itself.

Here your beating heart. Caged thirty-five years in this chest. Muscle, bone, blood, skin. All temporary. That is for certain.

She sighed so softly she felt, but hardly heard, the vibration of her vocal chords.

And what about our devotion to each other—you and I, Agostino? Has that already been lost? It pains me to think so. But if we live until whatever ripe age we live to be, when we die, does the devotion die then anyway? The church would have our souls exist, but would throw them in hell for our wanton actions, our sins of the flesh. Oh, perhaps not you, my love. For have you ever done anything wrong? Have you ever sinned? Aside from loving me, that is. Perhaps that is sin enough to send you to hell.

I don't believe the church is right. I don't. And I have to say, I hate God. But if the church is right, then there is no doubt that we will be separated in the afterlife. And I cannot bear that. I cannot allow that. I will not lose you.

She removed her hand.

The sun had long set and the lone candle in the room cast a shadow with dramatic effect. The contrast of dark and light, the stillness with which Agostino lay, and the rich blue and gold of the divan made the scene worthy of a Caravaggio painting— worthier still, of a Zanetti painting. After all, this man belonged to her.

She reached for a vessel of hearty red wine that sat on a nearby table and poured several ounces into a waiting goblet. She moved the goblet back and forth under Agostino's nose.

"It is your favorite."

He opened his eyes, sat up, and reached for the wine. He saw that there was only one cup. "What about you?"

"We shall drink from the same, but I've had my fill for now. Sip it. Savor it—as if it were your last."

She could say those words. He wasn't a suspicious man. If he were, he might have wondered about her meaning as well as the gentle tone in her voice. Lavinia was a strong woman, an outspoken woman. Gentle was not her approach to life. She guided the cup to his lips.

He swallowed—once, twice. She took the goblet from him and placed it back on the table before he could drink more.

"Please join me," he told her.

She didn't answer, but took hold of each of his wrists and pressed them to the divan. She leaned in, forcing him to lie back. Her face and his face were nose to nose. She looked into his eyes and could see that he had no idea what she had done. Light from the candle danced in his dilated pupils.

"You have not expressed your opinion of the painting," Lavinia said. "It is finished. Did you not notice?"

"*Amore mio*. You did not tell me, but swept me away with your charms. When I am here, I only notice you."

She stood, clutching the coverlet about her, and took the candle. She moved to a portrait of Agostino that was propped upon an easel. He adjusted his gaze to have a look.

"*Bellisimo. Bellisimo!* You have outdone yourself. She will love it." There was pride in his voice that Lavinia did not like. It was pride in the wonderful gift he would be giving the latest object of his affection, Catherine, not pride in Lavinia's prowess as an artist.

But his pride did not matter, she reminded herself. It was true that Catherine would love the painting. Lavinia had taken the money and done the work, but the painting would be delivered to the unsuspecting Catherine on Lavinia's terms. She had gone to great lengths to learn the last name of this Catherine.

"And the portrait of myself?" Lavinia said as she moved to a second easel that supported another painting. In it she looked a good ten years younger than she was now. She had given her eyes a haughty, piercing stare. The clothing was shear and seductive. One tender hand, the left, lightly touched her chest in contrast to the stark nature of the eyes.

"You are a wonder," Agostino said. "A woman, but still a painter of merit."

Lavinia's eyes narrowed. Even with all his years of knowing her, he still believed being a woman made her work inferior to that of a man.

"And you are a great healer—for the male of the species," she replied, coming back to the divan.

"What do you mean?"

She gave him a calculated smile, placed the candle on the table, and sat.

"Oh, of course," he said, tugging a lock of her hair. "How you do tease and yet it is true. I am one of life's mysteries. Why should I be blessed with the gift to heal? Why any man?"

Lavinia shrugged. She didn't bother herself with such questions. Why should a person be able to sing or play the piano or write music or books? Why was one man good at amassing money and another good only at having none? In her own case, why had she been born with the ability to paint if a woman was not to do so? From an early age her work had shown brilliance.

Her father had been a painter. Although not of great talent, he had been able to make a living, and he recognized in his daughter the greatness that was not in him. He might have reacted with jealousy and taken steps to thwart her talent except for the fact that he saw her as an extension of himself and wanted her to become known at the right time. He taught her what he could but knew she needed a teacher who was the best if she was to become one of the greats.

He devised a plan. When Lavinia was eleven he had her disguise herself as a male in order to gain access to the art world's premier instructor, Guiseppe D'Addario. The teacher had a reputation as a brute, one without fondness for females who thought they could do more than raise children and keep a house. But a task master was what Lavinia's father wanted. Soft words would not help Lavinia become a great artist. Little did he, or she, know that D'Addario's reputation had been understated.

Their scheme went undetected for just over three years before Lavinia's feminine charms became too difficult to hide, and once D'Addario realized Lavinia's true sex, it sent him into a rage. Lie to him? Belittle his stature as a master artist and teacher? A female in his class? He resolved to teach her a lesson she would not forget and it had nothing to do with art.

She fought him off, only to lose, and afterwards her father sued D'Addario in court for having deflowered his daughter. After a lengthy four month trial, Lavinia's father lost his case. A thumbscrew had been placed on Lavinia's right thumb and tightened to excruciating effect. It was the court's way of making sure a person told the truth. Did it never occur to them that a person would lie to stop the pain? Did it never occur to them to apply the screw to Guiseppe D'Addario as well?

She was publicly humiliated and the humiliation did not end with the trial. She was branded a lascivious woman even though she was merely fourteen and had been a virgin at the time of the rape.

In hindsight, even at that young age, she saw that the offensive label had its upside. She was notorious and notoriety helped to sell paintings. The experience may have been painful. It may have left her changed. But she was now a skilled artist and one of renown. She wondered if everything of value came with a price. She wondered if prices were always as steep as the one she had paid. She wondered if somewhere, unbeknownst in her sleep perhaps, she had made a deal with the devil to be a success.

She glanced at her thumb, long healed—not because of time, but because of Agostino—and rubbed it. Advantages aside, the rape and her attacker's acquittal had left her bitter and ruthless.

She did things that no one knew about. Hatred and rage burned within her belly and only three things soothed her: the presence of her beloved Agostino; being lost in the process of creating her art; and inflicting the pain she felt upon men. Yes, sometimes, when she was unable to contain herself, when Agostino missed a visit and when the creative process had been spent, she went into the city in search of appropriate victims.

And now Agostino had told her that she must share him with another. She wasn't naïve. She had probably shared him with many. But this was the first time he had told her about it. This was the first time he had shared a name. This new woman, this Catherine, meant something to him and that was a reality Lavinia would not live with.

Agostino's arm fell limp from the divan. Lavinia stroked his cheek. An "ahh" escaped his lips.

She stood up and dropped the cloth that had been covering her body. She was a portrait painter and the eyes of all the paintings in the room were upon her. *We are here for you*, they seemed to say. *We shall be your witnesses.*

Lavinia giggled like a girl, clasped her hands to her chin and did a little spin. This was to be her wedding night. Not in the traditional sense, but in a more lasting sense.

Agostino had asked her to marry him many times, but she had liked their arrangement as it was. He was hers and she was his. Of that, she'd had no doubt. Now the situation had changed because of Catherine. Now it was a marriage for all eternity that she desired.

Men were so clueless, she thought. Why did she love such a clueless man? For all the times he had been in the workroom of her villa, whether to pose for her, to look at the work she had done, have a cup or two of wine or to make love, he hadn't noticed that she'd arranged the paintings in a special way—with the portraits of the two of them at the core.

And if he had noticed, what would she have said?

Nothing. She would have shrugged and smiled cryptically.

Lavinia walked over to a full-length mirror and gazed into the glass. She appraised her body and face. She was forty-two, had years ahead of her to paint, but without the exclusive devotion of Agostino she felt she had nothing to live for. Her beauty had faded. Her hips looked too wide now and there was superfluous flesh upon her thighs. They dimpled in the flickering candlelight. Her breasts looked fine, but for how long? Time had etched shallow lines around her mouth and downward from the corners of her eyes. The blush in her cheeks had vanished and the once-rich, deep brown color of her eyes had dulled. Was all this the reason Agostino felt drawn to Catherine?

No one ever sees the physical changes as they happen, she told herself. No one feels eyelashes replace or fingernails grow. No one feels it when the brows begin to gray, or the jaw line wants to sag. It's the internal things you feel. It's the events that rip you apart that you notice. And any event that thwarts your plans for happiness helps mold you into something you never expected to be.

A thin moan escaped from Agostino's mouth and Lavinia's eyes shifted in the mirror so that she could see him lying on the divan. She watched and waited. He did not moan again. He did not move. The drug she had given him must have worked. He was breathing. He was unconscious, but alive. It was very important that he be alive.

She heard footsteps approach in the hall and her eyes went to the door. It was time. She felt her chest heave with excitement. The moon had waxed and the practitioner was here. She had one last plan to carry out—one last arrangement to follow through.

She lifted the goblet from the table and took a swallow. Pulling the coverlet around her, she sat on the divan. She engaged Agostino's right hand and entwined their fingers. She waited.

The footsteps stopped and there came a rap on the door. The rhythm: Tap. Tap. Tap. A short pause. Two quick taps.

Lavinia took a breath. "We are ready," she said. "You may come in."

THE ELEVATOR

Suzanne Holbrook-Brumbaugh

I stood outside the Carlton Towers Savings and Loan as near to the curb as possible, just like my kid brother Billy and I used to do some twenty years ago. My neck ached, and I felt slightly light-headed as I strained to count the windows leading up to the thirty-sixth floor. It wasn't any easier now than it was then. Everything just kind of blended together after the fifteenth. I awoke from my reverie when I heard someone calling my name.

"Is that you, Mr. Simmons? They told me you was a comin'. I was that excited, I was. It's been nigh unto ten years since I seen you last. Here, let me get the door for you."

I couldn't help but smile at the old doorman's enthusiasm. It was good to see him again. I had been away too long. He walked me to the elevator, chattering all the way, then insisted on pushing the up button "for old time's sake." As the doors closed behind me, those last twenty years dissipated, and I was once more a twelve-year-old child riding up and down, up and down, for hours on end with Billy.

"Okay, Billy boy. Where would you like to go this time?"

"Take me to the moon, Tommy. Take me to the moon."

Up we'd go, straight to the thirty-sixth floor, then plunge back down to the first, hoping no one would stop the elevator, wanting to get on.

"Hey, Billy. Why do you like to ride up and down so fast all the time?" I asked.

". . . it makes me feel like I'm fly-y-ying," he grinned.

As the ancient elevator jerked to a stop, I was suddenly thrust back to the present. *Wish you were here, Billy,* I thought. *You would love this. It all looks just the same.*

The doors opened, and just for a moment, I thought I had stopped on the wrong floor. The entire room looked, and smelled, like a florist convention. There were huge floral displays, and potted plants everywhere. Row upon row of well-padded steel chairs stood stiffly in formation, like soldiers waiting to honor one of their own.

As old friends hurried to greet me, my eyes quickly scanned this great hall. There it was. A small table, framed with roses and daisies, cradled the picture of a smiling young Air Force pilot. *Billy,* I silently cried, my eyes filling with unshed tears. *You always wanted to fly. Who would have thought it would lead to your death. Billy, the hero, shot down over Viet Nam. It was supposed to be a rescue mission—a medical evacuation. Why did it happen? I guess we'll never really know. But I'm here for you, Billy. Just like old times. I'm here, brother.*

The memorial service was real nice, but I was glad when it was over. As soon as I could, I picked up Billy's picture, said my farewells, and headed for the elevator. As I went to push the down button, I could almost hear Billy's voice calling, "One more time, Tommy. One more time. Let's take her back to earth."

I stepped into that makeshift rocket-ship, pushed the first floor button, and holding tightly to Billy's picture, plunged one last time to the ground below.

As I stepped out into the nearly deserted lobby of that huge old building, I was nearly flattened as two young boys flew past me and entered the magic of the elevator. I couldn't help but smile as I heard the youngest shout, "Take me to the moon, Danny. Take me to the moon."

CORNBREAD MUFFINS

Rica Gold

Mmmm . . . breakfast . . . .
I'm out of strawberries, raisins and bananas. All the stuff I like with walnuts in oatmeal would be missing. What else is there? A box of corn muffin mix looms in the cupboard, staring at me. It's been there awhile. I have an egg and some milk and some honey, I think to myself. Good deal... corn muffins and café latte for breakfast this morning will be a nice change. I'll eat grapefruit later to balance.

Corn muffins always remind me of my first love, Henry Kirk. I met him soon after I arrived my junior year in a high school out west, after coming to the United States. The dry, hot summer temperatures of the early September school day seemed to curl around me as he walked toward a cluster of the first few girlfriends who had welcomed me.

He was tall. His sandy blonde hair was cut in a "flat top" popular in the late fifties. He smiled at the others as he approached, a dimple breaking out next to his perfect, smooth lips. "Hey ya'll," he called out as all the girls' heads turned in unison and their smiles broadened.

Henry was from Texas, or his parents were anyway. He was sweet with a kind of corny, funny sense of humor. He had an older sister that we called Rita, although her real name was some long thing I could never remember. She was a Mormon, whatever that was. I just knew a Mormon didn't smoke or drink Coke. Rita was a lot older so I didn't pay much attention to that at first. She was already out of school.

Henry was on the football team. He carried the ball a lot, but I didn't know what position it was he played and I didn't really care. I just liked watching him. He kind of hung on the perimeter of the Catholic crowd, the first people to bring me into their fold socially.

I soon began to realize that the high school population seemed to consist of Mormons, the most popular kids it seemed, Methodists, the ones giving the Mormons a run for their money in popularity, and the Catholics, who appeared to be the underdogs when it came to standing out in the school. These divisions were further broken down into the jocks, the brains, the cheerleaders and flag girls, class leaders, square kids, science geeks and loners.

Some kids tried to fit in by joining clubs to have a feeling of belonging. One or two were actually altruistic and were friends with everyone, especially the exchange students who stood out, misplaced in the mass of people sliding by one another as we moved from classroom to classroom during passing periods. I knew I wasn't popular or pretty enough to be a cheerleader. After all I was a jock myself at my last school. My hair was cut short and I was athletic and loved running. I had just started wearing lipstick—some funky kind of clear tangerine stuff—that I didn't like much. That was it for make-up. So I tried fitting in on the school newspaper staff and my love of everything drama grew.

I'd only had one date in the tenth grade and that ended badly after the car my date drove broke down and we didn't get home until about one o'clock in the morning. My dad grounded me for the rest of my sophomore year. When Henry asked me out, I knew what true joy really felt like. We went to a school dance. I loved to dance and fortunately Henry actually *could* dance. When there was a dance competition though, I opted to dance with my younger brother, John. He was as good as I thought I was, but that was about as much as we had in common, I was sure. Later in life Henry would lament that my mother told him he better watch out because I was a "dancing fool."

After the dance, we went to the UDI. Everyone called it that although the real name was the University Drive In. I'd never been there. I sat right next to Henry in his old car as we pulled into a space next to the building with a metal roof that spread over six or seven other cars. A girl came to Henry's window and took our order. We got hamburgers and chocolate shakes. When we reached my house afterwards, Henry pulled me into him, his arms holding me warmly and kissed me long and sweetly. My heart fluttered so hard I was sure he could hear it. I knew I was the happiest and luckiest girl in the world. Hopefully he barely noticed when I burped from the chocolate shake while he was kissing me.

Henry and I started going to seminary classes for the Mormon Church at six o'clock in the morning before school. During the winter months it was cold and Henry would pick me up in the old Ford truck his dad had since passed down to him and we'd stop at his house for a super early breakfast. His mom would make scrambled eggs with spinach and cornbread muffins with honey and warm butter on them. The best breakfast I had ever had. We attended Sacrament services on Sundays and prayed together with our LDS classmates before some of the outings we went to. The Mormon crowd kids began to warmly invite us more and more into their activities. We became better known in the school. I was nominated for class representative and won.

When Henry gave me his ring to wear on a chain around my neck, I was officially his girlfriend. It was our senior year, and Henry became a part of our family. He was always around and went on family outings with us. I became more popular at school and was chosen as the Assistant Director for the senior class play. I began to spend more time on the school paper too. Henry and I got baptized by total immersion in the baptismal pool for the Latter Day Saints Church. I had to wear a kind of all white, cotton jumpsuit with nothing on underneath. I can remember what seemed to be a whole row of my Mormon male classmates waiting for me to be completely dunked. It was a very "see-through" material, I noticed as I passed a mirror in the dressing room after.

Henry was knocked out at a football game, suffered a concussion and many of us went to the hospital to make sure he would be alright. I sat by his bedside, holding his hand, jealously guarding the privilege I had of being his girlfriend. His popularity soared.

At school we went places together with other couples and on dates alone. We made out, and while enticed physically, never ventured past kissing and holding each other. I wrote in my diary that there was a good side of me and a bad side and I never crossed the boundaries (though Henry tried a few times). I wrote about it and the awakening sexy feelings I was having and how I knew Henry was feeling that way too in a letter to my good, far-away girlfriend, Carmen. Not having a stamp, I put the letter in the desk drawer in my bedroom. Sometime later, my father snooped in the drawer and read the letter while I was gone. He forced Henry and me to break up. I was no longer allowed to go out with him. I hated my father.

I spent several nights looking at the moon from my bedroom window sobbing. I loved Henry with all my heart, I was sure. I was devastated for months. For awhile Henry and I would look mournfully at one another passing in the halls, but soon he started dating one of the popular flag girls. I was devastated and felt humiliated too. I went on dates, but none of them interested me. I asked the Mormon class Vice-President to the senior prom. He accepted. I was nominated for Homecoming Queen and placed fifth. Henry was voted King. My senior year left me bereft. My heart was broken.

Henry married one of our classmates who I had never met, a quiet, southern girl. He became a heavy duty equipment operator after a stint in the Army. At high school reunions his tanned, lanky, muscular frame planted in cowboy boots always made it over to me for a dance and once, a kiss. He was a heavy drinker. Being a Mormon was apparently behind him . . . behind me, too. I no longer lived locally so I never saw him except every ten years at those reunions. We spent a little time talking at the last one. He had finally divorced and was alone. I was in a hurry to circulate and talk to my other classmates. When I left that night I saw Henry in the parking lot, his suede jacket close around his body, his cowboy hat squarely on his head. He was leaning into a car side window, talking to his ex-wife, smiling. He waved my way as I drove by.

When a letter from my mother arrived a few months later, a newspaper clipping fell out. The obituary described Henry as a wonderful father and grandfather, who played guitar and was a skilled craftsman of wood. Only sixty-six, he was adored by his grandchildren who loved listening to him sing as they had sat around campfires with him many times. He was survived by his sister, Rita.

I wish I had spent more time talking with him.

JUST ME

Patrick Wallace

I awaken in the middle of the night
to the sound of your voice,
only to discover,
It was just me.

The cool droplets I feel upon my face,
enhanced by the warm summer breeze were
really tears of joy – it was just me.

A french vanilla scent lingers,
With no apparent destination.
The sky adorns a sexy blue hue,
and I blush at the thought,
It was just me.

I'm guilty of being a dreamer,
sentenced to the confines of my imagination.
My mind, body, soul, and spirit divide the
Inheritance of what's left of *me…*

CALL ME GOD

Rocky McAlister

Call me God.

No, not me . . . the Guy in the big overstuffed chair on stage at the front of the auditorium; that's what He said after we all filed in behind St. Peter and took our seats in the auditorium.

My head ached, and I had to pee, but Pete said to hold it, that we had to complete our orientation before signing onto the Kingdom of Heaven; and, no he didn't have any sunglasses, and told me to just squint if the room was too bright. Yeah, it was easy for him to say . . . he was wearing these really slick aviator glasses that looked prescription.

But then a really cool Angels baseball cap with embroidered golden wings appeared in my lap and I snugged it down. That worked pretty well.

Now, I figured, all things considered in a cursory reflection upon my life, that just getting here was a plus, so I endeavored to persevere to hold my pee, but I did covet an aspirin.

The last "real" thing I remember was my face approaching the ground very fast and someone yelling for me to pull my emergency chute. At 200 feet, it seemed resistance was futile, and just closed my eyes and stopped screaming. Well, I think I stopped.

I mean, c'mon, I should've expected this to happen. My chute had this big dragon on it while everybody else had things like a Cowboys logo, a couple of soaring eagles and stuff. But oh no, mine had to have this dragon on it, and I kept telling them I didn't want that.

"Gee, how come, buddy. You afraid of dragons?" the instructor asked. I was the only one in class who didn't laugh, and I told him straight out, "Because sometimes the dragon wins." Now that I recall, I think I saw that on a shirt from some life insurance company.

Yeah, well, he thought that was cute, but he's not here in the white room waiting for God to speak. I should've done that tandem thing and ignore my buddies calling me a wuss.

I do have some regrets, though, like not listening to Margie this morning. She wanted to go shopping while I watched the boys. Was she kidding? The guys and I had this skydiving thing in the works for weeks. It was my chance of a lifetime. I also regret she refused my kiss goodbye when she left with the kids. She was sort of grouchy, now that I think back on it.

Anyway, one second I'm face-planting concrete at 125 miles an hour, and the next I'm standing outside the Pearly Gates with a bunch of other folks, who I bet were just as confused as I was to be here.

One guy kept feeling his chest for gunshot wounds he said he got from some cops during a bank holdup; he was really surprised to be up instead of down, you can bet.

I could tell the others were puzzled too and they sort of moved away from him and his gyrations, figuring he might rectify this mistake and they'd get taken down in the shuffle.

I was the only one with a headache; and I know, because I asked if anyone else had a headache or an aspirin and no one said yes. I guess I should've noticed the robes we all wore didn't have pockets, but I was a little dazed so I think a little slack was in order.

But ol' Pete seemed very disinterested in my condition. Apparently he doesn't know who I am.

So, anyhow, when we all get seated, pretty much everybody was quiet. Not too many of us were in a talkative mood, except the old guy who said he died in a hot tub with his young secretary. He was really grumpy and didn't care who knew it.

One guy did ask Pete if everyone had to wear the white robes, that they scratched, but when he never got an answer he looked pretty peeved about it and said something about the fashion sense up here being evil.

This guy, I'll call him Chuck, since I never did get his name, stayed mad all the way through this really cool choir act and didn't even clap when they finished and flew off. Even Pete's staring at him couldn't make him put his hands together. I haven't seen Chuck since God rose to address us.

Now, he didn't really get up or like out of his chair, mind you. The chair rose. I was applauding that when Pete shushed me and shook his head. But it was a great trick and I never did see any wires or anything, and He was a lot better than that guy in Vegas.

That's when He said, "Call me God."

Wow, what a great voice. I didn't see any microphones or even speakers anywhere in the auditorium, but His voice sounded like it was right inside my head. Inside! And just hearing it made my headache go away.

Anyway, He let His name sink in, and then pushed His big puffy sleeves up on his arms. I have no idea how He kept those sleeves up, which Pete whispered were flowing and not puffy . . . whatever, they didn't slide back down. Not during His whole talk. Oh, orientation, He called it.

"Welcome to Heaven, ladies and gentlemen."

I looked around. I was so surprised when I got here that I didn't even think about there being women here too, but there they were, lots of them.

I guess there were about five hundred of us in the room, and maybe a third were women. I tried to ask Pete if this was customary, but he ignored me. Again.

"Some of you are thinking you don't belong here," He said then, and there were a lot of heads bobbing up and down on that one, you can bet.

"My children, you all belong here. Trust Me on this. All that Heaven and Hell stuff was just to encourage you people to do your best while on Earth, be a team player. You know, that do unto others thing?"

He had that chair rocking all over above the stage, but He never seemed to be doing anything to control it; it just sort of swayed to His words.

"And that free will thing? Now, that's golden, and you'll all soon find out that the better your decisions were down on Earth, the better your assignment will be up here. Good works count."

That stirred up the crowd. Then some guy down in front jumped up then and argued that that wasn't fair, that we didn't know our behavior on Earth was going to determine our place up here in Heaven. That's discrimination, we should've been warned, he said. That got a lot of us laughing, like we weren't told about that all our lives? C'mon.

God was cool about it, though. He listened politely and asked the guy if he was a lawyer, and had he ever appeared before the Supreme Court, and this guy says yes, many times and that he never lost an argument.

I have no clue where this guy went, but if we thought the trick with the chair was slick, you should've seen our faces when this guy vanished. I guess he's with Chuck or something.

Anyway, the room got real quiet after that and God positioned His chair dead center above the stage. And then He sort of wiggled his fingers and the room's walls turned into windows. All around us. Holy cow! We were in space! The earth was way below and it looked so cool. And I wasn't the only one who gasped, I call tell you. It was spectacular and everyone said so!

"Do any of you want a glass of water or something?" He asked. Just about everyone raised their hand, and presto! a glass of the purest-looking water I ever saw just popped into my hand. I looked around and everyone was staring at their glasses of water.

"It's pure mountain spring water. Try it, you'll like it."

Man, did it ever taste good, but then I felt like I had to pee again and raised my hand. I wanted to see if He noticed me.

"Yes?" He looked right at me and I shivered all over.

"God, I have to pee."

"You do?" He cocked His head, kind of jauntily I thought. Wow, I didn't have to pee then.

"Thanks," I told Him straight out and in my best voice. He nodded, and I figured that even God likes to get a thanks once in a while.

"So, you're all probably wondering what this is all about. I'll keep it simple. Life on Earth was boot camp. You all were given opportunities to learn that following the rules I outlined for you were there for a reason."

He put his hand to His ear and nodded. "We originally had about fifty, but we edited it down.

"Anyway, the trials and tribulations you encountered over your lives were to test your mettle; victories gauged your humility, defeats your resilience.

"Your life was a string of parables . . . and yes, you got a sampling of them in the Bible, well the ones that didn't get altered over the years for a better market share."

He held up a pointer I hadn't seen before and He aimed it at a screen that appeared behind Him. He smacked it with His pointer then and zap! the screen filled with a picture of me! As a baby. Mom, dad!

I looked around and got the impression that everyone was seeing the same thing, only the picture was of them. That's really cool, I remember thinking at the time.

"You entered boot camp as a baby, and your parents were your drill instructors, just as their parents had mentored them and so on and so forth. You get the idea."

Everyone nodded, saying how great the pictures were and how wonderful it was to see the folks young again. Well, except the guy behind me; he complained he'd been an orphan and definitely had no fond memories of Headmaster Quint in Detroit and muttered how he could get that picture off the screen. God must've done something, because the guy relaxed and mellowed out pretty quick.

"You all grew up and learned, then graduated to adult and got to do the same for your own offspring. Although some of you too often shirked off your responsibilities on to your spouses."

Wow, I could feel His eyes drilling into my forehead. I thought I was going to get my headache back, but it didn't happen. I think I dodged a bullet on that one.

My life flashed by in pictures, showing me jumping off the roof in my Superman cape . . . breaking my arm.

"Everything you did resulted in either success or failure, and you learned something with each attempt at whatever you did.

"As I said, free will was the key and My way of determining how you made judgments and sought out solutions to problems, which as you all can see, resulted in you being here."

I have to admit, when I saw me standing in the open door of that plane, I shook my head. What was I thinking when I jumped out of that perfectly good airplane. What did I prove?

"You proved that your decision to leave that plane for a momentary thrill was not well thought out."

Now, I know nobody else heard that, but I saw lots of heads nodding that whatever they did to end up here was what He was telling them. This God guy was good.

"And yes, your family and friends will mourn your loss, and that too is part of boot camp. Everything you do has consequences. Remember that. If nothing else I say here today leaves an impression, take that truth with you to your next assignment.

"Think before you leap, Walter." His eyes were so intense on me that I wanted to duck behind the seat, but somehow I knew He'd still see me and I'd still feel He was directing His every word at me.

God rocked back in His chair and I thought He was going to dump Himself right onto the stage, but He stayed seated as it rotated completely around. I saw His sleeves not even budge, and seemed quite pleased when He saw our amazed expressions.

"That's gravity interrupted," He said. "You all will experience this new wonder, but then if you are at all familiar with space you know there is no gravity in space, well not enough to notice."

Some woman in back stood up and asked if she was still going to be an astronaut like she was back on earth.

"Lydia, my child, not only are you going to be an astronaut, but you are going to pilot your own starcraft and command a crew of twelve."

God then drifted up off His chair, and if anyone could pace in mid-air . . . well, He sure could.

"So, I'm certain that in addition to asking yourself how you made it here, let's go over some of the misconceptions some of my representatives have uttered over the millennia. Just to straighten out the record, so to speak.

"First off, you had to believe in Me to make it, right? Look around, half of you wondered if I really existed. Well, think about it for a second. You're here, I exist, and even that little bit of faith was enough. Period."

A glowing goblet appeared from somewhere and He took it in His hands and sipped from it, then left it hanging in mid-air as He continued to pace.

"Let's see, there were a bunch of floods but only Noah's made it to press; I thought it sent the right message for people to straighten out their lives or I'll do it again."

God looked way up in back. "Yes Charlie, I only flooded the world where people were taking notes. Didn't see any sense in flooding the whole place. Anyway, cleaning that up would've been a real headache."

"What about the virgins?"

We all tried to see who asked that question, but whoever it was no longer was with us.

"Sorry," said God. "He was in the wrong room."

God snapped His fingers then. "Now I know there are many religions. Except for some minor details and major misinterpretations, they all more or less try to prepare you for here."

He took a breath then. "And now I want you to meet my staff."

Two men appeared from stage right, drifted over to God, and then faced us. Man, these guys were slick looking too, but if I thought about it, God was a little taller than they were.

He pointed to the figure on his right. "This, of course, is my son."

Jesus bowed slightly, and extended His arms in welcome to us all, and darned if He didn't look just like a lot of His pictures. Wow, I could even see the scars on His wrists. I thought to ask why He hadn't fixed that, but decided against it.

"He's my right-hand in charge of day-to-day operations and personnel. Of course, I reserve the ultimate right to hire and fire." A nervous giggle swept the room, but it was over quick.

God then rotated to the left. "This is the Holy Ghost. He's in charge of combat operations and intelligence."

The Holy Ghost drifted forward and nodded.

"You'll hear that I can be tough, but if you're assigned to my unit, you'll be zipping all over the universe gathering information. It can be pretty exciting."

A woman two rows in front of me then stood. "Sir, why do you need intelligence and really . . . why do you have combat operations? I thought we'd left all that behind back down on Earth."

Jesus and Ghost faced God, then nodded in unison. God then faced us.

"Excellent question, Mary. My wife's name is Mary, by the way. A lovely name. Created it myself, actually."

When the throng began to mutter, He waved His hand and everyone quieted down. "Not THAT Mary. But she did select a couple of Marys to help my Son when He decided He wanted to visit Earth to help people learn the rules firsthand, and be a good role model. Set a living example, so to speak."

God looked at me again. "Yes, crucifixion was horrific, but it was His call to serve as an example of what it takes to endure . . . and your missions will contain perils. Trust me."

Ghost then glided forward. That's when I noticed he was wearing something under his robes, like maybe he was packing? Up here?

He looked at me and smiled. "Always be prepared. Life after death is full of surprises . . . and don't ever forget: We are at war with Evil, and have been for 4,000 years."

Wow, that goosed everybody, you can bet. Me too and I thought I was going to stain my robe, but God just chuckled and the feeling passed. Thank God; He nodded.

"Son," said God, motioning for him to take over the orientation.

Jesus held out his hands. "As you see, I still bear the scars of Evil . . . so endeavor to persevere.

"Now, you know all this stuff that there's a battle going on for your soul? Well, it's true. In fact, you're in your soul form now. Had you succumbed to Beelzebub and lost it during boot camp, you'd be in Hell's orientation hearing all about the virtues of Evil."

You can bet that got everyone squirming in their seats; I know I was sure happy to be Up instead of Down when pictures of fire and brimstone came on the screen and we could see people really hurting working in some kind of foundry or something. Big ugly dudes were whipping people, and man, there were a lot a flames and stuff.

Jesus eyed me. "Some of you are quite right that being here is better than being there. We are about to engage in the final battle for your soul, and that's the long and short of this war with Bub."

The room chuckled, and Ghost hovered forward. "We had several hundred names for the Devil to choose from when this war began, but we liked Bub because it annoys the Hell out of him."

Even God laughed at that, and the room shuddered. "He makes me laugh every time he uses that line."

"On a more serious note," said Jesus, "this is what you being here is all about.

"Finally," said a woman two rows in front of me. God glanced at her and wagged his finger. "Nancy, please, I'm not Henry."

Jesus strolled about the stage, well, about two feet above it actually. "Existence comes in three parts. Life On Earth, Life After Death, and then Life Eternal. It's our goal to have you all spend eternity here rather than enduring Bub's version, which is pretty nasty.

"As you saw, he's building his star fleet in foundries. Hot and sweaty even in your soul configuration," added Jesus. "And a lot of scourging." He cranked his shoulders at the memory.

"Here's the nitty gritty, people," said Ghost. "We have been building God's Legion ever since Bub left his assigned piece of the universe and came here carpetbagging God's souls so he could someday run everything . . . his way."

God then floated close to the front row. "By the way, this thing about me being omnipotent and that I can do anything is only partially right. If I had the power to stop Beelzebub, believe Me when I say I would have put a stop to his nonsense long ago."

"As it is," added Jesus, "Dad's just one of twelve Gods assigned a universe. But Bub's the only one with attitude. The others are staying out of it."

"So," said Ghost, leveling His stare at us, "don't go thinking that if you goof up, He's gonna automatically save you. The fact you're here goes to show that stuff happens."

God then outstretched His arms, and man, did that ever look imposing. "But I'm just a prayer away . . . just don't abuse the privilege," He said soothingly. "But we do have a wonderful health plan."

"And," added Jesus, "we have terrific mountain retreats if you need time to recover from injuries that aren't fatal . . . well, fatal again."

God looked at me again. "But you're all in My Legion now, and you all have a part to play in our battle."

Ghost leaned to His ear and whispered.

"Oh, right, actually you ARE parts of My starcraft. We don't actually build the ships; We create them."

He smiled at me then. "Your ship's commander will explain it all later."

Ghost then swept his finger across the audience. "But stay away from hull shield duty, so keep your noses clean up here and follow the rules."

Holy smokes! I grabbed the guy next to me and we shared a scary look as it suddenly struck us that this war between God and Evil was the real deal. I could get killed all over again? That sucked.

God soared about the room then, circling the perimeter; man, He had a flair for the dramatic.

"I know you're wondering where this all will end," He said, holding his arms out.

Wow, what a great image that made, Him winging above us and all. Gave me goose bumps, but I saw I wasn't the only one nodding and wanting to know.

"Victory over Beelzebub means you will move onto Life Eternal."

"It's on Eden, by the way," injected Jesus, "and a wonderful world to spend eternity. Lots of terrific things to do . . . forever."

God frowned at the interruption as Ghost punched Jesus on the shoulder, shushing him.

"Some will, alas, be lost forever during battle. But truly outstanding efforts, however, may result in some of you being rewarded with reincarnation to re-experience the human condition."

"What if we lose?" called out this really cute woman three seats to my right.

I think I was going to have questionable thoughts about her, but God put a stop to that. Man, He thinks of everything.

"Failure is not an option," barked Ghost. "Don't even think it. We have spent 4,000 years building this fleet to battle Bub once and for all out here, in this dimension, and we do not intend to lose."

"We will not lose," shouted Jesus, fisting the air.

"Yeah," added Ghost glumly, "or you'll all be making rope-soled sandals and you all know where that leads." God and Jesus eyed him, and shrugged toward us.

God returned to the stage then and hovered in front of us. "Your commanders will complete your orientation and issue you your assignments."

"Remember," said Ghost, "that you're in a different dimension here, so learn the rules, pay attention to your supervisors and be careful out there."

God retook his chair and then suddenly jumped up. "Oh, before I forget," He said, "this argument over Evolution and Creation that's going on back on Earth? Figure it out. You're here and Mr. Darwin is . . ." He eyed Ghost.

"Sabbatical on Galapagos," said Ghost. "Again."

Jesus then drifted to the edge of the stage. "Okay, Pop, if you're done."

God nodded solemnly. "Good luck to you all."

Man, why's He wishing us good luck? What the heck does He know that we don't? Everything, I heard inside my head. Wow.

"Okay, before we release you, please join us in our fight song."

A familiar marching band's trumpet-heavy flourish came from somewhere and I heard myself say, "Fight on."

God was tapping with both feet and nodding my way; huh, when did He change into a USC crimson and gold jersey?

No way.

He winked.

GHOST STORY

Virginia Hall

$\mathcal{A}$fter living in the same house for twelve years, Beth Martin was moving. She was cleaning, sorting, and packing. Her teenage daughter, Toni, spent the first weeks of summer vacation helping her mother. Boxes, labeled and sealed, were neatly piled up in the garage.

"I've had it for today," Beth said. "Let's head to the kitchen." Toni was quick to agree. After grabbing a drink, Beth brought out her address book. "Toni, I'm going to call and see if we can get a cabin at that resort I love. In a few more days, we'll be done with boxes."

"Fine by me, Mom," said Toni. "Seems like we've been packing forever."

Reservations were made for a week's stay in a one bedroom cabin, and soon they headed off. They spent the first afternoon settling in. The next evening, there was a bonfire down in the camping meadow. The fire was going strong when Beth and Toni joined the circle around the fire pit. Roasting marshmallows had to wait until the coals were ready. Someone suggested it was a good time for a ghost story.

For a few minutes, no one spoke. Then Beth said, "Well, it's not a scary story, but I could tell a real ghost story if you like." Everyone greeted her suggestion with enthusiasm, so she started.

"My story begins in early 1918. Billy Olsen, who grew up in the mountains just north of here, was going off to fight in the Great War. Before he left, he asked Emma Sue, his high school sweetheart, to marry him. He was blond, tall and slim; she was short, shapely and dark haired. They became engaged, and after

62

he left, Emma Sue wrote him letters and sent packages of cookies and candy. Once he was at the battlefront, Olsen didn't expect to get mail, but when his mail caught up with him again, the only letter he got was from his mother. She wrote to tell him that Emma Sue had run off with a traveling salesman. Needless to say, he was devastated.

When Olsen was back in the States, waiting to be discharged, the Army found out that he could type and put him to work. Then he got another piece of bad news. His little sister had died during the 1919 influenza epidemic. Well, he was so depressed he didn't want to go home. He ended up staying in the army and making a career of it. When he retired, he moved to Buckley, just down the road from here. He got part-time work in the general store.

Olsen bought a house at the edge of town. It was small, but comfortable. Then, after living there for a few years, strange things started to happen. The first odd thing was the occasional smell of something sweet—like gingerbread or cookies baking. It puzzled him, but didn't really worry him. When the footsteps started a month later, he was more upset. For a few weeks, nothing would happen, but then it would all start up again. Next, he started feeling soft breezes at unexpected times. It was very strange!

Now, while he had considered it, he hadn't mentioned any of this to anyone. He didn't want to be teased or sound like an idiot. The final straw was the appearance of a vision, something running away from him. It was always a glimpse of a white gossamer dress worn by a dark-haired spirit, a spirit that could disappear right through a wall.

The next time he was in town, Olsen announced to his friends, "I have a ghost in my house. It doesn't come too often, but. . ." Then he told them of all the things that had happened.

His pal Fred laughed. *"Oh, that's just Widow Jones. She hasn't haunted anyone for, oh, nine months or so. She haunts someone for a while, and then she's gone. Sounds like she's moved into your place."*

"Who's Widow Jones?" Olsen asked.

"Well, she came here right after the Depression. Her oldest son got a job in town and moved his mother and brother here. They all lived together; she did some mending and sewing to make a little money. We heard that her husband had left her, but she claimed she was a widow, so we called her that. She was fine until both her boys were killed in an accident. She took it hard and started avoiding people. Everyone felt sorry for her. She sold the house and moved into a tiny cabin, still sewing and mending. She didn't talk much but to thank people for their help, she'd started making gingerbread cookies. Any special occasion and there she'd be, delivering cookies.

Olsen said, "I always liked gingerbread cookies. They smell good, too. It's just spooky to smell them when there aren't any there."

"One sad thing is that Emma Sue never gave anyone her recipe," added Fred. "Everyone agreed that hers was the best."

Olsen was stunned. "Emma Sue, did you say? I was jilted by my fiancé when I was off at war, and her name was Emma Sue. She even used to mail me gingerbread cookies. Then she ran off with a salesman."

Fred said, "Looks like you have her now. I bet she'll never leave. You finally got her." All his friends laughed and laughed. And that's the end of the story."

When Beth had finished, there was a pause.

The lady next to Beth said, "That's a good tale." A younger voice added, "That's sad." Someone else commented, "I don't believe in ghosts, but I believe in ghost stories." By then it was time for marshmallows, and people started talking about the resort and local sights to visit. The fire was now just coals and the night was cool. Soon the party was over.

Walking back to their cabin, Toni said, "You never told me that story, Mom."

"Well, I just made it up."

Toni stopped walking. "What do you mean? You just made it up right now?"

"Well, yes. You must remember, after ten years of volunteering at Library Hour, I have lots of experience telling stories to children. Tonight I just imagined a setting and my main characters, one to be haunted and the other to do the haunting. The rest just came to me as I went along."

As Toni started walking again, she said, "Mom, you're amazing!" That ended the conversation, but as they reached their cabin, Beth heard Toni repeat very softly, "Amazing."

QUICK STOP

Bonnie Darlene

*A*lex snuggled up into a ball inside his warm, soft comforter while riding in the 'way-back' of his parent's station wagon. The constant drone and vibration of the car's engine lulled him in and out of a dream-like state as he sank deeper into the clutches of sleep. He awoke with a sharp jolt when his head knocked against the back of the front seat and the car came to an abrupt stop.

The rhythmic swishing of the wiper on the window let him know it was raining. Back under the covers he dove as he listened to his mother's voice coming from the front seat.

"Alex has been asleep for hours . . . do you think we should wake him so he can use the bathroom?"

"Oh, let the boy sleep." His father answered while yawning. "He'll be okay . . . besides he'd get drenched in this downpour. That's all we need . . . a wet whining little boy all the way home. But we'd both better get a cup of coffee if we're going to stay awake for the next four hours."

Both car doors slammed as his parents made a mad dash for the station's office. A minute later he heard the attendant putting the gas nozzle in the side of the car, turning on the pump, then, after a few minutes, running back into the dry office. Alex put his head up, fully awake now. He put his face to the window and looked towards the station's office. He could see his parents talking to the man through the large office window. He dove back under his covers and lay still for moment while thinking about what his dad had said to his mom.

"I'm nearly eight years old, I'm not little, and I don't whine!" He voiced out loud to a cold empty car.

Alex sat a moment, thinking, head still covered by the blanket. He popped his head out after deciding to sneak out of the car, use the bathroom, and get back in the car before his parents returned. He opened the door, jumped out, slammed the door shut, and ran towards the men's room on the side of the station. As he dashed by the office, he noticed his parents sipping coffee, but they didn't see him.

The bathroom door was locked. He put his ear to it and listened to water running inside. He shivered while he waited, leaning into the wall to shield his body from the falling rain. The handle clicked and the door swung open. A man came out, looked down and put his hand on Alex's damp head.

"Your turn, kid." He rushed by Alex and into the rain. Alex closed and locked the door. Looking around, he noticed that the bathroom was surprisingly clean, not like the other gas station bathrooms he had been in during this trip. When he finished, he washed his hands and headed out the door, taking a quick glance into the office window. Not seeing his parents, he ran towards the gas pumps. There were no cars at the pumps.

"They're gone! They've left me . . . I'm all alone."

Alex sat down in the rain between two pumps as panic overtook him. Tears trickled down his cheeks. He soon felt a firm warm hand on his shoulder.

"What's wrong son?"

A tall man with hands smelling of gasoline loomed over him. Looking up, Alex was only able to squeak out between sobs, "They . . . left . . . me!"

The man motioned towards the office. "Let's get inside out of this rain, son . . . before we are drenched."

Alex followed the man as they both ran. Entering the door, the man motioned towards a large desk chair.

"Have a seat, son . . . and don't worry about your folks. They'll soon realize you're not in the car and be back for you." He handed Alex some paper towels. "Here, use these to dry your hair."

Will they? Alex thought to himself as he dried his hair while still shivering, even in the warm office. *Will they be back for me? . . . How will they know where I am? Maybe Dad will be so mad he won't come back for me.*

He looked up into the man's kind face. Trying to be brave, he spoke out. "Sure . . . I'm not worried . . . they'll be back." His voice quivered.

"Hey, don't worry, son. Everyone in Barstow knows where Phil Pacina's '91 Mobil Station is. They'll remember it was just before driving over that large trestle bridge over the railroad yard.

"My name's Phil. What's your name, son?"

"Alex . . . my name's Alex."

"Well, Alex, I have a lot of work to do and I could use an extra hand tonight. Do you think you could help me out?" The man reached for a shirt that was hanging on a hook and handed it to the boy.

"Take off your wet shirt and put this on. I'll hang your shirt near the heater to dry." Alex quickly nodded his head, reaching for the warm dry shirt with a flying red horse above the pocket. He was soon busy washing the office windows, sweeping the floor, and stacking oil cans on a shelf in neat rows. In between jobs, he listened to Phil talk about when he was a young lad, back in Pennsylvania, spending summers on his Grandma Sara's farm in Belfonte.

Phil was a kind, older man, and didn't seem like a stranger at all. Alex was glad to have something to do. In between jobs, Alex would begin to feel anxious, but then he would look up into Phil's smiling face and soon he would be listening to yet another story about how Phil and his brother, Jim, drove to California in a Model A Ford after the stock market crash when Phil lost all his college money. When he first came to Barstow, in 1930, he worked on that bridge over the railroad yard. Soon he was hired as the desert reporter for the San Bernardino Sun newspaper while working as a night clerk at the Mel-rose Hotel.

Alex liked hearing about the *good old days.* The hours went by fast and he found himself curling up in the office chair and beginning to doze off, wrapped in Phil's warm jacket.

I guess I could stay with Phil if they don't come back . . . he seems to really like me, and could use my help. A tear slowly ran down his cheek. He soon fell fast asleep.

Alex had been sleeping for a couple of hours when he felt a gentle nudge and heard the sound of Phil's voice.

"Alex . . . son . . . wake up. Your folks are here! I told you they'd be back."

Alex opened his eyes to see Mom and Dad standing over him. Tears streamed down his mother's face as she reached for him. Dad's smile was the most welcomed sight the small boy could imagine.

"Alex, we thought we'd lost you! We got as far as Cucamonga and our turn-off at Foothill Blvd. Mom turned around, telling you 'Look at all the grapevines in the vineyard, Alex. They stretch for miles!' She reached over the front seat and tugged at the blanket, but you weren't there! We had to turn around and go all the way back over Cajon Pass to come back for you."

Mom cried out as she grabbed Alex, hugged him so tight that he could hardly breathe.

"We thought you were asleep under your blanket." His father's voice was gentle and reassuring as he reached for his son.

"You've got quite a boy there! He's been a big help to me." Phil tousled Alex's hair and handed him his dry shirt.

Alex's dad reached for his wallet in his back pants pocket. "I want you to have something for all of your trouble and for taking such fine care of our boy."

" I wouldn't hear of it. Alex has been quite a help to me. I should be paying him."

As they pulled out of the station, Alex pointed to the left and asked his dad, "Could we go back over the bridge down there? The one that's over the railroad yard. I want to see it one more time and tell you something about it."

Alex's father and mother smiled. The car pulled out, turned left and soon was driving over the trestle bridge. Alex rolled down his window and poked his head out.

"Dad, did you know that Phil worked on this bridge a long time ago? And . . . hobos used to ride on the trains during the depress . . . depress-shun? When the train stopped here, the hobos . . . some people called them tramps . . . they would walk to Phil's home. Phil's wife . . . her name is Helen . . . she'd give them something to eat."

"No, Alex, I didn't know that." Dad smiled again at his young son's enthusiasm. The early morning sun sparkled in the rain drops that danced on the bridge's metal trestle. The wind blew through Alex's hair as he peered out the open window. He could see the hills blushing gold from the rising sunlight. The world seemed changed somehow. Magical.

"Wait, Dad! Go back. Go back to the station."

"You forget something, Alex? Don't worry. We have to go back in that direction anyway to get home." After crossing the bridge he turned around and headed back over the bridge towards the '91 Mobil Station.

After their car pulled in, Alex glimpsed Phil walking towards the office. He quickly poked his head and shoulders out the window, waved his arms and yelled, "Hey Phil! I'll be back when I need a job . . . that is, if you can still use an extra hand."

Phil turned, smiled and waved while yelling back, "You do that, Alex! You do that. I'll be waiting here for you, son. Good help is hard to find these days."

MY BROTHER

John Margotta Ferrara

Dedicated to Lt. Col. Richard Pifer, U.S. Army Retired

I watch my brother as he sleeps,
His teeth are clenched and his mouth is tight.
Shadowy grimaces drift across his dreams,
My Brother has been to war, you see.

His lips move incoherently,
Meanings that wander and are lost within.
Lost it seems in a litany of fire and steel,
My Brother has been to war, you see.

In the sun we walk and talk,
We talk of weather and memories,
Of young girls, baseball and rainy days,
My Brother has been to war, you see.

His laughter is loud and without form,
At times words spill over his lips in a gush.
Yet, he does not laugh at the three-legged dog,
My Brother has been to war, you see.

I am not privy to the private thoughts,
Locked in a dark and private vault.
He holds the key to his own secluded hell,
My Brother has been to war, you see.

FEATURE STORY

M. M. Gornell

*J*ake guessed he was missing a decent sunset—but didn't much care. For years now, he considered happenings outside of work and *Arnie's* of little importance.

Besides, it was the third Wednesday of the month—in this case May—and tradition needed to be dutifully honored. He and his lifetime friend, Marcus, would eat, drink, smoke, and chew-the-fat in the back of the bar. In the dark, in *their* booth.

"Glad you could make it," Jake had greeted Marcus almost an hour earlier. "Would hate to have to eat by myself."

"Wouldn't miss it," Marcus agreed.

Now, Jake half smiled and unconsciously patted his stomach—*a good and filling meal*. He knew he should lose a few pounds, but he felt good, and easily ignored the reality he should weigh at least thirty pounds less. Fortunately, he'd aged well on other fronts—grey sideburns accentuating a full head of black hair, his face only slightly marred by the passage of time, and no neck jowls, *thank goodness*.

But with Marcus, Jake uncharitably mused, *I can see what the years have done.* Sure, his friend remained svelte, but time had bent his shoulders, thinned his hair, and marked his face with age spots and deep crevices.

Time spares no man.

Arnold "Arnie" Jr., proprietor and barkeep, appeared and placed fresh drinks on the table between the two men. "Might be nice to watch the evening sky, breath in the air," he said. "You know, see the colors. Lots of red this evening. Customers out front say it's real pretty," he eyed their ashtray, "and fresh."

73

Jake recognized the teasing twinkle in the eyes of the pleasant-faced and good-natured young man. For sure, it was probably true that outside the backroom of Arnie's Bar and Grill, *anywhere* in the valley, *anyone* who took the time to stop, look, and take in their surroundings would be rewarded. When he'd arrived, the rain, constant throughout the day, had finally stopped, leaving a near perfect clear-blue pallet across the horizon—ripe for a perfect sunset. And to breathe was to take in crisp Pacific Northwest Spring air, still moist from daylong rain. Indeed, even back here in the depths of Arnie's inner sanction, he could almost hear the Snoqualmie River, flush with the day's rain, rushing joyfully on towards the Falls.

Before turning and leaving, Arnie added, "There's also a rainbow stretching across the valley. Mount Si is looking pretty darned spectacular."

Jake nodded toward Arnie's retreating back. "Gets more and more like his grandpa every day, don't ya think?" He didn't wait for a reply. "But back to your question before our steaks arrived. Me retire? What the hell would I do?" He sighed heftily. "For goodness' sake, you think I should fence up everything and raise llamas?"

For a second, his deceased wife Deirdre's face flashed across his mind's eye. She'd been the one who wanted to "go rural," move to Josiah, buy land, have a huge spread. Deidre had also insisted on no fencing, wanting the wild critters to come in close.

"I'm still a city boy," Jake added, fighting down the catch in his throat that always came with her memory. "You know that." He and Marcus had been friends for over thirty years—both majoring in journalism—way-back-when in Chicago.

A million years ago, a million miles away. Now, it was back to just the two of them again. The rest of their friends and journalistic comrades accumulated over the ensuing years had moved on—or passed on. And, in two days time there would only be one. Marcus was retiring, maybe heading down to the Mojave Desert he loved, and often visited. The Wednesday night gang at Arnie's Bar and Grill would be no more.

"The 'in' thing, I hear, raising llamas." Marcus tapped ash from his cigar. "Me, I'm gasin' up the motor home and Fran and I are taking off and looking at California desert property." He paused a moment. "Guess I'm lucky," he finished softly.

"Journalists don't retire—they just die in their boots at their typewriters."

Marcus snorted a responding laugh.

Jake would sorely miss his friend. He could always count on Marcus to appreciate his smart-aleck comments. And more importantly, Marcus had helped compensate for his shortsightedness in office politics. He gulped more than half his drink in honor of their friendship.

As if reading his mind, Marcus said with a sigh, "You know they're at your heels."

"Nothing new." Jake smiled wryly. "The jackals are always nipping at me." He tapped his pack of cigarettes on the table, selected one, and lit up for the third time that evening. Then holding his almost empty glass in the air, he motioned to a passing Arnie for a refill. Bourbon and water on the rocks.

Marcus's tone turned serious. "I need to be sure you know what you're facing this time." He leaned forward and narrowed his eyes. "I'm talking about your new boss, and his two clones."

Jake watched as a thick trail of smoke from Marcus's cigar spiraled upward and almost got sucked into Arnie's new ventilation system—but not quite. They were breaking the law, and he knew it was a matter of days before Arnie lowered the no-smoking boom. "You think I don't know they want to get rid of me?" *I'm not blind.* "Nothing would satisfy them better than my retiring." He could see the three of them—his boss and two sycophants, dressed in their casual slacks and sweaters— so full of themselves. He made a self-deprecating face and added, "I have to give them their due, though. They're bright, they're enthusiastic, and some of their ideas aren't half bad."

"And they know how to use the computers," Marcus quipped.

They both laughed. Jake's new drink came, and Marcus ordered coffee to go with his cigar. They'd already devoured eleven-ounce steaks, baked potatoes saturated with butter and sour cream, garlic bread, and apple pie *à la-mode*. Out front, in the newly remodeled part of Arnie's, the "Light Cuisine" was the most popular. *Who knew*, Jake thought, *two dinosaurs were sitting in the back*—the familiar smell of old wood, smoke, and liquor their only company—and struggling to hold on to something Jake was hard-pressed to articulate.

After a moment, he said, "What are they going to do, fire me?"

Marcus looked down and rubbed his hand across the dark mahogany tabletop, still shining with a rich and deep vibrancy despite its years. He didn't speak.

But Jake understood. "You're kidding? They'd really try to fire me? Fire *me?*"

"I know." Marcus shook his head in sympathetic disbelief. "To some folks you are *The Sentinel*. Hell, you broke all the major stories the paper has run over the last fifteen years."

"Not recently."

"Well, so you might not be the hotshot reporter you use to be, but who is? And just because a man has a dry spell . . . ," his voice trailed off.

"Age discrimination," Jake mumbled.

"Hard sell, since you're eligible for full retirement. They wouldn't actually fire you, but, you know, forced retirement."

"The same thing."

"Yeah, the same thing." Marcus leaned across the table, and lowered his voice considerably. "At my retirement party, did you notice Marshall and me talking?"

Jake nodded.

"You know what we were talking about?" Marcus squinted his eyes, tightened his shoulders, and leaned in closer. "What he wants is for somebody to find out who murdered Eddie Holiday. He'd give his eyetooth to get an exclusive on that one. Yep, it would be a *Feature Story* alright." He relaxed and straightened himself. "The reporter solving that one could call his own shots for quite awhile in the future."

"Eddie Holiday," Jake repeated the name. Familiar, but he couldn't quite place the context.

"Mr. Edward Eugene Holiday," Marcus said. "You remember, just two months ago? Died right down the road from you. Car supposedly skidded off the ledge on Cedar Falls Road. The man nobody liked?"

In a flood, the incident came back to him. All the papers, especially the local rag—which he, the big city journalist, was rather fond of—had gone on and on with interviews of people claiming they'd known Eddie Holiday and how cantankerous, unfriendly, and sometimes downright rude they thought the man had been. But Jake didn't remember the murder part, just a tragic accident; driving too fast on a wet road, took the curve too fast. Jake had a lot of contacts out there, but not one had mentioned murder, not even Slippery Steve, who was always looking under rocks.

"You know, Marshall has ears everywhere," Marcus continued. "And when a man like Eddie, who made a lot of enemies, dies suddenly, there's bound to be some talk."

Not really, Jake thought. *A lot of unlikable people die suddenly and nobody gives a damn.* "Must be more than that."

Marcus smiled slyly. "Are you getting interested? Don't want you going out without a fight. Seems the ME can't say for sure what killed Eddie. Could have been from the crash, like a concussion or broken neck, or could have been from the flames. On the other hand, could *not* have been from the crash, like somebody knocked him on the head, or cut his brake fluid line— or both. You see, Eddie was burned up pretty badly and the car was a mess." He finished with a grimace. "Not much to examine I'm told, even with all the modern forensic doodads and tests."

Jake remembered the fire truck sirens. It had happened late at night, wakening him out of a sound sleep. *How could I forget?* "Did they use the State Patrol Crime lab?" he asked.

"Yep, and they came up with nothing."

"Who benefits?"

"Nobody, seems like." Marcus shook his head. "Had a million-dollar life insurance policy, but it went to some save-the-something-or-other foundation. No wife. No kids. No sisters or brothers. Parents dead."

"Insurance paid the claim?"

"Yep, and far as I know there's no suspicious adjuster out there hammering away on this one." Marcus fell silent and waited.

Jake lit another cigarette and stared into space for a moment. For twenty-five years he'd trusted his gut to tell him what to pursue and what not. It was like he could smell a story, especially a crime, but this one—nothing. Marcus was right; it could be murder. "I think I've lost the touch," he finally said. "I should have been sniffing around this myself." *No wonder they want to send me out to pasture.*

"Who cares." Marcus waved his hand. "Now that you've got the message. Get on it. Find out what happened to Eddie Holiday and put those punk kids in their place."

Jake wondered if outside their one last smoking booth, in the one last tavern in Josiah, the rainbow and setting sun had finally faded into night.

"And," Marcus added, "there are the small items of no brake or skid marks at the scene. And my friend, the little-known fact Eddie Holiday never drove at night."

***

"Come in," she said pleasantly. "I'm the caretaker, Sandra Towns."

Jake said, "Thanks," and stepped into the entryway. He'd talked to her the night before, explained who he was, said he wanted to do a piece on Eddie Holiday. She'd agreed to his dropping by; even said she had wondered why no one bothered talking to her before now. He'd ended the call somehow knowing he'd hit the jackpot. This woman was the key—he felt it in his bones.

This afternoon, in person, Jake found her smile warm, comfortable, and surprisingly agreeable. Middle-aged, round, and short, Sandra, however, was not what he'd expected. Indeed, he'd visualized someone younger, thinner, taller—sexier. He was disappointed—egocentric and unkind he knew—*especially* from a portly old dog like himself.

Her house looked remodeled, or was it technically a renovated barn? Regardless, he was *glad* for the quiet, *glad* to get away from her noisy dogs. From the start of the final turnoff, about half a mile before he'd reached the house, five or so canines had "escorted" him—running along the inside of the fence line, barking and yapping the whole way.

"Come on back to the kitchen-nook for tea," she offered. "You look like a coffee man, but I think this afternoon calls for tea."

A thin Calico cat appeared from nowhere and unsuccessfully attempted to rub against Jake's legs as he followed Sandra to her kitchen. Aside from the difficulty of cuddling moving targets— Jake's legs—the cat also seemed a little tipsy.

"Is your cat well?" he asked, while taking an offered seat at a large oak table. From where he sat, through a glass wall of French doors, he could see a large fenced area—maybe a couple acres, and rimmed with a thick hedge.

Sandra laughed. "She's love-starved, I think. And blind in one eye." She sat a tea service on the table. "You like cats?"

Something about the way she asked prompted Jake to answer with a quick and emphatic, "No." It wasn't that he *disliked* them, but he hadn't had pets since he was a kid. They tied you down, and when they died—well, he didn't like that part one bit.

She smiled. "Dogs?"

On cue, an old black and tan German shepherd awoke from his resting place in front of the kitchen stove, raised his head quite slowly, and tried to focus on Jake. His eyes were on the cloudy side, and grey hairs protruded from his snout.

"No," he answered again. "But, you evidently do."

The dogs that had followed along the road were now out back, mostly tussling and playing. One, though, a curious short and chubby black mixed-breed with a spotted tongue had taken station outside at the French door nearest Jake, laid down, and stared in at him.

Jake ignored her, somehow he knew the dog was a she, and said, "I'm not an animal person. I'm not really a tea person, either." It sounded ungracious, even to his own ears. But he hadn't driven halfway to Snoqualmie Pass to sip tea and pet animals. He was there to find out who killed Edward Eugene Holiday. Sandra, though, was not to be rushed. Tea and shortbread cookies first.

"Eddie was a great man," she finally said after they settled down across the table from each other, steaming cups of Jasmine tea before them.

Sandra had large brown eyes, a few age lines starting to tell their story, a generous mouth used to laughing, and thick black hair that framed her face like a bowl. *A pretty face,* Jake thought, then wondered why he had.

"You don't smile much, do you?" she said.

"What?" he asked, caught unaware.

"I know, sometimes it seems like there's nothing left to smile about. So many disappointments in life. But still," she stopped, her eyes piercing into his.

Jake refused to let her see "into" his soul, and said quickly and firmly, "I think Eddie Holiday was murdered." His interviewing style had always been snappy and direct, sometimes catching people unawares, surprising them, and consequently drawing out information a softer approach would not have gotten.

"You know that cat needs a home," Sandra said. "And that German shepherd over there. He's old and arthritic. And you see that little black dog looking at you through the door? Trying to find her a home, too."

What planet is this woman on? Jake wondered. He'd just proclaimed Eddie Holiday was murdered—and she wanted to talk about cats and dogs?

"That's what I do, you know. Find homes for all these lovely critters."

Jake didn't know what to do but play along. He knew in his gut this crazy woman would eventually say something worthwhile. "You probably think Eddie's death was an accident."

She was still looking directly into his eyes. "Of course not. Eddie never drove at night."

Then they sat in silence for what seemed to Jake an eternity.

Finally, Sandra spoke again, softly, almost musically. "I'm going to tell you some things. When I'm finished, you fit the pieces together however you want. It'll be your story, you tell it as you wish. I won't be telling anyone else Eddie's story. Ever. Just you, and just this once."

Jake held his breath.

"Eddie Holiday loved animals. He also hated people who abused them. Not many people liked Eddie because he usually spoke his mind. Most of us don't really want to hear the truth, no matter how much we proclaim we do."

"But the animals, well, the animals loved Eddie. And he loved them. We've had up to thirty cats here, and, oh, maybe twenty dogs. We've rescued birds, pigs, skunks, raccoons, geese. You get the idea. And all of 'em, Eddie and I, we found them good homes."

"And we've gotten by with help from volunteers, donations, hard work. We were happy. Eddie, me, and the animals."

Then Sandra smiled and winked. For a blink of a second, it made her look childlike and innocent. "Don't get me wrong, we weren't romantically involved, but we were good friends— *friends of the mind*, if you know what I mean."

He didn't really, but kept quiet and waited.

"Eddie often said he worried about what would happen to the animals 'after he left.' That's the words Eddie used for dying. He never could use the word, *die*, even after they told him."

"After they told him what?"

"That he had inoperable cancer. Pancreatic I believe it was." She looked away for a second, her eyes moist.

"I'm sorry," Jake said. He genuinely was. Deidre had died of cancer. This, he understood.

"Eddie Eugene Holiday's death was not an accident," she said. "Neither was Eddie murdered. Do you understand?"

He asked softly, "Did Eddie's insurance policy pay a premium for accidental death?"

"Yes."

"That would take care of a lot of animals."

"Yes. Yes it would."

Then Sandra told him about how hard it was to get all the fencing in. *And* he told her about all his years at *The Sentinel*. *And* she told him about the llama that spat in Eddie's face, *and* the horse that kicked Eddie in the butt. *And* he told her about thirty years of marriage with Deidre.

They talked through the afternoon. They talked through dinner. And they talked well into the night.

***

Jake stood next to his brand new wheelbarrow for a moment, making time to take in the morning. The all night rain had stopped, and a frail morning sun, slowly but most assuredly gaining in radiance had started its path across a pallid sky. No anomalous rainbow greeted him, but still, very nice indeed.

He breathed in deeply, filling his lungs with spring air, still moist but containing a promise of dryness. Jake was confident a respite from the damp was in the cards. He saw in the distance, Mt. Si, uncluttered by the low hanging morning clouds that were so fond of shrouding its peak.

Nearer, the Snoqualmie River rushed on as usual. Its sound, distant, but comforting. And where he stood, for the first time, he viewed, he inhaled, he experienced Deidre's land—now his land. And there, in that second in time, he knew and understood he'd made the right decision.

"Ah, Deidre," he told her across time and unknown dimensions. "You'd be proud."

Jake lit a cigarette, then put it out after one puff—wondering for the zillionth time if he would ever be able to quit. Then slowly and resolutely he pushed his wheelbarrow forward, heading to the edge of his property. He'd start right in front, begin at the beginning. *The way it should be.*

Sandra was coming over that evening, a quiet dinner, some music, congenial conversation. And tomorrow, Marcus and Fran were visiting with Route 66 pictures from the Mojave Desert.

Jake would never ask Sandra if Eddie committed suicide alone, or with her help. Either way, it was insurance fraud, and he didn't want to know. *Pursuing this story was over.* Eddie Eugene Holiday died an accidental death—on purpose; and Jake Andrew Banks had retired on purpose—accidentally.

In his wheelbarrow was a roll of six-foot high wire fencing, a couple four-by-four wooden fence posts, a pair of heavy gloves, and brand new wire cutters. He decided to haul what he needed little by little, rather than drive the truck down across the lawn.

As Jake walked forward, a small black dog with big black spots on its tongue ran circles around him and the supplies he pushed. To their rear, an old black and tan German shepherd, legs stiff with arthritis, but nonetheless functioning just fine, followed at a slow but steady pace. A calico-spotted cat with only one eye, tail standing high, brought up the rear. *All friends of the mind.*

Jake smiled.

UP IN THE AIR WITH NO WHERE TO LAND, YET!

Robert Foster

I usually have my feet planted firmly on the ground. My career gave me the chance to do something that fueled my passion. As an elementary school principal, I enjoyed seeing students learn and grow. I was thrilled to see new teachers blossom into highly efficient facilitators of learning. Often, I was able to help parents deal with issues, such as learning disabilities in their children that were difficult to face. The look on their faces as their child started to become successful in school was worth any effort I gave.

Feelings of being successful in my career were deeply satisfying. It gave me a boundless amount of energy, or so it seemed. Long hours of work sped by quickly. The results of my work propelled me further. A vague but calm sense of success was a foundation that gave me a real sense of stability in my life.

Working with teachers, parents, and students added to my collaboration with other administrators in giving me a sense of belonging to something bigger than myself. This educational community brought me real satisfaction.

I knew one day I was going to have to retire and let go. The thought of that day seemed like a mere reflection in a passing moment. In the back of my mind, I was preparing for this day two or three years in the future. Everything was running according to plan. My world was going to change soon, and I had no clue that a swift change lay dead ahead.

The actual details of this change are irrelevant. The events were beyond my control. Political actions in education are usually like that. I do confess to being angry. It felt like I was placed in a corner, forced to make a decision that was not something I wanted to do yet. In my mind, retirement was still years in the future. Reality was far different. The tethers of my life were cut very quickly. I had no clue as to the ramifications that early retirement brought into my life.

Gone were the long hours of work to help children learn and grow. Gone were the hugs and appreciation they gave so freely. Teachers that were like my daughters kept in touch, but my daily influence on their career was no longer there. I was unable to help parents in their time of need. I no longer belonged to an educational community. My passion was drained. Success was but a memory. Life was depressing.

My balloon was released to float in any direction the wind blew. The tethers no longer kept my feet planted firmly on the ground. I bumped into trees, rocks and hillsides struggling to gain control of my life. I floated high in the air and dragged low, almost touching the ground. The direction of my life was at the whim and will of powers over which I had no control. It seemed that my efforts were useless in trying to stabilize my balloon as it careened through the air, providing a bumpy ride.

Many books are written about retirement. The reality of retiring is something that is quite different from what is written down to help you through one of life's major transitions. My challenge is to find a suitable landing place where I can tether my lines to the ground securely. I need to locate a place to plant my feet firmly on the ground. This place will not be working in schools again. The economy is such that good positions are hard to find. My retirement was most likely a move to reduce the school district's budget. There is no pleasure in knowing that I am not the only one going through this dramatic change.

Now my balloon is floating through life. I have gained enough control to avoid the harrowing experiences of depression and helplessness. My search for belonging, success, and the motivation that drove my passion in life have eluded me so far, but not entirely.

I have been able to cast out a few lines in search of a landing field. The gym has helped me meet other retirees who have a goal to be healthier and stronger. This goal is aligned with one of my new goals. Joining a group of retirees in counseling has helped me keep my focus on finding the right direction to steer my balloon. Writing a book that deals with an educational theme has provided me with a degree of satisfaction. It also helps to fuel my passion in life. These are all good initial attempts to create my new life so that it is satisfying.

I am still up in the air in my balloon. Finding a place to land has not happened yet. However, I will find it!

SHUTTLED
(for Jeffrey)

Rusty LaGrange

If wings that soar
men to the moon,
could hover soft
and touch my cheek,
then I, too wish
the ride be swift
and dauntless carry
my eyes up too,
and view the earth
through cosmic tears.

The voyage in my heart
beats strong. Soon the time
will tell, when astronauts
devoured skies beyond
our Universe.

HAIKU TIME

Michael J. Hawley

The clock ticks and ticks.
Here today, gone tomorrow.
Time will never stop.

DID YOU FORGET?

Hazel Stearns

nn MacCallum was in the moderate stages of Alzheimer's. This week, she had threatened one of her grandsons with a pair of scissors, called her daughter Kate's office at least 150 times with no recollection, and developed a new habit of spitting food on the floor. Each day seemed to bring something new. This morning, Kate had answered the phone to hear her mother's caregiver say, "We have a problem. Ann's sneaking cigarettes into her room at night and smoking in bed. I found burned matches on the carpet and butts in an ashtray on the bedspread."

Kate pulled into the driveway at her mother's house with mixed emotions. Ann was no longer the person she had known...no longer the tough controlling woman who had spanked her, coached her, taught her . . . no longer the woman from under whose thumb she had longed to escape as a child. Instead, the once hard-working, strong-willed woman was spiraling toward a vegetable state. She couldn't help herself, and her family and friends could only stand by and watch the deterioration.

Not visiting her mother made Kate feel guilty. Seeing her made Kate feel angry—angry that after a lifetime of struggling to gain dignity and respect, a human being could be reduced to a glassy-eyed, zombie-like creature who spat food, drooled, needed diapers and, most of the time, recognized no one.

At the door, Kate greeted the stout sixty-year-old caregiver. "Hi, Ethel. How's she doing?" Inside, Kate unloaded her things on the kitchen counter, out of her mother's reach, the way she would to prevent a baby from taking her keys or ransacking her purse.

"Pretty good," Ethel replied. "She ate a banana, drank some milk and swallowed a few spoons of Cream-of-Wheat before she pushed her bowl off the table." She shook her head and smiled.

Somehow, Ethel always remained cheerful, though Kate didn't know how. Kate knew she could never give her mother the care and compassion she needed and marveled at the people who did.

Kate pursed her lips. "Well, we have to do something about her smoking habit, but I don't know what. I hate the thought of taking away her cigarettes. They're the only thing she looks forward to."

"I know," Ethel said. "I'm just afraid she's going to set fire to the bed with her in it. How long's she been smoking?"

"Forty years, three packs a day. She chain-smoked right through breakfast, lunch and dinner. She's really hooked. Before the Alzheimer's, I tried everything to get her to quit but she wouldn't. And you've probably noticed that hardheadedness is *not* one of the things this horrible disease diminishes."

As if on cue, Ann MacCallum shuffled her way across the living room, stooped from osteoporosis and holding on to her squeaky walker. She stopped and looked at Kate. "Who are you?"

Ethel spoke up. "This is your daughter, Kate. She's come to visit."

"I don't think so," Ann said, sarcastically, and stared at Kate. "Push your hair off your forehead; you look like a rabbit peeking out of a brush pile. You're too thin too; you need to gain some weight—not as much as her, though." She nodded toward Ethel when she made the last remark, and then turned and pushed her walker down the hall to her bedroom.

Kate raised her eyebrows, twisted her mouth, and watched her mother walk away. She wondered if it was her imagination, or if all Alzheimer's patients had their faults magnified. Speaking her own mind and offering her opinions, whether asked for or not, had always been an unpopular trait of Ann's. Now it was more out of control than ever.

Kate thought of all the things her mother had forgotten, except for the rare moments of recall: the names of her son and daughter, brothers and sisters—all of the extended family—and even her late husband of thirty years. Strangely, she still remembered Kate's father and their marriage of thirty years. But that was this month. The short lucid periods stretched farther and farther apart.

Kate stared out the window for a moment, remembering the way things used to be and all that Ann—and the family—had lost. Even something as simple as meals together had changed because of her mother's new spitting habit. Besides that unappetizing practice, another odd thing had happened. Ann no longer liked the same foods that had always been family favorites. Pasta and enchiladas were in; roast beef and chicken-fried steak were out. Kate drew a deep breath and let out a long sigh. With so much gone, it was too bad Ann's smoking addiction hadn't disappeared with everything else.

Something clicked in Kate's mind. She spun toward Ethel. "I have an idea."

The caregiver jumped at Kate's abruptness, and then listened wide-eyed as Kate quickly laid out her plan.

"Oh, no! Ann will be *furious*." Ethel was chuckling now. "Do you think it'll work?"

"What do we have to lose?" Kate laughed. "I'm going to check on her, and then I have to run some errands."

Kate walked to the bedroom and looked at the frail, wrinkled little woman now asleep in her mother's bed. She leaned down and kissed the stranger's forehead. A lump in her throat sent tears to her eyes.

She quickly returned to the kitchen, picked up a stack of bills, her purse and keys, and hurried to the door to avoid talking. Hoping her voice didn't crack, she called over her shoulder, "See you tomorrow, Ethel."

***

The next morning Kate drove across an area called The Mesa where acres and acres of potatoes and onions once grew. She crossed Danbury Street and dropped into the canyon where she and her brother, Mitch, rode bikes as kids, leaving home just after dawn to escape their mother's never-ending work list. Kate climbed up the other side of the gorge, remembering that the street used to be dirt and known only as the *potato road.* In her mind, she saw herself and Mitch pushing their bikes up the steep hill, dripping with sweat, on their way to play at the dump—the place their mother called dangerous and insisted they never go. Driving on the pavement to her mom's house was like rolling over a tape that had recorded her history—a history chock-full of her mother.

Kate knocked and Ethel opened the door with a jovial, "Good morning!"

"Hi. I can't wait. Tell me what happened." Kate dumped her purse and keys in their regular spot without taking her eyes off the caregiver.

Grinning, Ethel said, "I did just what you told me. I picked up all the ashtrays, in the house and on the patios, and threw them into the outside garbage cans. Then I searched the whole house, every nook and cranny, for cigarettes, matches, and lighters. I thought I knew where all of her hiding places were, but she had some creative ones—in her shoes, under the extra rolls of toilet paper in the bathroom, and even some in the woodpile on the porch. I put all of them in the outside trashcan too."

"What happened? What happened?" Kate smiled in anticipation.

"Well, she got up and, as usual, started looking for a cigarette. She yelled, 'Hey, you! Come in here! Where are my Belairs? They were right here next to the lamp when I went to bed!'"

Kate grinned broader as she pictured the scene. "Then what?"

Ethel chuckled. "I did what you said. I put a puzzled look on my face and said, 'Belairs? You mean cigarettes? You don't smoke, Ann—don't you remember? You quit four or five years ago.' I kept my gaze steady and tried to be convincing." She chuckled again. "I guess we really shouldn't be laughing, but . . ."

"Yes we should. If we didn't, we'd be crying all the time. That wouldn't help my mom—or us. You go right on laughing, any time you can. Now tell me. What did she say? Was she mad?"

Ethel shook her head and continued. "It was your mom's turn to be puzzled. She looked at the nightstand again for her cigarettes. Then she tugged on the bedspread, smoothed it, and looked for her ashtray. She stared at the bed for a minute, and then flounced to her dresser and jerked open the bottom right drawer. I could tell she thought she was going to *show me*. She rummaged through the scarves, did it again, and then stood. She looked deflated. I felt so sorry for her and so mean."

"I know how you feel," Kate said, all traces of smiles and grins gone. "She has nothing else left—not even memories." Tears sprang to her eyes.

"It's okay, honey." Ethel patted Kate's shoulder. "I know this is best. You had a good idea. It's better than being hateful and just taking them from her, or trying to talk to her. She can't understand and she won't remember."

94

"You're right. I'd never forgive myself if she caught on fire because I couldn't stand to be the *bad guy.* I can even hear what she'd say to me right now: '*Stop being a baby, Kate, and get on with it.*'"

"I know." Ethel squeezed Kate's arm. "It'll be all right, you'll see. Now why don't you check on her—I think she's sleeping—and then run along. Get away from here for the day. I can always call you if anything comes up."

"I think I'll take you up on that. Thanks." Kate gave Ethel a hug and then checked on her mom. Ann was sleeping and a soft snore filled the bedroom. Kate knew her mother would never want anyone to see her like this . . . mouth hanging open, hair uncolored and wiry from the exposed gray, and no makeup. She had always been fastidious about her looks. Kate kissed her forehead and pulled the door almost shut on her way out.

***

Across the mesa and down the canyon the next morning, knocking on the door and bringing forth Ethel and her cheerful *good morning,* dumping her purse and keys on the high countertop, all gave Kate a feeling of déjà vu. This routine had barely varied for weeks; only the caregiver had changed. But if Ethel agreed to stay, even that would become permanent. She was the best thing that had happened for Ann's wellbeing.

"Good morning! Anything new to report?" The day away had rejuvenated Kate. She felt almost as upbeat as Ethel always sounded.

Ethel started laughing. "Remember it was *you* who said we needed to laugh to get through this."

Kate nodded. "Why? What happened?"

"Well, last night, the grandkids came over—your Aaron and your brother's daughter, Clare—and relieved me while I went shopping and home to visit my family for a few hours. Wait till you hear this!" She wrestled to get her laughter under control.

Her humor was contagious, and Kate started laughing too.

"Aaron filled me in when I got back—Oh!" Ethel stopped talking and walked to the door. "Here he is now. I'll let him tell you. Hi, there!" She held the screen door open for Aaron.

Kate reached out and hugged her youngest grandson. "Good morning! What are you doing out so early?"

"I wanted to check on Gramma Ann." He grinned at Ethel. "She was acting kinda *funny* last night."

The caregiver laughed and said, "I just started to tell your Gramma Kate about that—but you do it."

"Okay." Aaron laughed. "Well, ya know we're out of school for summer vacation, right? So Clare came over and we painted birdhouses all afternoon, then we asked if we could walk over here and visit. We were kinda bored, ya know? So we were watching TV with Gramma Ann when, about seven o'clock, she stood up and said, 'Okay, kids. Time for bed. Turn off the television.'

"At first I thought it was a *joke* because of the time, and then I saw she was *serious*. I elbowed Clare and we begged and pleaded to stay up awhile. We didn't bother to tell her we weren't spending the night. Well, Gramma finally gave in and went on to bed.

"A few minutes later, we heard the squeaky walker, and she came back down the hall. She stopped and glared at us and said, 'I told you to shut that TV off and get to bed!'

"I told her, 'No, you didn't, Gramma Ann. Don't you remember? You said we could stay up.'

"I was *really* mixed up for a minute, but then my cousin, Clare, reminded me about our grandmother's problem.

"Gramma said, 'Are you sure I said that?' I told her yes, I was sure, so she said, 'Okay, but just for a little while.'

"Gramma Ann really looked funny, but she turned the walker around and went down the hall.

"A little time passed and she came back *again*. Her mouth was in that tight knot she does, and this time she was *really* mad. She yelled at us—*really loud*!" Aaron mimicked his grandmother's expression. "She said, 'Do I have to get the flyswatter? I told you two to go to bed!'"

Ethel and Kate were laughing so hard they had to hold their sides.

"Let him finish! Let him finish! It gets even better." Ethel's laughter wound down and Aaron continued.

"We both said, 'Gramma! You said we could stay up!' Clare's face was all scrunched and mixed up, and I knew mine must look the same way. We looked at each other, and then looked at Gramma. She was stooped over that walker, and her head poked out toward us—you know—like a turtle's. Her face was fuming mad. We didn't know *what* to do.

"I tried again. I said, 'What's *wrong*, Gramma Ann? Don't you remember telling us we could stay up?'

"Gramma said, 'No, I don't.' She let her hands slide off the walker and they just hung by her side—and her shoulders kinda dropped. She seemed to shrink even smaller than she was before. She asked me, 'Did I say that?'

"She looked like she was trying to remember. I went over and put my arm around her and told her, 'Yeah, Gramma, you did.' She turned away from me and she looked real sad. She let out a big sigh, and started walking back to her room mumbling, 'Well, okay . . . if I did, I did.'

"I called her and said, 'Wait, Gramma Ann. I have a plan.' I grabbed a piece of paper and scribbled my idea on it, and then handed it to her.

"She read it out loud: 'I Gramma Ann said it's okay for Clare and Aaron to stay up and watch TV until 11 p.m.' There was a line where she could sign her name.

"Gramma smiled at me and said, 'A contract is a good idea, Aaron. That's the way all business should be handled.'

"I couldn't believe it! Gramma sounded just like she used to, and she used my name. Anyway, I told her, 'That's right, Gramma. That's what you always told us.' She signed and then said we had to write our names too.

"I told her that if she got up again, she could read the note and she'd remember.

"I'm laughing now," Aaron said, "but I didn't laugh when I was with Gramma Ann. I just put my arm around her shoulders and walked her to the bedroom." His face straightened and he said, "It was really good to hear her voice the way it used to be."

"You're a good grandson, Aaron." Kate gave him another hug. "Why don't you go in and see her; maybe she'll remember you again."

When he was gone, both women laughed and agreed that all of the business talk in the family's homes had paid off. Ten-year-old Aaron had used a contract to solve his and his cousin's problem.

"Ooohhh," Kate said, ". . . it feels good to laugh. It's such a stress reliever. It's too bad Alzheimer's has to be the stimulus for it. Speaking of Alzheimer's, tell me what came of the cigarette fiasco."

"Well, she asked for a Belair several times during the day, but I just held to the same story. Twice, I found her bent over the kitchen stove with a burner turned on, trying to light a *stick match* that she was holding between her *lips*. I was afraid her hair was going to go up in flames. That's when I removed the burner knobs and waited until she wasn't looking to put them on a high shelf out of her reach. The good thing is she never argued or got mad when I said she had quit smoking several years ago."

"I can't believe it worked. What a relief." Kate drew a deep breath. "I hope she stops asking and searching for cigarettes pretty soon, but with her addiction, it may take a while."

"Oh, I don't think so." Ethel laughed again. "Aaron forgot to tell you Ann's parting words. Remember—he and Clare didn't know anything about our trick.

"He said, 'When I walked Gramma Ann to her room, I asked her where her cigarette was. I told her I'd never seen her without one.

"'Gramma Ann stopped and looked at me like I was a kook. She said, "Aaron, I gave up smoking four or five years ago. Did you forget? "'"

AT THE EDGE

Rusty LaGrange

It wasn't too long ago that I sat quietly on a damp picnic bench, hugging a steaming mug of coffee, and watching the desperation of a mother with four screaming children. They were grimy and she was shutting down. Emotionally she had given her last try at something that wasn't working. I could see it in her eyes.

The site would not have been so amusing if she had been in her own backyard or even at the dirt lot of the local park. In this case, she was camped next door. We shared a water spigot that dripped all night and a mangled trash bin.

Camping, for me, was a way of life. Real camping meant you were out in the elements, where the lack of pavement exists, but cement barbecues and a pit were your kitchen. I liked taking each day's weather as it came. I didn't camp often, but I enjoyed going when time offered me its bit of leisure. Crisp mountain mornings or deep desert sunsets, it was all a welcome release from the daily grind, but not for some campers.

My neighbor had obvious difficulties with the basics of camping. Their unblemished tent leaned precariously toward their smoldering campfire. A mound of camping gear, flung from their car late last night, still resembled a packrat's nest.

While the children continued to scream at each other, an industrious little chipmunk stealthily tugged on an opened loaf of bread lying under their picnic table.

I remembered that before I had any children, I had promised myself not to be one of those camping moms who fed the kids cold cereal, helped them on with their damp sweatshirts, and tossed them outside to fend for themselves. I'd seen enough of that. On the other hand, I wasn't going to be a mom who scrubbed the grill spotless or swept out the tent three times a day.

I just wasn't going to do it.

Camping taught the basics of nature to children as well as adults. To strive to be a good camper meant that you had succeeded in understanding why you went out and enjoyed the outdoor adventure in the first place. I tried never to complain about the bugs, or the grit in the sandwiches, or the water in the lunchmeat. It was the experience of doing it that I craved. So, you could imagine my chagrin to see the jar of peanut butter open on the table with yellow jackets calling in for landing instructions. Not many city folk had really taken to the backwoods. It seemed more an inconvenience than an adventure. But for me, what better way to strip the tensions of the world away, like shedding a girdle at the end of the day. All the daily deadlines, the nagging, the incessant noise of my traffic commute, seemed petty when standing in the deep shadows of a stately redwood.

Your daily priorities changed to meet the essentials of life itself: gathering firewood, searching for drinking water, hooking a fish or two, planting a tent in an isolated meadow with good drainage. And, when your tasks were complete, the reward was kicking back to the soothing sounds of creatures in the underbrush and breezes tumbling in the treetops, thick with the aromatic duff of the forest.

This woman missed the point and I wanted to go straighten her out. I wanted to tell her that children at camp created a fieldtrip and science lab rolled into one. A youngster in the wide-open spaces is the epitome of imagination run amok. Believe me, while chasing butterflies or hunting down toads, you can't help but be a kid once more. Finding a red worm on your own is pure joy to a child. And, yes, even running for cover after thinking you had seen a bear in deep shadows was at least exhilarating.

So why was I here, parked next to the Rugrats meet the Transformers with a manic-depressive Mom at the helm? Because the weather had turned nasty and I was torn between flashflood watch in the back country or holing up here in Camp World USA for the duration of a quick-moving storm.

As I self-consciously spied on my neighbor's plight, I mentally made a checklist of all the things I would never have done. Placing a dozen eggs on the cooler chest and asking the middle child to get the baby's bottle from the cooler, for instance. I probably would have assigned the oldest boy the task of sorting the camping gear to find useful things, such as coats and hats for each of them, instead of allowing him to play with a hunting knife. Keeping the toddler busy with sand toys would give Mom time to diaper her littlest one. A freestanding child backpack would serve the dual purpose of holding the baby off the ground and giving her some exercise so Mom could cook breakfast. There were ways to cope.

So maybe my scenario conflicted with her family's reality. Meantime, mom-next-door had a mess on her hands, and the yelling continued. I even caught myself visualizing their ride in the car; it only sent shivers up the nape of my neck. They had arrived in the dark during a dumping of spring rain. I had to give them credit for the tent being erected, at least.

Although I conjured up an idealistic camp, I knew that best intentions, even camping, seldom follow a true course. It reminded me that even my own father, in haste to push on through the night to our destination many years ago, became so tired that he finally conceded to setting up our rented 1960s tent trailer in a remote flat spot at two a.m. At early light, we awoke to the odd whirring sound of an engine and found our perfect camp pitched on the end of a landing strip. We never packed so fast in our lives.

So maybe it was her best intentions to pack up the kiddies for a camping weekend and let Dad go out early on a fishing trip. He could probably use the peace. Maybe she was the best little camper in the state and she was just having a meltdown day. Maybe their trek across the country was nearly over and this was the final stretch toward home.

I finally gave up guessing and ventured over to her side of the spigot. I believe I caught a look of despair mixed with a tired smile.

"Isn't camping fun?" I coupled my opening line with a wince.

"I wish I was camping. This ain't my idea of camping at all," she said, brushing her hair back with a sticky hand. "I just had enough of life at home." Her tone was sour.

"Oh. You're not camping."

"No, not really." She turned back and realized her children were perched quietly on the picnic bench staring at us. Their focus was not out of entertainment but of terror.

"Don't worry, kids, I ain't going nowheres." She turned back to me. "You see I had to leave. I just had to…"

Her voice trailed off, but I knew she had more to say. I gave her my best consoling smile and waited.

"'Cause my husband was beating me and the kids. Things had to change. Since I don't have much money on me, I figured camping would be easy." Then she laughed, "Boy, was I wrong."

Boy, was I wrong, I muttered to myself. I let go a little chuckle as a reflex to her misfortune, but not for the reason she left. "It's probably the best reason to go camping," I smiled.

"I guess. 'Cept he was the one that always went on camping trips. This is his stuff," she grinned, licking grape jelly off the back of her finger. "I don't even know what to do with it all."

"Then maybe you could use some help from a well-seasoned camper, and maybe an extra hand with your children," I said, feeling a bit humbled that I had accused her of being an ineptly bad camper.

As the first drops of rain slapped the pavement, it turned out that she was a sensible woman. The kids were terrific, wide-eyed and enamored with nature's grandeur. Their eyes followed every move as I set the tent back on all four corners and found the sleeping bags, lantern, and clothes.

After the light rain let up, I took a short stroll with the two older children. We found spider webs glistening with diamonds, yellow banana slugs hiding under cupped leaves, and two papery cocoons ready to open. Although they tried to be happy, they seemed sullen and apprehensive to stray too far from their mom's watchful eye, but they really tried to be happy. The children had never been camping before. I hoped they would try it again under better circumstances.

I enjoyed burnt hot dogs and watery potato salad, told ghoulish stories around a toasty warm fire that night, and wished them all sweet dreams when I finally wandered past the spigot to my own camp.

The next morning I packed up and waved at the children as I rolled slowly down the asphalt trail. Doe-eyed and eager to wave, they had survived their second night in better condition. They lined up, their muddy-toed sneakers poised over the lip of the asphalt that marked their territory. They were safe, together as a family. Her children found security as long as they were within eyesight of mom and no farther than the edge of the pavement. I would never see them again, but it felt good knowing that I had a hand in giving them a chance to survive. And, that I had helped give the love of camping another chance as well.

PRISON SONG

Gregory D. Caruth

Cha-Chink, Cha-Chink, Cha-Chink . . .

Sing the keys slapping against the correctional officer's thigh.
Momentarily everyone looks. But only a few recognize the
sound . . . only a few recognize the melody of freedom.

Lost in the symphony of jingling keys, I deeply inhale a breath,
full of patience, and the will-power to deal with another day.

Another day of constant racket. Toilets flushing, loud laughing,
arguments over TVs, dominos, card games and the irritating
cackle of the overhead loudspeaker.

Another day of trying not to cross the deeply etched color lines
of racism.

Another day avoiding frivolous conversations full of exaggerated
war stories and lies.

Another day waiting on the familiar chime of keys that master
every door of my destination . . . but not my destiny.

You see, in prison, keys manifest into credentials of power. Steel
symbols that represent freedom, and mobility. They separate the
keeper from the kept.

But when you find yourself listening to the jingle of those keys, without a set of your own, you'll come to understand the true meaning of patience, and appreciation . . . which comes along with the years of being removed from all things mankind.

I used to familiarize freedom with a bird, or a plane.
But now . . . after this life changing experience, it will always be the beautiful harmony of . . .

Cha-Chink, Cha-Chink, Cha-Chink!

FRIENDS FROM THE BASEMENT

Thomas Kier

Hi, my name is Jacob. My fourth-grade teacher gave us a writing assignment to keep a journal and write in it a couple of times a week. Then we could pick the best parts every two weeks and write a page or two to turn in. The best part in my journal so far happened to me just yesterday afternoon.

I don't know if you could feel the earthquake two days ago where you live, but at my school everyone had to hide under their desks for a while and there was dust coming down from the ceiling. Sandra got some in her hair and it stayed there for the rest of the day. Me and my friends laughed at her. She's pretty but she's stuck up, so it serves her right. Then she cried and had to go clean up in the bathroom. I felt a little bad, but it still serves her right.

Our house is kind of close to the school, so the earthquake was pretty strong there too. Now we have a new crack in the floor of the basement that runs from one corner all the way to the other one. My dad says it's because of the cheap-ass construction company. I'm not supposed to use that word, but I don't see a problem because Dad uses it, so why shouldn't I? So there! ASS! That felt good. Besides, my new friend says there's absolutely nothing wrong with it.

Did I tell you I made a new friend the day after the earthquake? But I think he's trapped in his own house and I think his house in right under ours. It must be because of that cheap-

107

ass construction again; those dummies built our house right on top of one that was already there. And now I can hear my new friend because he can shout up through the crack in our basement. I tried to tell Mom and Dad to go down there and listen, but they said they were too busy. Then they looked at each other with that look, you know the one. It's the look that says, *We think our son is lonely and maybe a little crazy, but we can't say it out loud.* It's the same look they used when I had an imaginary friend five years ago. But this one is real. I don't care if they hear him or not. That just makes him more special to me.

When I first wrote about my friend in my journal, I spelled his name like this: Lijun because that's how it sounds. But he told me it's spelled like *Legion.* I asked him how he knew how I spelled it anyways, but he says that doesn't matter and we need all the time together we can get so he can teach me some new games. I like new games. He usually has a lot to say, but I can't spend too much time down there because Mom worries about me. She said I always have a weird look on my face when I come back upstairs. I'm just trying to understand all the details of the games. Legion says it's important to get it right, and I'll be a baby if I don't get it. I don't want him to think I'm a baby.

Legion says I have to learn how to use new tools. Some of them are tools that we already have in the house or in the garage, and some of them are just drawings that I can put on the floor or the walls. I don't know how drawings can be tools, but I don't think Mom would mind me putting my drawings on the walls as long as I just use a little tape. When I was first in school, she would put my baby drawings on the fridge anyways. Well, that's enough writing for now. I'm going downstairs to listen to Legion some more. He's always kind of funny. Sometimes he says big words that I don't understand, then he just laughs and explains it to me in English.

***

It's been four days since I last wrote here, but I write in my other journal every night. Legion says it's a good idea because it will help me remember how to play the games he says are so much fun. I asked him if I could invite Tom and Billy over to play the games with us, but he says it's not a good idea right now. I have to learn all the rules first. Then we can play with more people, and maybe even have a party. I told him I felt a little lonely, so he started doing different voices for me and said I could pretend he was a bunch of different people. That helped a little.

Sometimes when I'm down there, it's like I forget how long I've been there. Mom will come home from work and wonder why the house is all dark, then she will call down the basement stairs to see if I'm there. Sometimes it takes a few minutes before I can even hear her. Then I remember I forgot to have my snack or start my homework or anything. I feel a little guilty, but Legion says it's OK and that pretty soon he will be talking to Mom too, or maybe he will have me talk to her and tell her just what he says. That part confused me a little, but he's always telling me not to worry and that he'll never let anything bad happen to me again.

When I was little, I had a spider bite that I got down in the basement. It swelled up really big and made me very sick. Mom and Dad didn't care about it at first until I threw up during dinner, then passed out on the floor. They told me later that they had to call an ambulance and rush me to the hospital. I think maybe they still feel guilty about it.

Legion says he knows all about it, and that he's been watching me a long time. He says don't be nervous because that would be *counter-productive*. I already knew how to spell it, but he told me what it means. I remembered in just one telling. I think I'm understanding him better and that he's helping me learn a lot of new stuff. That's good. I hope he'll teach me stuff we don't learn in school. Then I can know more than Tom or Billy or even stuck-up Sandra. It will be our secret, just Legion and me. He says it's all right to have secrets, and that not too many people would understand why we have to keep this stuff secret. So now the fact we have secrets is a secret too. Cool!

***

Legion's been telling me a lot of stuff I should know. He says kids don't usually learn this stuff until they're older. I told you he was good for my education. He's teaching me all about how our bodies are put together. He calls it *anatomy*. Anyways, there are pressure points in our bodies and in our heads that could make a person sick, or pass out, or even die if you wanted them to. Legion's been showing me maps in my head. He also includes *all* the parts of girls as well as boys. Seeing some of those parts makes me feel funny sometimes, but Legion says that's OK and that's the way it's supposed to be. When I'm ready, he's going to show me why boys and girls are different and what they're supposed to do about it. But first I need to know how to disable anyone who tries to stop me from playing Legion's games. That's my first assignment.

I never realized how many ways a person could hurt another person or how easy it is to make sure the other one stops living. Just like my parents almost made me stop living when I had the spider bite and they ignored me. Legion says maybe it is time I made them stop living. I started to cry and said I would miss them a lot, but Legion says he can make me believe they're still alive in my own head and that I could even see them anytime I wanted to. Then he made me believe I could actually see him reach out from the crack in the floor of the basement. Legion has a lot of hands, and those hands grabbed me and held me down for a minute. They didn't look like people's hands at all. Then he let me up and said he was just playing around with me, and that it was too late to be scared because that game was all over. After that I realized it was totally dark in the basement and I wasn't sure how I had seen any of that at all. So Legion put a little light in front of me that led me to the switch on the wall, and I turned on the lights.

Then Mom was upstairs and starting dinner so I left in a hurry. Legion said I'd better be back tomorrow or he would make his hands grab me anywhere I was and pull me down into the earth with him. I couldn't sleep that night. The next afternoon, Legion showed me a little movie about older boys and girls using the parts of themselves that made me nervous, and he helped me feel what it would be like. I'm not scared anymore. If he can do that for me again, I will do anything he tells me to do.

***

That wasn't even bad. Legion helped me, and he was right about me believing that my parents could still be alive, well, at least that my Mom could still be alive. I never cared that much about Dad anyways. Sometimes on the weekends he would get drunk and yell at me a lot and even hit me. So I'm not going to miss him and Legion says I don't have to believe in him ever again. But anytime I start missing Mom, Legion says he can make me see her and hear her and even feel her kissing me goodnight. So it's not even going to be lonely here.

I thought I was going to have a lot of work digging a big enough hole in the backyard for two grown-up bodies, but Legion just told me to drag them down into the basement and he would take care of it. It was some work, but they rolled pretty good down the steps once I got them started, then I got to watch

Legion's hands reach up and pull them down inside the crack. That was a good trick! I don't even think I'll be afraid of his hands anymore. It's like when Mom used to spank me for doing something wrong; she said it was for my own good. Legion says the same thing, and I trust him. He promises to always be good to me.

Legion says there are people outside our family that need the same treatment that I gave to Mom and Dad. I asked him if I would get caught because it wouldn't be done inside our house and maybe other people would see. He explained to me just how I could get these people to follow me inside an abandoned building or into a dark alley, and all I need to do is tell them to help me find my lost puppy. Legion says if I do everything he tells me to, I can even have a puppy someday. I hope it's as real as he makes Mom for me now. This sounds like it will be fun!

***

Today was my next assignment. It wasn't as bad as I thought it would be. Legion said it was all the bad people of the world that I am taking care of. He has never used the word "kill" but I know that is what I am doing. I think it's all right if you are making the world a safer place. Legion should know; he tells me all about what horrible things these people have done or are planning to do. He knows a lot more than I do, so I have to keep trusting him. Besides, I don't want to be pulled down into the crack in my basement. That would be worse than what I am doing to the people that help me find my "puppy."

Afterward, I went to the basement to ask Legion what to do about the bodies. He said he already took care of it. Then he came out of the crack looking like an older girl this time and he took off all her clothes and we had fun together. It was even better than what he had promised me. I'm so glad I'm such good friends with Legion.

***

I think I like power tools the best. I've used all kinds of knives, hammers, saws, even a big screwdriver one time. But power tools, even the ones with the rechargeable batteries, seem like I'm doing a real man's work. And that's what it is. Legion tells me so all the time. I am making the world a safer place. I guess I would be like a policeman and a fireman and an astronaut all rolled up into one. That's good. I like my job and I like the rewards. The girls are always there waiting for me, and my puppy never leaves my side. Now it's even more believable to the people I "take care of" because Rusty can run on ahead and whimper and bark like he really is lost or stuck somewhere. Legion always has the dog do whatever I need him to do.

I think the people that help me find Rusty are getting smarter, or maybe Legion just had me doing the dumb ones first until I got better at the job. It also seems like maybe Legion is getting stronger. I don't know what he does with the bodies, but I never see them around even if I go back to the same place a few minutes later. I've seen some newspaper headlines about missing people, but that's just been recently. When I first started, the people I was saving the world from looked like no one would miss them anyways. They were all bums.

I have to take a good long nap now almost every day after school so I can be awake during the middle of the night to do my job. Sometimes I have bad dreams, but Legion is there in my mind to comfort me when I wake up. I wonder if he's just doing his job the same as he has me doing mine. I hate to think what his boss would look like. One time Legion got mad when I didn't do a person just right and they almost got away and when I saw

113

him come out of the crack, he was the scariest thing I ever saw. But it only lasted a second, then he was just telling me that I had to be more careful. That's the day he gave me Rusty. It was like he was making up for scaring me.

So far, I haven't had to do anyone I know. I'm not sure how well I'd be at killing people that knew my name. I mean, I'm sure my teacher is a good person. Yesterday, Legion had me do a man in a police uniform. He told me the man was bad because he wasn't a real cop and he was just pretending. I wasn't sure, but I thought of the girl that might be waiting for me in the basement, and I actually enjoyed the feel of the power drill vibrating through bone while the blood splashed up onto me, warming me. The nights are getting colder, you know. In my dreams after, the warmth of the blood and the warmth of the girl who lay with me became one and the same. I think this might be my purpose in life. I'm so glad I found Legion.

***

It's almost time, and I can't wait! Legion has promised me that after only a few more jobs, he will be strong enough to come out of the basement for real. He says he will be a part of me. Me! I can't believe he chose me!

He says that the feelings I get when I'm with the girls and the love that I have for Rusty and even the comfort I used to get from Mom will all be there inside me and will be even stronger and better than I could ever imagine. All I have to do is agree to be a part of him and he will be a part of me forever. Doesn't sound too hard. I already like working for him. This just seems like it would be easier and better than what I'm doing now.

I think I'm just about done writing in this journal. The other one was just for practice, I guess. The teacher told us weeks ago that we didn't have to do it anymore, but I was used to it and

Legion said when I get everything right, we will burn this thing together. A bigger journal makes a bigger fire, right? So I'm writing a lot.

Hopefully, in less than a week, we will be ready to join together. I want it to happen before school lets out for the summer. This will be a *sweet* summer!

Well, I have to go and talk to Legion some more. It shouldn't be long now. See you in the basement!

DESERT BUNNIES

Anne Heimbeck

*W*hen I lived in Las Vegas and was looking for a job, I discovered an opening in Caliente, a little town in southeastern Nevada. I invited my friend Lois to ride along with me. Lois knew exactly how to get there, so she said, and since I didn't, I listened to her.

As we sped along, I saw a sign for Pahrump pointing that-a-way. That didn't seem right, and I questioned her. She insisted all was well. "It's okay, just keep going."

I did, and eventually, we stopped to check directions because it felt to me like we should be there by now. Lois went inside the gas station and came back with the information that we were on the right road.

Soon it got closer and closer to my appointment time, and I became more concerned. We were in the middle of what seemed like Nowhere, Nevada, with nothing but desert cottontails running around. We came upon a large motor home parked on the side of the road. I pulled over and asked if they had a map of Nevada. They did, and we discovered that we were on the exact opposite side of the state from Caliente. It would be impossible to be on time for the appointment.

Cell phones were not prevalent in 1995, and I hoped we would come upon civilization soon so I could call the little school to make amends. Mind you, it was all vast, open desert.

Then we saw it, a large sign indicating an establishment, and lo and behold, there was a phone booth right in front of it.

But hark! A large, rather rapid-moving semi pulled into the place just before we got there, and I just knew that truck driver

116

was stopping to make a call. But we were in luck, because he went around to the back of the buildings, leaving the phone booth to us.

I jumped out of the car to phone my contact in Caliente. I apologized and rescheduled for the following week. Lois had stayed in the car and from her vantage point she had a view of the front door.

When I returned to the car, she pointed out the little sign above the doorbell. It read, "Ring bell for pleasure." That is when I realized what the big sign on the road had read. We were at the Cottontail Ranch. And yes, I guess the truck driver did stop to "make a call."

THE GUARDIAN

J. P. Newcomer

On the roof of the world, beyond the highest mountain range, lies a little-known land of mystery, harsh beauty and magic. This is the home of the Guardians, the Protector Gods of this high and barren steppe. These Protectors of Innocents are known as the Yamataka. It is said they are sent through the Buddha Gate to combat evil. Their painted and gilded images occupy a place of honor in each of the monasteries in this high land. In order to appease their infamous temper and seduce them into granting requests, the faithful are known to bring offerings of distilled spirits, hoping that after drinking, the Yamataka will look more kindly upon their needs.

The wind freshened, blowing steadily from the west, from the troubled lands beyond the Gate. Robert felt his hair rise and brush against his forehead as a new gust surged across the valley. It rustled through the swamp grass and forced the tall reeds at the river's edge to twist and bow. The boy glanced up from his task of building a fire. "Strange wind," he said.

"Aye." Robert nodded. *Strange, indeed! As strange as the land from whence it comes. As strange as this youngster's blue-silver stare.*

They were camped to the north of the river's mouth on a high, sloping patch of barren ground. Two scruffy oaks stood nearby, leaves rustling in the unexpected breeze. The waters below assumed odd shapes—new swirls and eddies. The fire,

118

which was built of reeds and grass and a few sparse twigs, released a smoky plume.

"Spooky how it came up so fast, huh?" the boy muttered, giving him a knowing glance, as though privy to fears other than his own.

Robert evoked a mirthless smile. This boy had grown increasingly perceptive as time passed and required little need for extended explanations. In itself, this was a good and special quality that Robert had come to value, yet there were times when it made him uneasy. With the untarnished wisdom of his mere eleven years, Tim had come to know the subtle shades of his Guardian's moods, his likes and dislikes, perhaps even his unspoken fears. Robert dismissed the thought in irritation.

"What does it mean, Rob?"

"Have you forgotten so soon how to build a proper fire?"

"No, man. No." Tim gave him a sideways glance and scampered off in search of more dry twigs.

Robert used the respite to breathe in the strange gusts of air and test their mettle. This was a dry, demanding wind, difficult to inhale, painful to release—more than an erratic breeze, more than a change in the weather. This was meant for him and none other. This was the Guardian's Cup, bitter with bile and full to overflowing. *Not this boy. Not now. I can't lose another one.* The wind flattened Robert's shirt against his chest and threatened to uncoil the rawhide whip stuffed in the belt loop of his faded jeans.

The boy returned with his arms loaded with twigs and set to work on the fire. His face was expressionless, but his eyes blinked rapidly. "So how come you're actin' so weird all of a sudden?" he asked in a soft, insolent tone.

Robert was pleased with the insolence. Maybe this one is ready, he thought. *Let him be ready, Lord of Time. Let me not fail again.* "It is time for the testing, Tim," Robert whispered.

The boy seemed not to hear. He poked at the fire with a long stick, nursing a thin flicker of flame to life. "I don't like this wind," he muttered.

"Nor do I." Robert watched as the sun sank upon the swirling waters and the wind fanned the fire. *Easier to speak of the wind than the task at hand!* "It is time for the testing," he repeated. "Do you understand?"

"No." The boy caught his eye. "What is it, man? What's wrong with you? Don't get creepy on me."

"You shall come to understand many things."

"What things?" The boy glared at him, eyes bright with terror and welling tears,

How best to deal with this? How? Robert considered his options. *Hold him?*

No! Tim wouldn't take kindly to that. Better to be honest, Robert decided. "Tonight I shall restore your memories," he said.

"Huh?" Tim shook his head from side to side like a wounded buck shaking his antlers, waiting in confusion for the pain to stop. "What are you talkin' about, man? Look, whatever it is, I don't want any. None—nada—zip. You buy?"

"Zip?" Robert didn't understand zip, but he understood this boy. "Sit, now. Watch the fire."

"No, Rob. No." But the boy sat cross-legged before the fire, as ordered, and Robert sat across from him, watching his pale face reflected in the struggling flames.

Robert concentrated on gathering his strength. It was a tightening process, a bundling of emotions into cramped spaces where they could feed on the dry, gusting wind and the memory of the high land from which he came. *None, nada, zip. Could those be Gods? Gods which abide in this strange half-life, half-world, half-boy, half-man? Or like a zipper, maybe, holding all the evil inside?* Now there were flame-lit tears on the boy's cheeks and Robert knew this would not brush easily on the Gate.

This would press hard. "You must remember now, Tim. Let it come."

"No. No."

"Yes, boy. You can do it."

"I can't. I don't know how."

"You do."

"He hurt Lilly. That's all I can remember." The fire flamed, dancing in the boy's soft eyes.

"Your sister?"

"Yeah."

"Just her? Not you?"

"Me? Oh, some, I guess."

Lies. Frightened lies! "Just some?" Robert asked.

"I can't remember."

"You can."

"I don't want to. Don't make me."

"You must."

"Don't do this to me Rob. Please!"

"It's what I came here to do, Tim. You know that." *I cannot give you back your life painlessly. Did I not warn you, child? Did I not prepare you? Who's being tested here?*

"You're supposed to protect me. You're supposed to be my friend." The boy raised his head and the wind-whipped fire reflected his rage as the memories collected.

"Maybe you're just like him," he hissed.

"I'm not like him." Robert rose, circled the fire and dropped to his knees beside the boy, breathing in the angry words. This was the Dawning—a tricky place where they could slip away from you like silken phantoms—and the Gate would clang on your empty arms. *This boy must not slip away.*

"He used to get in the bathtub with me," Tim said in a small controlled voice. "I must've been seven or eight."

"Good. Go on." Robert remained impassive, fighting the impulse to gather the boy in his arms.

"At first when he'd rub himself up against my leg, I thought it was a game. Later, it got to be less fun, but it was still OK. I mean I could handle it, you know. But then, he went after Lilly."

"What did he do to Lilly, Tim?" *Of course, I know. We both know.*

"He made her cry."

"And what did you do?"

"I had to stop him—she was just a baby—barely five years old—I had to make him stop."

"And how did you make him stop?"

Tim was sobbing. "They were in his bedroom," he said. "Lilly was crying hard and I knew he was doing something bad to her and Mom had taken off with this other guy and there was no one to stop him but me, but I was too scared."

"So what did you do?"

"When it was all over, he got into the tub—laid back to soak—like he always did—and called for me. He acted like nothin' had happened. I had the scissors behind my back. Lilly was still crying."

"And then?"

"Then I noticed the blow dryer on the counter right beside the tub. I turned it on and threw it at him"

"Tell me the rest."

"When it hit the water, he let out a scream and rose up like the devil, himself, with the hairs sizzling on his chest and his arms reaching out to me. I thought he was gonna get me, Rob, some kind of hairy monster, chokin' and shakin' and smellin' like burned toast, half in and half out of the water, comin' right at me. I still had the scissors, but I couldn't move. It was like I was frozen and I was thinking if he touched me, I'd die, too."

"But you didn't die."

"No. He kind of wobbled and sunk back into the water and I guess that's when I figured out that he was the one who was gonna die. Water sloshed out of the tub and I knew I wouldn't need the scissors anymore. Then I noticed Lilly standing in the doorway, still crying, and right then I knew I was done."

"You're not done."

"Why are you doing this to me Rob? Why?" The boy raised his head and his cheeks were streaked with tears.

Robert drew in his breath. *Always the same question. Always!* "You must reclaim your past in order to realize your future," he intoned, giving the standard answer, knowing it wouldn't help. It was the only answer he knew.

"What future?" The boy was on him, balled fists lashing, sobbing. "We both know I got no future."

Robert pulled the flailing child to his chest. "Your future is upon you! You must not judge yourself so harshly." *You must not fight me to the death. Not yours. Not now!*

The boy howled and raised his arm, brandishing an imaginary weapon, plunging it again and again into Robert's chest. This was the scissors, meant for his father.

Is this how you planned it, boy? In a mad frenzy, screaming and sobbing and watching the blood bubble and froth at your father's lips? I am your father, also. Have you forgotten all I taught you so soon, child of the wicked blade? Robert held the child and rocked him slowly, thinking he might be getting too old for this, wondering if he might be losing his edge.

The boy struggled. "Le'me go, you creep," he yelled as he thrashed. "Le'me go!" Blows rained against Robert's neck and shoulders until he was forced to pin down the pummeling hands.

"Hush, child. I won't drop you. Be still now."

Tim glanced up at him. "Drop me? What are you talkin' about? What kind of Guardian are you anyway?"

Robert smiled and ran his fingers across the boy's damp cheeks. "A poor one, you think?"

"Yeah. Awful!" Tim wiped at his nose with the back of his hand and pulled away in embarrassment. Robert watched him carefully. The wind continued to build in intensity and the fire leapt and hissed. Robert withdrew his whip.

"What's that for? You gonna beat me?" The boy said it half-jokingly, but stared at the uncoiled strap of rawhide in apprehension.

"Not you, Tim." *Can you really believe such a thing, child? Of course you can! Will you never learn to trust again?* Robert could feel his stomach tighten and convulse.

Rob?" The air stirred around them.

"They come," Robert said solemnly. "Can you not feel their presence?"

"I can feel something." The boy's tears were gone and his breath came in heavy gulps. "What is it?"

"We must fight them."

"Who?"

"We must fight them now."

The shadows were advancing. Robert cracked his whip. Tim withdrew his knife from its sheath, running his thumb across the honed steel. Robert had taught him how to keep a razor-thin edge. Robert had taught him many things, but nothing to prepare him for this night of gusting memories.

There were faces now—faces in the fire—faces in the wind. The boy began to scream and lash out with his knife. Robert could see them coming—those he'd lost. First there was the girl, Mary Jo, thirteen—and all-woman—with jutting breasts and a pregnant belly. With her, he'd been pre-ordained to failure from the start. His superiors should never have assigned such a case to him. They never did again.

Robert flicked his whip and her vision vanished although he could still feel her teeth at his throat, her angry fingernails racking his cheeks. Next, Joel came. *No. Not that one.* The smile was still there—the barbed eyes. *Use the whip, idiot. Use it!* 'Member me, buddy? Joel was saying. 'Member how you let me die? Let me drop like a stone? Right out of your arms, you let me drop. And you were supposed to take care of me—fix me up right. Well you fixed me alright. You fixed me up real good, buddy.

Tim was screaming. *Now, or it will be too late.* The whip cracked and the ghost vanished. Robert was panting. Tim rolled on the ground as though fighting an unseen opponent, his knife slashing in a giant arc. "It's OK, boy," Robert said, breathing hard. "We're done here. We can go back."

"Back? Back where?" The knife was still. "I thought you were gonna die, Rob. I thought they were gonna kill you. I couldn't stop them." The boy shuddered.

"But you did, child. You stopped them." Robert knelt and held the boy to his chest. "Neither of us shall die this day," he intoned as he rose to his full height. "Put your feet on the chair, Tim. You see it? It's right beneath you now. All you have to do is put your feet down."

"No." The boy's eyes filled with new awareness. He began to struggle. "Now I remember," he hissed. "That chair ain't there. Right after I rigged this hangman's noose and strung myself up, I kicked that chair over. I'm dangling! Can't you see that? I'm swinging from this rafter like a bloody sack of potatoes and I want you to let me go. I didn't ask for no damn Guardian, man. Let me swing."

"No more talk," Robert ordered. "Put your feet on the chair. We have set it upright."

"That's nuts. I kicked it away."

"It is as I say. You must choose."

"Look. They got me locked up in this friggin' nut house and they'll probably never let me out. I knocked off my father, man. Don't you think I gotta pay for that, Rob? Do you think I can just walk away?"

Robert was losing his patience. "You have already won your release, you stubborn child," he said. "I am your father now and you shall not die like this. Not if I have to hold you here forever." Robert supposed he could do that. It was his right to make such a decision. Of course, the risk would be great, since all worlds have timelines and given parameters. Sooner or later the chair would dissolve—the Gate would dissolve. They would both fall! *A mad threat, you fool!*

"What if I don't care?" Tim stammered. "What if I don't give a rat's ass about any of it?"

"A rat's ass?" Robert didn't understand.

The boy turned his head to give him a scornful glance. "Man, you're so out of it! So friggin' hopeless." His lips twisted in a jeering smile yet a hint of softness flickered in his eyes.

Robert watched in wonderment and relief as the scuffed toe of Tim's sneaker edged toward the upturned chair. He released the knotted bed sheet from Tim's throat and tossed it over the rafter to which it had been attached. The sheet slid harmlessly to the floor, fluttering as if trying to sprout angelic wings. Tim slid from the chair to slump beside the limp shroud, staring up at him in disbelief. "I don't get it, Rob," he whispered. "What's going on here?"

"You have won back your life." Robert said slowly, knowing his time was short. "But that can't be!" Tim gaped at him. "Once you start swingin', you don't stop. What is this? Some kind of kinky dream?"

Robert shook his head, feeling himself fading. "Remember the wind and the fire," he said, knowing the boy would remember nothing. *Turn your rage to perseverance, child. I shall miss you.*

Robert knelt beside the sleeping boy, bending over to kiss him gently on the forehead. The Gate was falling. Quickly, Robert gathered the knotted bed sheets in his arms and stepped backward, listening to the whistle of displaced air as the Gate approached. "You won't be needing these, anymore, Tim, " Robert whispered.

The Gate descended with a clang.

THE VIEW POINT

Curtis Yarbrough

S am and Charles are two good friends that differ as night and day. Having known one another for what seems like forever, their existence is characterized by one debate after another. Sam, the perpetual optimist, always sees the glass half full. Charles, the eternal pessimist, sees it half empty. These two friends, inseparable as they may be, are always contrary to one another.

Los Angeles, California. The weather is just wonderful. It is absolutely refreshing outside. They are taking one of their customary strolls through Athens Park on 120th Street and Broadway. Today they are debating *viewpoints*, and how to see things properly.

"I'll tell you my friend, each and every day is brand new for me," Sam says. "Ahhh!" He exclaims loudly. "I am so refreshed—just plain o' thankful to be alive."

"I hear ya, I hear ya," Charles gloomily states. "It's the same ol' stuff, S.O.S., if you ask me. I've got the same ol' job. The same ol' boss. The same ol' raggedy broke-down car—just the same ol', same ol'."

Staring at his friend in awe, Sam mockingly searches behind Charles, as if he's really looking for something. After finishing his mock search, he just as dramatically places the back of his hand against Charles' forehead, leaving it there for a few seconds. With a sigh, he says, "Humph."

Looking at his friend as if he's lost his mind, Charles asks, "Humph, what?"

Without hesitation, Sam starts in on him. "I noticed that there's no oxygen tank trailing behind you, and that you have no accessories hooked up to your nose or mouth helping you breathe."

"And?" Charles sarcastically asks.

Not missing a beat, Sam goes on. "And when I felt your forehead with the back of my hand, it is obvious that you are not running a fever—you are not sick at all. In fact, you are the picture of health and well-being."

Coming to a complete halt from the walk they're enjoying, Charles impatiently says, "Look man, what are you getting at?"

Visibly pondering his question, Sam carefully responds by saying, "Did you say something about same ol' *job*, and same ol' *boss*? Did you mention a *car*? You actually have a vehicle! Think about the people in this world that have never owned a car, and then consider all the folks who can't afford the insurance necessary to drive the car that they do own. Look at the economy for just one moment. Unemployment is at record high in some cities. Homelessness is raging out of control, with no relief in sight."

Charles seems to consider carefully the points just laid out by his dear friend. With stress lines appearing in his forehead, he says, "Sam, why do you have to raise such a fuss about everything I say? All I'm trying to get across to you is that *for me*, it is the same ol', same ol'."

Showing his pearly whites, Sam says, "Look around this beautiful park. We've been coming here for years. We were here just yesterday. Nothing is the same, although on the surface it appears that way. The people are different. The workers that tend to the park are different. The whole demonstration all around us is different in just one day."

With a chuckle Charles says, "My friend, you are too philosophical for me." They continue their walk.

They arrive back at the apartment complex where they live. Sam is ready to go up the stairs to his unit, but he is curious and fascinated with the activity going on at the liquor store down the street. For the life of him, he can't see the action from where he's standing. Sam continues up the stairs. As he ascends higher and higher, he becomes amazed at the view.

"Charles!" he yells out.

"What, man?" Charles says with exasperation. "I've had enough for one day. I'm going to call it an evening."

With unbridled excitement Sam says, "Come here, dude, and hurry up."

Reluctantly Charles starts up the stairs. The look he's giving Sam would peel chrome off a bumper. Nonetheless, he keeps on climbing.

With a gleam in his eyes, Sam points toward the corner of their street. In full view lies the liquor store with all the activities for everyone to see. Quite obviously a robbery has taken place. It appears that the robbers were caught at the scene. The absence of emergency medical personnel lets us know that no one was physically hurt. All the commotion adds up to typical neighborhood drama at its finest.

"Wow," Charles exclaims. "You can see it all from up here. I wish I lived upstairs and had this view."

In the midst of a full-fledged epiphany, Sam notices that the sky is clearer from this vantage point, and that the sounds of the neighborhood are more pronounced.

Turning to Charles, he asks, "Do you remember a verse that says, '*I see the end from the beginning*'?"

"Yeah, I remember something along those lines."

"Well, how could anyone see the end from the beginning without being elevated above whatever it is they're looking at?"

"You have a point there, Sam." Charles wistfully observes. Turning admirably to his friend, he says, "Every now and then something slips past those soup coolers on the front of your face that actually makes good sense."

"Thank you, sir, thank you," Sam says with a bow. "I just love these life lessons that we always get from the talks we have. By simply changing our *point* of view we didn't need to wonder what was going on. By changing our angle, we had a proper assessment of what is going on . . . even a full block away."

Slapping Charles on the back, he goes on to say, "We must have the proper perspective, or we are doomed to make erroneous assumptions."

MESSAGE

David Tisdale

There was a message that I was trying so hard to convey,
When I sealed up these words to send them your way.
Like a message in a bottle, these words that will follow,
Traveled far to your reach, like the shores of your beach.
And I'll be praying it's received in the same manner it was sent,
That it captures my emotions to the extent it was meant.
For surely I know, all too often, that a message deferred,
Meaning can get lost at the cost of my words.
Should that be the case, should these words seem a waste,
Just remove everyone, and put my heart in their place.
Because that's the only message that matters,
if all else should fail,
Words may not do justice, for a love on this scale.
One that, if you believe in me, will forever remain true,
This message is clear. All of my love is for you.

ANOTHER YEAR OVER

Jen Bayless

My *Smiley*, your mommy is sitting down five nights before the start of 2012 to record the year that you left us. I must say that there was anxiety at play during December. I was scared that if I didn't close the year by writing to you, that I would begin 2012 forgetting you. What comes to mind, my sweet girl is the Christmas song sung by Celine Dion, which has the words "Another year over . . ." Mom loves Celine's music.

While taking Scooter and Turner to your park in Hesperia, a moment of stark reality hit me. Although the Christmas decorations were exactly the same, they took on a different meaning. This year brought a warm beauty, gorgeous weather, which was so opposite to the winter weather afforded to you the same time last year. Bridget, this year the park was devoid of two key elements, you and the snow. On this Christmas day, we took Turner and Scooter to the park, and someone was sitting by your veterans' plaques—experiencing heartache too.

Bissie, I don't want to see all the Christmas decorations be taken down, as it will be a sign that next year we won't begin the year with you by our side; instead we will just have memories that become foggier as the clock ticks. I told Dad today that it would be wonderful to have another husky, as I miss you so much. I feel guilty that I can't seem to feel the same connection with Scooter and Turner. There isn't a day that goes by during this Christmas season that I don't miss you.

It has been very difficult to feel the same way about life, Bridget. I don't even feel the same about your vet. It's different

133

when I go in there, and I don't want to stay too long. When I go there, it still feels as if I am coming there to have consultation about your issues. It is very difficult for me to figure out whether or not I should begin a new relationship with another veterinarian service near home. I don't know if I can feel the same about life without you, Bridget.

My biggest comfort this year, since your passing, has been the pet loss family on the internet. Their pain begins with the devastation, the wondering how we will live without our fur babies and ask when the tears will stop. All I could tell them is to cry until they do stop, when the wound becomes less raw. Not having you here has made me more of a recluse, and not as eager to be away from home. I think that I am healing, but it isn't easy to say goodbye to a relationship of fourteen years. Since you have passed, I seemed to have withdrawn somewhat, and being at home, having quiet times means more to me than when you were alive.

To return to another year over, it's inevitable that we be reminded that we are supposed to be preparing for a whole *"happy new year."* Personally, I think this whole happy idea is fake. No matter if it's called happy New Year, pain, loss and healing cannot possibly be fake. Happiness is something that is ideal or temporary. It is fleeting, and it really isn't about fireworks and party hats. A new year brings some new beginnings, which are up to you, but it can't erase your suffering. I really do not look forward to being wished "Happy New Year." I think it's really one of humans' failing attempts to be real. It may be another year over for many, but it's not the end of me longing to have you back, Smiley. It's difficult to have the same panoramic view about life that I had while you were alive.

As this year closes, so do we move past the initial loss. The passage of time helps us to let go as well. This doesn't make sense, but it's how I feel about the idea of 2011 coming to a close.

***

A New Year brings some beginnings, and it is up to each of us to make the best of our situations. However, the grief monster will still be there. The grief monster will be there, unpredictable in all its shining glory.

And so, as the ball drops in Times Square, may I wish those of you who have lost a *"furbaby,"* not a happy healing period, but a more insightful time as we journey through the pain.

HOME IS WHERE THE HEART IS

Marilyn King

$\mathcal{M}$y dad had "itchy feet." Even with a large family, he couldn't settle down in one place for long. Because we moved so much, to this day I get the feeling that it's time to get the brown cardboard boxes out and start packing. It got under the skin. I blame my dad for the many excuses I've used over the years for picking up and moving to another house. I inherited his "itchy feet." I work hard at keeping myself rooted in one place longer than a year. I didn't want my children to live the life I had as a child, not knowing what it was like to be rooted in a town you could call "the old stomping grounds." It helps that my husband has no problem "staying put."

As children, we had our ups and downs as all kids do. But, if I had to do it all over again, I wouldn't choose to be in any other family. It was a heck of a ride. We seemed to always be barely just getting by. Daddy struggled to provide for all of us, but we lived a very rich life because we had each other.

House #25
4171 Lewis Street, Fresno, California

By the time my parents had been married seven years, they had moved twenty-five times and added child number four to their household. At 8:45 a.m. on a Friday morning, December 9, 1949, Marilyn Vernay LeRoy was born. A native of California, I would learn through my growing up years that there would be

136

many more places to live; some would be my favorites, and some not so good.

My parents had four daughters and three sons. I was the fourth child either way you looked at it. Fourth from the oldest child down, or fourth from the youngest child up, right smack dab in the middle of the most wonderful family in America.

My siblings have fair complexions, but I was born with olive skin, dark ringlets and hazel eyes. And no, I wasn't the milkman's daughter. All of my mother's family had fair complexions. Most of my father's family had olive complexions. Some Spanish blood sneaked in there somewhere along the line.

I later learned my parents wanted another boy for my brother, Johnny, who was two years older than I. But Johnny (John Charles LeRoy) found I was a good playmate. We played cowboys and Indians, army guys or just about anything he wanted to do.

Our family was not your typical family, if there is such a thing. We moved anywhere from six weeks to three years, all the years I was home.

***

Dad, Jack Henry LeRoy, was born and raised in Santa Rosa, California by a meat cutter, Martin Peter LeRoy, and his wife, a tiny little gal, Tillie Mae Grigsby. Dad was the oldest of thirteen children.

Mom, Verdean Gwendolyn Fisher, was born in Great Bend, Kansas to John Sylvester Fisher, who died when she was four, and his wife, Verna Violet Smith, a widow who raised three daughters by taking in washing and ironing for a living. Mom and her two sisters, Dolores and Doreen, grew up in a small rural town learning to help Grandma make ends meet. Once old enough, at the age of eight-years-old, each of the girls had to do their share of washing and ironing. When they reached their teens, they went out and found jobs to contribute income for the family.

Grandma set her sight on Grandpa Roy Powell when he worked at the Santa Fe railroad station. She would bag a lunch for him each afternoon and wait for the train to pull into the depot. She didn't charge him for the lunch. Grandma hoped that in time he would return her affection. They say the way to a man's heart is his belly. It worked. After ten years of living in a home with no man in the house, Grandma married Roy Powell, and life eased for mother's family knowing food would be on the table.

When Mom turned eighteen, her aunt Zella had a stroke. Uncle Ed wrote Grandma and asked if one of her daughters could come to Ocean Park, later known as Santa Monica, California, for the summer and help care for her. Mom was glad to go. Uncle Ed's house was on Pier Avenue, four blocks from the beach. Coming from a rural farm town, this would be a nice change.

That summer, 1942, World War II was in full swing. My mom's cousin, Enid Fisher, had heeded the call for women to work at Hughes Aircraft. She worked long hours and could not be home to care for her mother. On the weekends, Uncle Ed could be home to care for his wife, Zella. Weekends were one of Mom's favorite times. She and her cousin, Enid would go down to the Ocean Park Pier. It was like a carnival year round. The long pier had a Ferris wheel, Carousel House, roller coaster, restaurants and a dance hall. This is where my parents met. Dad was working for the defense plant in Venice Beach, and Mom was taking an evening break from her summer job.

There was a dance hall on the pier. If a couple wanted to dance to the live band, they had to purchase a token from the ticket booth. The tokens were twenty-five cents each. There was a slot in which to insert the token on the turnstile. Once the token was inserted, the turnstile would allow access into the hall. Mom said Dad just kept putting the tokens in the turnstile to get another dance with her. Three months later, September 5, 1942, they were married. House number one was in Venice Beach, next door to Ocean Park.

While World War II raged on, Dad left the defense plant and joined the Army Air Corps. It was during the war that my older sisters, Deany, (Verdean Louise LeRoy), and Rene, (Rene Marie LeRoy), were born. My parents moved several times because Dad was stationed in different bases while in the Army. Then he was sent overseas. Mom took little Deany back to stay with Grandma and Grandpa Powell in Great Bend, Kansas. By then she was expecting Rene, who was born while Dad was in France. When the war was over, my parents continued their adventure of moving from one house to another. When Dad got out of the Army Air Corps, he went to work at the meat markets.

My grandfather was a meat cutter. He taught four of his eight sons to be meat cutters. It was a risky business if one were not inclined to tip the scales. This brings to mind the picture Norman Rockwell did of the little woman with her finger under the scale to push it up, while the meat cutter behind the counter has his finger on the top of the scale pushing it down. Many of the places my dad worked encouraged a few ounces be added to the price of meat. In the early days, the scales did not display a digital screen on the backside of the scale for the customers. It was a keen way for the owner of the meat market to add profit to his coffers. That was one of a dozen reasons why my dad moved on to work for other meat markets. He was not willing to cheat the customers. Once the boss found out, Dad was out the door.

***

In the early years of my parents' marriage, Grandpa and Grandma LeRoy got a divorce. At that time several of my aunts and uncles were still children themselves. My uncle Bill, who was one of the older boys of the thirteen children, found a place for Grandma and five of the younger kids to live. It was a friend's home. It wasn't long before Grandma and the kids realized the living conditions wouldn't work. Grandma didn't have a place to go, and her five youngest children were scared for the first time in their lives. They had always lived in a house with both parents where life seemed secure. Now they didn't know what would happen to them. Where would they live?

When Dad learned of their dilemma through Uncle Bill, Dad told him to bring Grandma and the kids to our home until something better turned up. Uncle Bernie was the oldest of the five youngest children. He said that when they walked through the front door of our home, the first thing he saw was Mamma sitting on the couch holding baby Johnny. At that moment, something warm and good washed over him. He knew everything was going to be all right. To this day, Uncle Bernie remembers the way Mamma's hair was combed, the dress she wore and the smile on her face when they came through the front door. That moment was stamped on his mind and his heart forever. It was a moment that gave him hope.

***

By 1950, another child was born to our family, my sister Tess. It would be ten years before two more brothers would complete the family of seven children. Mom had other babies who were either miscarried or who died at birth. She delivered all of her children breech, feet first. Tessie, (Theresa Ann LeRoy), was a twin. Mom lost her twin in the fourth month of her pregnancy. The doctor had Mom stay in bed until Tessie was

140

born. He feared Mom would lose the other twin if she resumed keeping up housework and tending the children. Grandma Powell came out and helped Mom with the children until the baby was born.

Tessie would become my playmate for life. We were only one year apart, and she eventually became my ears because at the age of three, I became very sick. I had an intense fever for several days. My parents later learned I had scarlet fever. It starts out as a form of strep throat, but can cause ear infections, among other symptoms.

It wasn't long after I recovered that I began getting spankings for not listening to Mamma. She never beat us kids, but we did get the whack on the behind if we didn't mind. She would tell me to pick up my toys, or go get Johnny, or any number of other things, but because she was behind me, I didn't know she was talking to me. She thought I was just being a testy three-year-old. It was too soon for her to know I had lost most of my hearing from the scarlet fever. She didn't understand why her good little girl would not behave when told. It wasn't long before two-year-old Tessie figured out that I wasn't hearing Mamma. She would tell me what Mamma said. Even though Tessie was a year younger, she understood that I didn't hear.

From then on, Tessie had a loud voice. It wasn't her fault. She learned early on to speak loudly when we played. She was my saving grace. We played together all the time. She was around when anyone was speaking to me. She'd make sure I got it when people spoke. She learned my body language and easily picked up when I was at a loss for what was being said. She would lean over and tell me, to my face, what someone said. To this day, she still does it. Bless her heart.

It wasn't until I was in the first grade that my teacher figured out very quickly that I had a hearing problem. I had lost fifty to seventy-five percent of my hearing. Mom felt terrible. I remember her hugging me and telling me how sorry she was for all the spankings she gave me for being disobedient.

By then, I had learned on my own to read lips. If someone faced me while speaking, enough sound accompanied by the movements of their lips got me through most of what was being said. I did, however, miss the ways words were pronounced. When I became an adult, I learned the high-frequency fibers in my ears had burned up with the scarlet fever. Intense fevers can cause hearing loss.

***

Tessie was a 'rascally' kind of little girl. She fought for what she wanted, maybe because she was the littlest of the bunch. I'm not sure why. But she would wind up on top of me punching me and fighting. She would dig her little fingernails in my forearm leaving four small welts, or she would bite me. I think I was four and Tessie was three when Grandma told me, "Don't just lie there and let her tear into you like that. Fight back!" I don't know why I didn't want to fight back. Maybe I was afraid of hurting her. It just wasn't in me. But when Grandma coached me to fight back, I did.

It was quite a shock for Tessie to get back what she had been dishing out. For me, it seemed such a violation to dig my fingers into her soft flesh. But not for long. I soon found satisfaction in fighting back. She learned that the days of using me for a punching bag were over. Lying there and taking it from her came to a halt. It is one of my "stand out" memories of Grandma coming to visit. I was liberated, maybe too liberated.

When we got older, every so often I got brave enough to pull a chair out from under Tessie. She'd hit the floor only long enough to jump up and the race was on. We ran around the house with her chasing me to get even. I never learned my lesson. She would always let me have it back twice as hard.

***

Some of our favorite times were when Grandma Powell came to visit. Grandpa and Grandma would ride the train from Kansas to California and visit us for a week or two. Mom wrote Grandma letters telling her how much she missed her. Then Grandma would come. All eyes were peeled on Grandma's suitcase when she came through the front door. We kids knew there would be treats inside that brown suitcase. I can still see it in my mind's eye. We would hover around Grandma as she opened her luggage and wait with anticipation as she brought out a "goody" for each of us. It was usually candy and a small toy. As a child, candy only happened on special occasions. One of those special occasions was Grandma's visits.

Grandma had always called Mom the sentimental one of her three daughters. Mom had a way of talking that held all of our attention. She would tell us her dreams in such a way that she could always make us want whatever Mom wanted. She had the most gentle and sweet spirit of any woman I have ever known. I don't remember anyone ever disliking her. Growing up, my friends would call her "Mom" and tell us kids they wished they had a mom like ours.

Mom would tell us stories of her growing-up years. Back then, we didn't have television. It was a special time when Mom would sit us kids down and tell us her stories. We loved it. She had all of our undivided attention. Sometimes, if she had a mind to, she would let us kids come into her bedroom and sit on the bed. Then she would open her bottom chest of drawers, and one by one bring out her treasures, little pieces of Mamma's past. Something from when she was a young girl, like her gold tassel from her graduation cap (that later came up missing), or something from when Daddy was in the war.

Mamma would usually take a little longer telling us stories about when Daddy was in the war. She would hold up the half-dollar-sized cigarette lighter made from two coat buttons from one of the prisoners. My dad was a prison guard in France, among other positions in the service. He didn't see the men in the cells as only war prisoners. He saw them as husbands, fathers, brothers and sons. He noticed their boots were in bad repair, or a prisoner didn't have a coat. Dad would slip in a pair of boots, a coat or sometimes a candy bar to cheer up a prisoner.

He was known throughout the prison camp as the guard who cared. When World War II ended and the prisoners were released, they lined up and saluted my dad. They shook his hand and some of the men made something for my dad with the little they had. The button lighter was a gift from one of the prisoners. Every time Mamma told the story, my heart would swell so big I felt it would burst. I was so proud of my daddy.

Mamma's bottom drawer gave us a peek into her and Daddy's past. And she had a way, in her sweet voice, of telling us about it. We loved being around her.

Many of her stories were about Grandma, what it was like growing up in Great Bend, Kansas. She made Great Bend, Kansas sound like the next best thing to being in Heaven. Grandma was a strong-willed woman. She *had* to be in the depression days, raising three little girls on her own. The stories were endless, and we would listen, wanting to hear more.

House #26
Two-room motel, Fields Landing, California

At the time of my birth, my dad worked for Garzon's Meat Market in Fresno. He was a union member. When a meat market strike was called, Dad couldn't work. He had to carry a sign and picket the market. When the meat market strike was over, the owner of Garzon's Meat Market was fit to be tied. He gave Dad a hard time. Dad saw an ad in the paper for a manager position in Eureka, California, near the Oregon border on the ocean. By then I was a year old.

Dad applied for and got the job. He rented two rooms at a motel just outside the town of Fields Landing, California until he could find us a home to rent in Eureka.

***

Eureka was the town Dad lived in as a boy when he was nine years old. Grandpa LeRoy managed a meat market. At his tender young age, Dad helped contribute to the income of the house. Bib tankers and boats would pull into the harbor. Dad and his friends would pick wild blackberries and sell them to the cooks on the ships. Dad also took a wagon and gathered driftwood for their wood stoves. It was Dad's job to cut cords of wood for the cooks. Every day after school, he would go out to the backyard of his home and chop wood. Now we were back in his boyhood town.

***

Neighbors in a motel room next to ours, Crit and Lilabelle, had a daughter and a son. Sometimes our two families ate together and made minced egg sandwiches and whatever they could put together to go with them. Some folks called their sandwiches 'deviled eggs.' But more times than not, Mamma called them 'minced-egg' sandwiches.

One evening some of the motel renters went crab hunting. They got a big load of crabs and built a fire in the center of the motel square. Then they set a big tub filled with water over the fire and boiled the crabs. All the motel renters sat outside and enjoyed the meal. Mom said the crabs were sweet and delicious. It was a memory that showed the bright side of living in a motel.

The landlady of the motel had five children. Every day at suppertime, she would stand outside her office and call her children by name to come home, starting with the oldest child and working down the line to the youngest.

House # 27
3126 Montgomery Street, Eureka, California

By 1951, we moved into house number twenty-seven. I was two years old. The house was by the woods. My sisters, Deany and Rene, and my brother Johnny would take buckets and pick salmonberries in the forest. They were called salmonberries because they were the color of salmon and looked like large blackberries. Sand fleas got into the house and drove the family crazy. I remember Mom telling us how awful they were, and how she had to keep putting lotion on us to soothe the itching.

Dad bought our first boat while living on Montgomery Street. It was twelve feet long and not too wide. It had an outboard motor. He painted the boat white and trimmed it in navy blue. Then he painted Mom's name, 'VERDEAN,' in navy blue along each side.

One Sunday, my folks decided to go fishing in the Pacific Ocean. They asked their friend's daughter to babysit their five children. The girl they sent was around fifteen. Dad and Mom intended to be home before six p.m. They stopped at McDonald's and bought a bag of hamburgers and french fries. They brought Coca-Cola along with their fishing poles and tackle box. They wore Army life jackets in olive green.

They took the boat out into the ocean about five miles. Dad caught two big salmon and Mom caught three big red snappers. Another big salmon took off with Dad's fishing pole! They had a great day. After a good part of the day had gone by, they noticed that other fishing boats were headed for shore. It was then that Dad noticed that white caps were forming in the water. The water was beginning to move into swells. Boy, my folks headed for shore as fast as they could. They only had a small outboard motor and it wouldn't go very fast.

The swells began to pull their small boat high into the air. All the water below was way down. Mom said she felt like they were on a mountain looking down into a valley. When the boat swooshed down into the bottom of the wave, all the water around them was very high. This continued until they made it to shore. It took a very long time. They had only gained a small amount of progress between swells.

It was 9:00 p.m. when they reached shore. Both of my parents had been praying and asking God to save them and bring them safely home to their children. When they finally got home, they found that the babysitter was so upset at their coming home late, that she had taken scissors and cut the eyelashes off all five of us kids. We were crying, and my sisters were telling Dad and Mom how scared we all were.

Mom was angry.

Dad said, "Don't say anything." He gave the girl $10.00 and took her home.

Mom said later, "That girl was so happy with the $10.00, I bet she sang, 'Stay all night–stay a little longer.'" That was the one and only time my folks hired a babysitter. Where they went, we went.

House number twenty-seven was the house where the landlady's daughter pushed my brother Johnny down onto a jagged piece of cement. It cut the skin just above his eye. It bled so much Mom thought it had put his eye out. She borrowed a neighbor's telephone and called Daddy at the meat market. They got Johnny to a doctor. To this day, he still has the scar above his eye.

Eureka has a cold, damp climate. In the summer, we all had to wear long-sleeved sweaters. We were getting sick with pneumonia, and my baby sister Tessie was not able to eat any baby food. Mom would put thin amounts of Pablum cereal in her bottle of milk to get some nourishment down her. Tessie's legs got so weak that she couldn't push up on them. Mom's doctor told my parents if they didn't get her to a warmer, drier climate, Tessie would die. It was time to get the brown cardboard boxes out. We were going to move!

THE DREAM

Virginia Hall

She was slim, blonde, smart, and heading off to college. There, she fell in love with a fellow student and, since it was the 50s rather than the 60s, they married so they could live together. They finished college, found jobs, and had two children. For their fifth wedding anniversary, he gave her a diamond wedding set to replace the simple gold band he'd exchanged at their wedding. Around the time of their tenth wedding anniversary, he asked for a divorce. She tried to dissuade him, but to no avail. He married the other woman.

She struggled financially and emotionally. Because of her job, she received no alimony and he rarely paid child support. She dated a bit, but it was years before she fell in love again. She lived in Ventura County, and Max lived in San Bernardino County. They didn't see each other often. Finally, after years, she and Max married in her family's backyard. He lived in the desert, but she was used to a world with green in it, so they moved to the mountains. She quit her job, rented out her house, and started a new life.

She found a job, taking a large pay cut, and helped her daughter adjust to the change in their lives. Her daughter and her new husband vied for her affection and attention, but in time life smoothed out. They traveled every summer, enjoying happy times. He'd put his arm around her shoulder, and say, "You're the best thing that ever happened to me." Then, four years later, he died of a heart attack. She was alone again, a widow in her early forties.

Not long after that, her car broke down in a parking lot; it was sitting in a new puddle. A nice man stopped by, looked under the hood, and saw that the car had a broken hose. He took her to get a part and fixed the car for her. She had no intention of seeking romance. Enough was enough. But, when he called her at work a few weeks later, she had to at least return the call. Eventually, she relented, and he came up to the mountains to take her out for dinner. It was another slow courtship, and she couldn't say "Yes" when he asked her to marry him. She asked him to wait, and he did. Finally, she said "Yes."

It was after they were settled into the house they'd bought together, that she had the dream. She rarely remembered her dreams, and only the ones so terrible that they woke her up. In this dream she and Max were driving down the mountain in Max's little white car. She said, "You know, I married again."

He said, "Yes, I know. It's all right." Max dropped her off where she used to work and she stood there, watching his car drive off, getting smaller and smaller. She thought, *Well, that's that,* and then she woke up.

To her surprise, there were tears on her face, and she could still replay the whole vivid dream. The next day, she told her new husband about the dream, which still brought her to tears. He hugged her, and said, "It's all right." And it was.

IF WALLS COULD CRY

Patrick Wallace

Portraits of the days of old are no more,
leaving the walls as my only companion.
We talk and reminisce, while redefining loneliness;
We laugh, we cry, without any particular reason why.

Tonight I'm cold, and the walls offer comfort.
They assure me that new portraits will present themselves;
New works of art that mirror the Picasso era.

While I'm sleeping the walls pay close attention.
There were many things that happened inside these walls,
that they're way too classy to mention.
As I roll over in my sleep, searching for inner peace,
I feel the moisture from within the walls,
and discover they also weep.

THE ECHOS OF A WHISPER

Gregory Caruth

'm from a small town, where everyone knows everyone. A place where morals, a sweaty brow, and southern hospitality are the ways of life. A place where a firm handshake and a smile meant that you were a man of your word. And indeed a friend. A place where your neighbors were considered more than just someone that lived next to you. They were family and friends. A place where you could leave your windows open, and your doors unlocked at night. We were more than just a neighborhood, we were a community.

This community was a place where a hot plate and a good night's sleep was just a door knock away. A place where struggles and hardships meant unity and togetherness. This neighborhood was like glue during the midst of hard times.

As I was growing up, it was easy for me to believe that everyone who called themselves a friend was indeed one. But things changed around here.

"Hey Bobby Ray," a middle aged man with an oil-stained T-shirt, worn cut-off trousers, and callused bared feet yelled.

I stepped off the front porch wearing my usual around-the-house work attire. A withered straw hat, tattered demi overalls, and old grass-stained work boots. Giving him the once over, I thought to myself, in all these years ol' Buck Earl hadn't changed a bit.

"What's goin' on Buck Earl?"

"Nothin', but the hands of time," he replied with a distant look and a harsh southern accent.

I followed his gaze to a group of teens down the street, hanging out in a yard that was littered with trash. Loud music was playing, as they danced and sang along with bottles in their hands and marijuana joints in their mouths.

"Man, Buck Earl," Bobby Ray said, still staring down the street. "What happened to this community?"

Buck Earl shrugged. "Here it is. You got young kids strung out on dope. Carrin' on like they ain't got no type of sense or home trainin'. I know you heard what happened to ol' Arthur Lee 'bout a week or two ago. Earl, I tried to talk to him 'bout messin' round. But he just wouldn't listen. Anyway, he was on his way back from that ol' juke joint down there in Possum Creek. He was full of that devil juice when a group of young hoodlums roughed him up, and took what was left of his change money, that he saved up from cuttin' grass all week."

"I declare," Buck Earl interjected. "These kids today just ain't got no respect for they elders, or nobody Bobby Ray," he said, mopping his brow with the back of his left hand. "An I sho' hate to hear that happened to ol' Arthur Lee. But you know how bad his mouth is. 'Specially when he got that juice in him. He'll let his mouth get him into somethin' that his ol' marrow rump can't get him out of," he added chuckling. "You know I ain't lyin', Bobby Ray!"

"An speakin' of the devil—here come ol' Arthur Lee now." Buck Earl added. "Look at'em, with that bottle in his hand. Probably some ol' cheap Night Train," he laughed. "You know befo' ol' Dr. Huckleberry passed on, he say—that Arthur Lee is the only chile he know who come out the womb with a bottle of moonshine in his hand."

Bobby Ray cackled as Buck Earl continued.

153

"Sho' did, Bobby Ray. You know I ain't lyin'," he exaggerated. "Look here, I'm fixin' to get on up the road," Buck Earl explained, shifting his weight to his right foot. "Cause you know last time Arthur Lee came 'round here with a bottle you had to call the Fire Department to pry my arms from 'round his neck." Buck Earl laughed and shook his friend's hand.

"Boy, I tell ya . . . you ain't changed a bit," Bobby Ray said, smiling as he shook his friend's hand. "You be sure to stop by here, sometimes this evenin'. I'm throwin' some of my famous BBQ on the grill. Momma's comin' over today and she been on me all week 'bout havin' her some BBQ when she get here."

"Wouldn't miss it for nothin' in the world," Buck Earl said, rubbing his stomach.

"Alright, Buck Earl," Bobby Ray said, looking in Arthur Lee's direction. Bobby Ray walked to the middle of the street after he saw that Arthur Lee had stopped in front of the group of teens. Sensing that something was wrong, he attentively started walking in their direction. The closer he got, the more he could hear Arthur Lee's slurred yelling.

"Boy, I wish I was just ten years younger," he paused, balling his fist up. "Cause I'll go to all fo' of your sorry asses," he yelled in the midst of staggering, "at the same time!" Arthur Lee waved his fist in the air like it was a lasso.

"Well you keep on runnin' your mouth old man, and I'mma give you a reason to wish you were twenty years younger," one of the teens shouted.

"Well, come on over here, boy." Arthur Lee staggered. "I'mma cut you every way but loose," he said fumbling with his pocket. He sat his bottle down on the dirt road, and stood there swaying.

Bobby Ray had seen enough. He hurried over to stop a fight before it even started. Arthur Lee reeked of alcohol, and it spewed from his pores. He was dressed in a wrinkled red and black flannel shirt, faded cut-off Dickie Khaki's, and a pair of muddy black boots. His hair was sandy red, and matted as if it hadn't been combed in weeks.

"Alright, Arthur Lee," Bobby Ray interrupted. "That's enough man. What's goin' on over here?" he asked, knowing who the real trouble maker was.

"Bobby Ray, these little mothersuckers think I'm some kind of fool," Arthur Lee slurred as he bent to pick up his bottle of Thunder Bird.

"He is!" another teen yelled.

"You see what I'm talkin' 'bout," Arthur Lee exclaimed looking at Bobby Ray. "They think I don't know that they're the same ones who robbed me the other night. They look—and sound—just like the little punks who did it," Arthur Lee slurred.

"We haven't done a thing to this old bum," one of the teens vented. "Besides, what would somebody get if they did try to rob him . . . Alzheimer's!?" The group of teens erupted in laughter at the joke.

Bobby Ray laughed himself. He knew Arthur Lee was still sore about the incident, and would blame any crowd of teens in sight. So he did what he thought was best. "Come on down to the house, Arthur Lee. I'm fixin' to throw some of my famous BBQ on the grill while you sit back and enjoy yourself. I know you're hungry," he said, hooking an arm around Arthur Lee's shoulder and guiding him in the direction of his house.

"Bobby Ray, you know I love that BBQ," Arthur Lee said slowly walking towards the house. "Ya'll little thieves better count your blessin's, cause if my friend been two seconds later— ya'll ass was grass!" he yelled over his shoulder.

"Psss...that old man gonna make me hurt him," one of the teens that wore his pants hanging off of his buttocks said, walking towards the street.

Back at Bobby Ray's, Arthur Lee saw that the lawn was overgrown, and needed to be cut. His only motivation to ask was a quick opportunity to make a little money for his next bottle of wine. So he inquired, "Grass looks like it needs tending," he slurred, staggering to Bobby Ray's rocking chair that sat on his wooded porch.

"Yeah, I've been doing a lot of working this week. I ain't had time to get around to it, but I'll get it done sometime this weekend," Bobby Ray added, grabbing a bag of charcoals, and a box of matches from the wooden box on the side of the porch.

Arthur Lee continued drinking, as he took sip after sip. Bobby Ray's mother arrived, a beautiful woman in a yellow sun dress with a flowery design, yellow sandals, and a yellow bow tied in her streaky grey hair.

"Hey, baby," she cried as Bobby Ray embraced her warmly.

"Hey, momma," he responded like a puppy who had just seen its master. "We're gonna be rollin' here in a minute," he said gesturing towards the grill that sat in his front yard.

"I've been waitin' all week for these ribs that just fall off the bone," she said with hand animations. "A few more minutes ain't gonna hurt nobody," she added, turning her gaze on Arthur Lee who was slumped over in the rocking chair, bottle still clutched in his hand.

"Hey there, Arthur," she said with her slight southern accent. "I see you still touting that bottle around. Liquid foolishness,' she added in a frustrated tone. She took a seat in the rocking chair next to him.

"Yes, ma'am, I am," he said unenthusiastically. He knew that she was about to lecture him.

"Well," she began, adjusting her dress below her knees. "Just like it was a time to pick the bottle up—it's a time to lay it back down, son. Ain't you tired?" she asked, as she shifted in her seat. "Tired of lettin' that bottle control your life because all you do is waste your hard earned money on that stuff, son. And all it do is bring out the worst in you." She stared deep into his bloodshot eyes. "Baby, you got to be tired."

Arthur Lee sat despondent. He stared at Bobby Ray's mother and lowered his head. "Ms. Thompson—I mean, yes ma'am. I get tired," he said in a pitiful voice. "But the only thing I can turn to, to wash my pain away, is my bottle." Arthur Lee said yawning, and raising the bottle of Thunder Bird to his lips to take a sip.

"Well," she began in a caring voice. "When you really get enough…I know who you can call to wash your pain away," she looked up towards the sky.

That was the last thing Arthur Lee heard before he drifted off into his drunken slumber. The BBQ sizzled on the grill as the zesty inviting aroma drifted in the air.

"Uuummm, baby," Bobby Ray's mother remarked. "You sure got it smellin' good 'round here," she said watching him on the grill.

Bobby Ray smiled.

"Bobby Ray," she called.

"Yes, ma'am," he answered respectfully.

"Baby, I've been around a long time, and have seen many things. I've watched you, Buck Earl, and Arthur Lee grow up from when ya'll was babies," she said as she shifted her weight in the chair. "And…" she hesitated. "If you don't remember nothing else I tell you today, baby remember this. Never listen to the foolishness. A pair of lips will say anything, baby. But pay close attention to a person's actions. They tell you everything you need to know. Everything," she stressed, giving what she just said some time to marinate as Bobby Ray took a slab of ribs off the grill and into the house.

Suddenly, there was a faint scream coming from down the street. Ms. Thomas looked in the direction of the sound, and saw Buck Earl being surrounded by a group of teens.

"Bobby Ray," she yelled hysterically. "Buck Earl is in trouble out here. Hurry up, baby."

Bobby Ray ran out of his house, stumbling over a lifted plank on his porch. "What is it, momma?" he said, flinging the screen door closed behind him.

"Them kids down there is about to jump on Buck Earl!" she pointed at the crowd down the street.

Bobby Ray ran, grabbed a 2x4 that lay on the side of his house, and headed as fast as he could to Buck Earl's side. "What in the world is goin' on out here?" Bobby Ray demanded half out of breath.

"These kids still fired up over some mess that Arthur Lee started earlier," Buck Earl tried to explain. Suddenly, a look of fear washed over his face. He realized what he had in his hand as he stared down the barrel of semi-automatic pistol that one of the teens withdrew from his pocket.

"Lord, have mercy," Bobby Ray yelled as he dropped his plank. The people standing around began to duck and hide behind cars, and you could hear a pin drop. He looked around in shame, and spoke in a low tone. "What happened to this community? This used to be a place of peace. A place where families were joined and generations were made. A man could walk the streets with his head held high, and never have to worry about being mugged."

People began to rise from cover. The teens began to look around at each other, as the young man with the gun lowered his weapon. "Now look at it," Bobby Ray continued. "You kids on drugs hangin' in these here streets, when you should be in school. Snakes all around us, it looks like. There just ain't no character in this community no mo'."

The people murmured as the crowd began to disperse.

"Let them people alone," another kid who stood in the crowd said, tugging at his friends, one by one.

Buck Earl looked at Bobby Ray and smiled.

***

I wish I could be a kid again. I've long since left that small town. And have come to realize just how crucial the word "friendship" really is. It's a word not to be thrown around lightly. And it doesn't apply to everyone in your life. It could mean the difference between life and death.

People we befriend—we let into our house, introduce to our families, and open doors for them to love or hurt us. It was easy as a child. Now that I look back on my life, I realize what my mom was trying to tell me that crazy day Arthur Lee passed out on my porch. I can hear the echoing whispers of so many neighbors that tried to lead me down a path of righteousness. I'm glad I listened.

THE COPIER

Jim Elstad

"George, take the prisoner into room one." Harrison walked down the hall, around the crate holding the new copier, and into the break room. He poured two cups of coffee and yelled, "Cream and sugar right?"

"You're finally getting it, thanks. Get a cup for Jason."

"Only if he'll cooperate. If he's gonna wait for his lawyer, his lawyer can get him a cup."

Inside the interview room Jason, an eighteen-year-old wanna-be street hood, perked up at the mention of coffee. "I ain't gonna wait for any lawyer. I ain't done nuttin. I'll take my coffee black."

Harrison came back carrying a tray with three cups, coffee, sugar, and creamer, all while carrying his organizer under his arm and a pen in his mouth. "All right, you answer a question and we'll give you a cup; the more answers, the more coffee."

Jason nodded. "Sure, ask away."

George held the pot in front of Jason, "Where were you last night? Don't lie, we know the truth."

Jason rocked back and forth in his chair. "Weeelll, I was walkin' down the street mindin' my own business when this guy jumps me and beats me up. Now, pour my coffee."

George filled a cup, put it to his nose and savored the aroma. "Ah, this is the best I've ever tasted." He glared at Jason, "What street, what time, give me a description of the guy."

Jason folded his arms, "You lied, you said if I gave you an answer you'd give me coffee. I ain't sayin' nuttin till I get some joe."

160

Harrison filled a cup half-way and placed it in front of the prisoner. "Okay, half an answer, half a cup."

The skinny man grabbed the cup and rolled it in his hands. "At 4:30 last night I was walking down Main Street and this guy jumped me. He drew his knife, I drew mine. We fought, I won, I …."

Harrison stroked his beard, and interrupted, "That's not how we heard it. Are you sure that's the story you want to tell us?"

"If that's how you want to play it I want a lawyer. Ain't gonna say another word until he gets here."

Harrison stood, "Excuse me, I'll be right back."

Ten minutes later Harrison returned with a piece of paper, the operations manual for the copier, and a helmet.

George hid his surprise. *What's the boss come up with now?*

Harrison slid the paper in front of Jason, set the manual and the helmet aside. "I had the tape recorder going while you were telling us your lies," he paused and tapped the paper. "Read and sign this to verify it's true."

Jason stared at the paper, ran his finger down the page. "Where do you want me to sign?"

The Chief Detective pointed to the bottom of the sheet. "Right here."

George put his hand in front of his mouth to keep from laughing.

Jason signed and shoved the paper back. "I want my lawyer."

Harrison pushed the paper away and picked up the helmet. "This is an accessory for our new copier. Here's the manual for you to read, but when I…" He held the end of the cable attached to the helmet. "When I plug this in, the copier will print a picture of your answer to every question. You won't have to say a word. It's like we searched you."

Shocked, Jason cried out, "I don't believe you! That's the craziest thing I ever heard. What do you think I am? An idiot?"

Harrison smiled, "Didn't think you'd take my word for it. Here's the manual." He opened it to chapter seven, and flattened it. "Take your time, this is important. I wouldn't try to trick you. This new copier has the new mental feature."

Jason ran his thumb down each page of the chapter and looked up. "It's amazing what they can do. I may as well tell you everything."

Harrison winked at George while looking at Jason. "If I put the helmet on you, I don't have to wait for your lawyer. If you give me a statement without your lawyer present, I get in trouble; unless you put it in writing that you'll waive your right to a lawyer."

Jason's eyes flitted back and forth between them. "I changed my mind. If you use that machine on me who knows what else you'll find out? Then I'll really look foolish."

An hour later, as Jason was led away, George burst out laughing. "Boss, you never cease to amaze me. You knew he couldn't read, that he'd pretend to understand. I don't know where you come up with these ideas."

KNICKKNACKS

June Langer

The shelf
  My father built it after retirement

An East Indian bronze bell
  My mother bought it as a souvenir

A pair of old vases
  Belonged to take-charge Aunt Viola

Two china cups and saucers with rose buds and gold trim
  Mary's antique shopping

A hand-carved, wooden bird
  My husband enjoyed giving me little things

A tiny teacart
  Doll house furniture—I like miniatures

An alabaster toothpick holder
  A gift from a neighbor from her trip to Mexico

A sea shell from my grandmother
  I hear the ocean when I put it to my ear

A small glass slipper
Inheritance from my other grandmother

Thoughts and memories as I dust and rearrange.

THE LAST TIME

Janis Brams

$\mathcal{H}$ er lids were paper thin, like Japanese lanterns lit from within. They were closed. I studied her face. It was hard to look another place when she was still here, just a touch away from the heavy wood chair I pulled close to her bed. As I reached out to smooth stray strands of hair, I noted the narrow blue lines that ran like threads from the top of her lid to her faded lashes. Her eyes had always been a prominent feature, one that we shared, mother and daughter. People called them bedroom eyes. Beneath those thin flesh shades rested two blue pools. They were bright but not always clear. Sometimes I found it hard to see inside her, to what she thought and what she felt. She was my mother, but she rarely shared her secrets. As I sat on that sticky leather seat, I wondered, is she afraid? Does she regret? Does she feel at peace?

She sat in bed, propped up with pillows. The mattress was raised to help her stay upright, a comfortable position, and one that allowed her to breathe. The last three years had been full of uncertainty. Aortic stenosis had weakened her heart, leaving her breathless at times and fatigued. Now, the lights were soft, and the room was private in anticipation of the inevitable. This hospital stay was young, just a day or two. Her flowered robe, a cotton housecoat, draped the single other chair that occupied this space, and a vase filled with daisies sat on her bed stand. There hadn't been time yet to bring by her pictures or collect the get-well cards from family and friends.

For the moment, she breathed with little effort. Her chest moved up and down, and she opened her eyes. "Are you still here?" she said. I nodded because nodding was the best I could do. "It's getting late, isn't it?"

"It's not so bad," I said. "I'm not ready to leave just yet."

Her lids lowered. I glanced down at my watch and, mesmerized, studied the hands moving round. Suddenly, a desperate feeling triggered inside me like floodwaters rising, and I willed her awake. Talk to me, I whispered. Tell me the secrets you kept, the secrets Dad shared when a wall stood between us that neither could breach. It was a wall that grew gradually, each brick a forbidden topic. I was your daughter, a teen, who wanted to know you, but you were a puzzle, a puzzle missing pieces; understanding came hard. I learned about your Mother who died young and the time you spent away, living with an aunt whose name I don't know. Dad told me about the burned out tenement you shared with your father. But they were Dad's words not yours. What was it like, Mom? Was it that time in your life that marked you, leaving you vulnerable and given to periods of sadness? Standing in your bedroom doorway, I watched you, seated in a chair staring at the screen of your tiny TV. A larger one stood in the living room, but you sat alone, blinds closed, immersed in soap opera lives. When I came home from school and said your name, you didn't answer. Just the soft orange glow of the TV set welcomed me home.

Her eyes stayed closed.

The others—my sister, my brother, and their families—had gone back to their own homes, places where they could face their grief or put it off a while longer. My home was not close by. It was 3,000 miles west, light years away from this chair, this bed, and this last time. Michael, my husband, and I decided to leave the east coast to have a life adventure. It was to have been a temporary relocation for our baby girl and us. I'm not sure that our choice to stay on in the California high desert had been conscious; rather, days had accumulated until years passed. We

166

had all settled into life, exploring, studying, working, and meeting friends who functioned like the sisters and brothers who lived so many miles east. "What did you think about all that, Mom?" I asked. But she was asleep and could not hear me.

The round clock face that sat on her nightstand said ten o'clock. How had it gotten so late? Michael was out in the family waiting area, his idea. This was a gift, this time alone with my mother. Her hair, bleached orange like a fallen leaf, had grown thin. Did I ever really know her true shade? Week after week when I was little, she walked to her salon for shampoo and set or cut and color. Sometimes we walked together, and I sat and watched or played pretend. Orange…it brought me back to their visits, Mom and Dad's. When the girls, our girls, were little, Nana and Papa would come for weeks, sometimes a month or two. Leaving what was familiar made Mom a willing player in our out-West adventures. I pictured her now, climbing a steep hill overrun with pumpkin-orange poppies. Our oldest daughter sat down among the flowers, while the youngest stepped between them. Mom, proud of her climb, stood at the top of the hill looking over fields and fields of orange blooms. Michael smiled and nodded, "Good job, Mollie."

I remember watching her, my Mom, standing in a field of flowers, smiling, sharing the moment with my girls and feeling their joy. She could do this now, and I was thankful but sad that this kind of abandon was never ours to share when I was a girl.

The nurse appeared, ready to do vital signs. Mom woke and sighed. She had drifted down in bed, so we each took an elbow to lift her, to help her move around. "How are you doing, Mrs. Alper?" the nurse asked. "Are you thirsty?"

She nodded, and I reached for the plastic cup with a straw inserted. "Here, Mom." I was glad to help, to do something that seemed to make a difference. But she only took a sip, and I thought how little she needed to sustain her. She wasn't always that way. There were times when she needed lots from Dad and us to make her smile. "Your Mother had it tough growing up," Dad said when we took our walks. What stopped her from sharing? Why dig a moat that no one could cross? Did she savor a memory, recall an event, or reflect on a moment from her own life story? I wondered what she was thinking now. What part of her history was she holding on to?

She was quiet. Her eyes, a watery blue, wandered the room, avoiding mine while the nurse finished. Why hadn't I asked? Why hadn't I pursued her years ago? Tell me, I could have said. While her life before Dad was a taboo subject, every so often, we sensed what it was. Gussie, her sister, came to supper most Fridays with tales about her nights in the city, dancing at the Rainbow Room, a New York hot spot. But when the Rainbow Room fell flat, she was bitter, living a poor life in the city projects while her sister shared the top floor of a two family house with a husband who loved her. Gussie complained and we listened, captives at the dinner table. Mom's responses were sparse. Even then her thoughts seemed locked up inside her, unable to find a way out.

"OK. We're done now, Mrs. Alper," said the nurse. We smiled at one another. "Your daughter's staying late tonight," she said leaving the room.

Mom followed the nurse with her eyes, bedroom eyes, hooded and heavy. For a moment, the room was silent, and I remembered the long ago times that were silent as well. When I came in late or argued with my brother, she grew angry and wouldn't speak. She gathered them up, her words, like jewels from a treasure box and stowed them away until the crisis passed and her anger subsided. I felt panic rise inside me. Had she gathered them up and put them away this time forever? Then she turned and looked toward me.

"Where's Michael?" Mom asked.

"He's out in the waiting room reading." I glanced at the clock on the wall behind her and hesitated. It was late but not too late. I wanted to share a time we had together when what we did, not said, was what mattered. I should have asked if she remembered the trout, when Dad went with us and we took the girls fishing. They caught the fish, but we had to clean them. We did it together, scaled them and chopped off their heads. We stood there over the sink at desert dusk. My Mom, the soap opera aficionado, staring out with me at a huge ball of feathering pampas grass caught in silhouette against a purple sky. Pioneer twins from Newark, New Jersey, dressing trout. We laughed while they slipped from our hands into the mess we'd made. They were trout, just trout, but I wanted to tell her how special they were; they were part of that moment that would always be ours. Instead I said, "He thought we'd want this time alone together."

Some days, I return to that night in August. I picture Mom as she looks away, and I hear her words. "Janis, I think that you should go get Michael so we can say goodbye. I'm tired. You have an early flight to catch tomorrow." I want to acknowledge the courage that took and thank her. I have other "thank-yous." I want to thank her for nodding in approval when we showed off our desert treasures, like the thorny monsters we called Joshua trees or the thick- stemmed white blossoms that reared their heads skyward from the yucca plant. I want to thank her for reaching out to my girls despite the thousands of miles between them and for embracing the adventures we planned for her, the mountain cabins, the beach walks and the sand dune hikes. I want to say thank you, Mom, for the excitement in your voice when I called on Sundays, for accepting the life Michael and I chose, and for loving us all as best you could.

The last time I saw Mom was midnight. The sky was dark but studded with stars and a hazy orange moon hung there. She whispered I love you in my husband's ear. Then we hugged. "I'll be back, Mom, just as soon as I can be."

I bent over so our faces touched, and her eyes were clear and blue. "Have a safe trip," she said as she dropped my hand. When I looked up, her lids were closed, paper thin, like a Japanese lantern lit from within.

SUNDAY NIGHT DINNER

*H*e did it again.

-Sit still, you did enough today, he told her.

She really hadn't done all that much. She had thrown a couple of loads of wash into the machine and later into the dryer. Didn't even bother hang out the wash on the clothes line, and she knew how much he liked his stuff air dried, flapping in the wind. After a late breakfast of pancakes and eggs, she hadn't given much though about dinner, which was not unusual. It was the end of the month, budget was thin. Chances of going out for dinner were slim. Football on TV would be their entertainment.

-Watch the game, I'll throw something together, we won't starve. -he told her.

In a half hour the aroma was irresistible.

-Open us a couple of beers, goes good with this Mexican grub. Gimmie' ten minutes and we can dig in. -his voice floated out from the kitchen.

They had Spanish rice, refried beans, those little beef tamales with a few black olives all smothered in a mild red chili sauce. Sliced avocado, tomato and cold asparagus spears made do for a salad. She was hungry and ate. It was not a happy meal; it just pissed her off more than ever.

171

CHROMO AND ROLLIE

Bobi Sullivan

$\mathcal{M}$y dad had a beautiful pet rooster, his feathers shiny red and green and his tail tall and full with golden feathers gleaming in the light. Those colorful feathers stood up higher than that rooster's comb, arching like the plumes around the thrones of the great kings in the movies.

Mom's pet, a rare German Green Roller, was in the canary family, but unique. I named her Rollie from the way she sang. Her song was curvy, like a train going up and over the hills. The clear, pure notes rose from low, vibrant tones to high, sweet, soft trebles. Rollie's songs never failed to raise goose bumps on her listeners!

Chromo, Dad's rooster, never left our half acre yard. Every evening Dad would spend time with Chromo, stroking his magnificent wings and they'd both make funny noises to each other, not like a man and a rooster usually sound, but like a foreign language only they knew how to speak. Then Dad would say, "Good night, fella" and Chromo would fly to his special branch in the almond tree outside my window to roost.

Rollie had the run of the house. Her cage door was always open. The food and water were there, but she only sang when she flew high and sat on the beams that braced the fourteen foot cathedral cedar ceiling in our living room. I always thought that she flew up there to pretend she was free and in the woods. But what did I know, I was only ten and Mom always told me that I had a vivid imagination!

One day the piano movers propped the front door open to replace our old piano with a new one. Without warning, Rollie flew at their heads. She seemed angry. The men tried to catch her, but she flew right smack out the door. Exactly what I would have done. I yelled, "Go, Rollie, Go!"

Mom was devastated. Her shoulder was the only one Rollie ever perched on. Oh, she would sit on top of my head and pull out strands of my long hair and then fly away, but she never stayed contentedly on my shoulder the way she did with Mom. I think that bird knew I was a kid and wanted to tease me. When I played the piano or sang, Rollie sang with me. She liked me, I knew it! Mom laughed and said, "You and your wild imagination; she's only a bird, doing what birds do!"

I was miffed, both for myself and for Rollie, so I sassed Mom. "She only comes to you because she knows that you're the mama and the mama feeds us, so we 'Have to be nice to Mama!'"

I'm not going to waste time telling you what I got for that bit of rebellion. Besides, I'm digressing from my real story.

That night when Dad went out to say good night to Chromo, there, perched up on the branch of the almond tree, was Rollie! What a sight: that green canary snuggled up next to that rooster. Rollie was tiny, not much larger than a sparrow, and she looked particularly small next to Chromo, even though Chomo was only a Banty. A Banty is much smaller than a regular-sized rooster, but even so, the difference between Rollie and Chromo was quite comical. I knew Chromo was small, but I also knew he was so much smarter and better looking than a regular rooster, so he and Rollie together seemed perfectly natural to me. After all, I'd seen all sorts of odd-looking couples in town: short with tall or thin with heavy, even young with old. So, to me, there was nothing wrong with a rooster and a canary being a couple.

Hearing Dad's whistle, Chromo swooped down and gave him a quick peck on the cheek, then launched off, flying right back to

Rollie's side. Dad smiled and said, "Atta boy, 'bout time you had a girlfriend. You're a handsome fella. I'm not even gonna try to tell you that you two are an unseemly pair or that she's not your type. Whadda I know, huh?"

Dad tiptoed into the house and softly called my mom, "Come here, hon. I want you to see something."

Mom rushed to the door. Dad motioned her to be quiet and walk softly. It was a full moon that night and all three of us could see clearly. I had the best view from my bedroom window in our loft. Chromo and Rollie were eye level with me.

They were nuzzling each other. Rollie pruned his feathers with her beak and Chromo chortled, I swear he did! My window was open—I know what I heard—no matter what Mom said. Mom always said animals were just animals; they didn't have a soul or anything like people. That's called animism—one of the big words she was always sending me to the dictionary to look up. Animals don't think and feel like we do, she'd say, but I don't see how anyone looking at Chromo and Rollie together could continue to believe that.

The night was so still that I could hear my dad whispering to my mom. Whadda they think, I'm deaf, dumb and blind just because I'm only ten? Anyway, Dad says, "Look Hon, Chromo's kissing Rollie's neck just like this." And he proceeded to demonstrate Chromo's behavior with my Mom. Yuck!

Boy was I embarrassed. There was my dad and mom imitating two lovesick birds—necking at their age! The birds were cute, but your own parents? Eeuuww! I closed my window and went to bed.

The next morning, Chromo woke me up crowing. He was still in the almond tree with Rollie snuggled beside him. And that rooster crowed loud and long every morning after that. If it was a hazy, no sun day, he'd crow when a car drove by with its lights on. And Rollie sang and warbled. It went on for weeks. I don't know about the neighbors, but we loved it! Mom and Dad always put food and fresh water out for both of them. I thought it would be that way forever, or at least until I grew up, graduated, and got married.

But one day Mom decided she wanted us to have our own fresh eggs, so she brought some Banty hens home. She didn't trust them to stay put in our yard like Chromo and Rollie; she clipped their wings so they couldn't fly. They laid eggs and Mom was happy for a while, but she wanted Chromo to come down out of the tree and roost on the ground on a rack she built. She wanted him to do his 'thing' with the hens, too, so they would make baby chicks. Of course, I love baby chicks, but we're talking about Chromo, not a breeder with no heart or soul. I was disgusted.

Someone had to argue Chromo's case for him. "That's what happens to kids in foreign countries. Will you try to force me to marry someone, just so that you can have grand children? How could you Mom? How could your separate Chromo and Rollie?"

"Don't be ridiculous! They're not even the same species, child. You're smart. You know creatures have to be with their own kind. I'm going to clip Chromo's wings so he learns where he belongs."

"No! I won't let you!"

Mom spanked me and locked me in my room. Then she tricked Chromo with a special treat and caught him with the swimming pool net and clipped his wings. Rollie and I watched in horror. She flew in circles around Mom and Chromo while I grabbed a chair and broke out my window. I didn't care what Mom would do to me. I yelled at Chromo, "Run, fly, run!" But it was too late. Mom was swift and the deed was done. When Dad got home I was still sobbing. I overheard Mom explaining what went on and ending with, "You need to give your spoiled daughter a severe talking to. She needs to grow up."

A little while later Dad came in my room. He hugged me and wiped the tears off my face while he quietly explained, "Sweetheart, the world isn't always a kind place. There's a lot of pain. We humans—especially grownups—don't always see things or feel things the same way children and animals do. But know this, your mother loves you and believes she did the right thing. You don't have to agree with her, but you do have to tell her that you love her anyway. And you have to repair the window. I'll teach you how."

For days Rollie flew around Chromo and the hens. She could not or would not land on the ground among the Bantys. She stopped singing. Chromo would look up at her and flap his wings but he couldn't get off the ground.

Then, one day, she was simply gone. Day after day I looked for her. I saw Chromo looking too. I was sure she had wondered off and died of a broken heart, or a night owl had caught her and ate her because Chromo wasn't there to protect her. People said it was just my over-active imagination at play again, because everyone knows birds and roosters don't think or feel, but Chromo stopped crowing and only walked up to Dad when Mom wasn't with him.

Before she disappeared, Rollie never went near my Mom again, either. Just once she perched on my head, but she didn't pull my hair. She was sad. I cried. They say I'll understand when I'm older. Well I'm older now; I'm eleven. I still can't forget about them.

I dreamed the other night that Chromo's feathers grew back and he flew into their old branch on the almond tree and he crowed and crowed until a green ball in the sky swooped down and Rollie returned to perch next to Chromo. And she sang.

PATCHES

Linda Bowden

I'm made of patches
Of different shades
And sizes of material,
Triangles and squares.
I'm so complicated,
Intricate.
Each detail,
Flowered and patched.
I'm a blanket
Of years and experience,
Of patches of this time and others,
Woven together one by one.
I'm a quilt of most beautiful,
Delicate patterns and such,
Of stitching neatly in rows,
Of lace lined patches.

VEGETABLE WARS

Jenny Margotta

The fat, sleek aubergine sat in the middle of his kingdom like some vegetarian Jabba the Hut, his dark purple, nearly black skin glistening when the occasional light hit the unblemished splendor of his rotund form. Slowly, regally, he opened his eyes and peered into the recesses of his cold chamber. He was hungry. Yawning, he bared his huge, white, razor sharp teeth. Should he just snack at this point or go for a full meal? Snack, he decided. His eyes swiveled around him in a 360 degree arc – this was one of the abilities that kept the aubergine at the top of the vegetable hierarchy. It was nearly impossible for anything to sneak up on him.

He smacked his large, bulbous lips as he eyed the possibilities. *Oh good*, he thought, his human underlings had been shopping, filling his domain with a multitude of succulent choices. His gaze landed on a small herd of Brussels sprouts, cowering in the corner. They would make a very satisfying crunch as he wolfed them down. No one would miss them—they were as disliked in the Vegan world as they were in any other. Silly, quivering, useless little balls of nothing. Crunch. Smack. Gobble. Gone.

Ah! Good start. Now what? Something perhaps that will put up a little fight would be nice.

King Eggplant eyed a row of asparagus, attempting to marshal their defenses against the far wall. He'd give them plenty of time to prepare—it was part of the game. Finally the asparagus were perfectly arrayed in a tight fighting wedge, the tallest one front and center, ready to defend the poor green onions and the larger, but equally indefensible, shallots behind them. *Oh, this is going to be so much fun,* thought the King.

Slowly he started spinning his firm buttocks on the hard surface of his world. Faster and faster he spun, suddenly pushing off with one short leg. Quickly he rolled across the floor, hitting the center of the asparagus formation with a tremendous crash. Strike! The spears tumbled around him, broken and smashed. Before they could regain their feet, they were devoured, head first. Their stalks made such a pleasant cracking sound as they were sucked into his mouth.

Now that His Purple Majesty had started on his repast, he decided he was definitely too hungry to just stop at a snack. *More,* his huge belly demanded. *More food!*

The King turned his eye toward the beets. Silly things, trying to hide behind the inert, green, bodiless globe of lettuce. The lettuce might have the biggest head in his kingdom, but that didn't translate into a brain of any consequence. King Eggplant rarely bothered attacking the lettuce; the effort wasn't worth the reward. But he liked beets and he wanted some—now.

He planned his attack as he rolled toward his target. The lettuce, its nap interrupted by the commotion, opened one lazy eye, then closed it and began to snore once more, knowing it had nothing to fear. Once past the lettuce, the Eggplant rushed the beets, crushing them against the hard side of his plastic kingdom. Dark red juice splattered the walls and ceiling of his world like some out-of-control Jackson Pollock legume. In two huge gulps, the beets were history.

His Royal Glutton was on a roll now! He tore through the carrots, leaving minute orange shreds of skin like a trail of autumn leaves in his wake. Red, green, and yellow peppers succumbed with hardly a whimper. The large sweet onion slid down his cavernous craw, the tears in its eyes only making the victory taste that much sweeter.

Wasn't there anything that could put up a fight? While accustomed to final victory, nevertheless, the King appreciated a challenge once in a while. He rolled back to the center of his kingdom, surveying the carnage on all sides. What was left to consume?

He'd munched his way through the Brussels sprouts, asparagus, carrots, three kinds of onion, the beets, the peppers and even the gingerroot. Still his huge appetite called for more.

Oh, what's this? In the far corner, wrapped in a blue net bag . . . King Eggplant stared. He blinked and looked again. Fear filled his eyes and his huge, nearly sated body began to quiver. *NO! No, it's not possible.* How could his human underlings do this to him? Didn't they realize what they had done?

Garlic. Dreaded garlic. As he watched, the netting parted as the garlic kicked itself free. Slowly the outer layers of papery skin began to fall, rustling as they fell away to reveal the sleek, seductive bodies beneath. The garlic cloves slid into the middle of the carnage-strewn battlefield. With a rush, they charged the Eggplant. As quickly as it began, the battle was over.

The King is dead. Long live the Vampire garlic.

ATTACK OF THE MARABUNTA

Anthony J Enriquez

"Don't do that," Grandpa said as Boy kicked over an ant mound. "You're going to get stung." As the ants scurried about, Boy was impressed at what he had caused. Beth his older sister, told him to get away from the ants and to stomp his feet on the ground, thus knocking any ants off his shoes.

"You don't want to get them angry," Beth said. "There's no stopping them when they come after you. I've seen movies about them. The ants eat cattle, horses, dogs and people! They go for the ears and eyeballs." Boy felt a chill go through his body as he thought of ants climbing in his ears and biting his eyes. Ohh! That was scary.

Beth smiled at Grandpa and said to Boy "Yes, once ants start marching, there's little you can do to stop them. Usually, it takes a strong rain to wash them away."

Grandpa then said, "The only other way to stop ants is with fire. You need oil or kerosene to stop them. I saw a movie in which Charlton Heston stopped ants by burning up the jungle; and even then, he needed river water to wash them away. For a little mound like this, charcoal lighter fluid and a match should do it. Charlton Heston called the ants Marabunta."

Boy whispered to himself the dreaded word, "Marabunta."

Grandpa and Beth took Boy into the house and for a while all was forgotten. They ate lunch; then Boy took a nap. After the nap, he watched cartoons on the TV. Beth snuck out of the house with a cup in her hand. She went to where there was an ant mound and scooped up half a cup of ants and dirt. Beth then went inside the house to Boy's and her bedroom. She pulled back the covers and sheet of Boy's bed and poured the ants and dirt onto the bed. She then pulled up the covers. Going to the kitchen, Beth rinsed out the cup and put it away. She laughed as she walked away.

Later that evening, the children's parents came home from work. Since it was Friday night, Dad bought home a pepperoni, olive, mushroom and cheese pizza. After dinner, Mom asked what movie they were going to see on the DVD player.

Dad said, "With Pop's suggestion, I thought we'd see a classic. It's called 'Them!' It's about giant ants. That's all I'll say."

"Yeaa!" The kids replied in unison.

As they saw the movie that night, Boy imagined he had a machine gun or a flame thrower and took on the ants. After the movie was over, they watched the news and then got ready for bed. Beth was the first one to say good night; she got into bed, closed her eyes and waited for the fun to begin. Mom and Dad both kissed Boy and Beth good night, then went outside to look at the stars and talked. Boy snuggled into bed.

All was quiet for a few minutes; suddenly, Boy started jumping around in bed. He jumped out of bed, rubbed his legs and stomped his feet. Then, he rushed out of the room. Beth laughed quietly, then, hearing Boy coming back to the room, she closed her eyes. She heard a squirting sound, opened her eyes, and saw Boy put a can of charcoal lighting fluid on the floor.

"No!" she screamed as Boy threw a lit match onto the bed. Woosh!!! The bed was in flames. Beth jumped out of bed, grabbed Boy and ran out of the room screaming, "Mom! Dad!! The house is on fire!"

Everything seemed to happen at once. Dad grabbed a fire extinguisher and ran to the children's bedroom. Grandpa looked out his bedroom, turned back to grab Fluffy the Cat, then ran outside with the children. Mom grabbed her cell phone and dialed 911 as she went outside. Grandpa threw a screeching cat into the car. From there, he grabbed the garden house from the front of the house and pulled. Suddenly, he stopped. Grandpa grabbed his chest, stumbled and fell to the floor. Seeing this, Mom screamed and ran to him.

Beth grabbed Boy, started shaking him and yelled, "Idiot! See what you've done!

Boy knew why his grandfather was down on the ground; just as he knew why the fire had been started and why his legs had been bitten. Boy whispered out loud to his sister, "Marabunta!"

PROSTITUTION IS A LIFE CHOICE . . . OR IS IT?

Frances Smith Savage

hyllis saw the couple as they approached her small apartment. Instead of waiting for them to pound on her front door, she ran to the bathroom, swished on the shower, stuck her head under the water, stripped off her clothes, grabbed an oversize towel, wrapped it tightly around her head, leaned over the sink and inserted her brown contact lens. By the time someone tapped on the bathroom window and called her name she had turned off the shower and wrapped her heavy robe securely around her body.

"Who's there, what do you want?" she called out. She recognized one of the women, but the other was a mystery.

"Phyllis, it's Mrs. Powell from the housing authority and we need to speak to you."

How'd they know it was Phyllis? She thought, but answered that she would meet them at the front door. She unlocked the door and opened it wide. The couple walked in and looked around. Phyllis watched the mystery woman as Mrs. Powell asked another question.

"Are you here alone? Where's Sally?"

"What's this about, and who are you?" Phyllis asked the other woman who looked into the kitchen and started down the hall toward her bedroom. "Wait, you can't go down there, who are you?"

"Phyllis this is Miss Newhart, and she's Vice Principal at the high school. Sally missed school again today, where is she?"

"Sally spent the weekend with our aunt, they had car trouble and weren't able to make it back in time for school."

"Have you talked to your aunt this morning?" The Vice Principal asked the question. She apparently didn't believe Phyllis.

"Yes she called because she knew I'd be worried."

"Where does she live?"

"She lives in Crestline, and her phone doesn't work in the mountains."

"How'd she call you then?"

Oh oh, Phyllis thought, *I'd better be careful.* But she said, "She called me from her house because they couldn't get the car started this morning."

"Sally has missed a great deal of school this year. Can you tell me why?"

"I know, I've been fighting with her to get back to school, and she promised that if I let her go to Aunt Margaret's house this weekend she would make sure she got to school."

"How old are you?" Miss Newhart said.

"Why are you asking me so many questions? I really don't think it is any of your business how old I am. I am of age, and I help my sister. Our parents died last year in a car accident."

"Well, I'd like to see you and your sister in my office as soon as possible."

"Why?"

"Because I can see you have problems here and I want to help you."

"I work hard and pay my rent on time every month."

"Where do you work?"

Phyllis didn't answer her question, and was ready to ask the women to leave when Mrs. Powell stepped in and said, "Phyllis *has* worked hard after her parents were killed. I can vouch for them both. I'll talk to Sally Anne and help get her to school regularly. The girls have had a tough time this past year. In fact Phyllis was in college and came home to live with her sister."

The vice principal didn't stop there. She demanded, "You must bring Sally Anne into my office tomorrow, or I'll contact Mr. Adams. He'll look over your apartment and find out the reason Sally has not been to school. He'll also want to know Sally's legal guardian. Do you understand? Tomorrow, not the day after, or next week. Tomorrow! Do you understand?"

Phyllis replied, "Yes."

"You may not understand that it is the law that children attend school, and the parents or guardian, if that is what you are, can and will be fined and even face jail time."

Phyllis shook her head and refused to utter another word.

After they left Phyllis realized her hands were shaking. She waited for them to ask which college she attended, and who was the aunt that she never mentioned before. *Thank goodness for Mrs. Powell, I'll have to call and thank her.*

The couple left. No one but Phyllis knew the truth, and she worked hard to keep it that way. There had been no dead parents, no aunt, no college, and no job, and in actuality no Sally.

Phyllis looked much older than her fourteen years. With her long dark hair that swirled softly over her shoulders, her brown eyes, and when she applied black eye liner and mascara she aged by at least ten years. While Sally with her short blond hair and blue eyes never wore makeup and continued to attend school unless she was too tired or simply not interested.

No one realized that they never ever saw the two girls together. When pictures appeared online across the country they claimed that one girl was missing. If they compared the pictures with Sally, they may have seen a resemblance.

186

She invented Sally because in order to live in the housing projects where rent was cheap, they wouldn't accept a single young woman. It worked for almost an entire year, but now they questioned her guardianship of Sally.

Phyllis quieted her shaking hands as best she could. She should have been at work, but was too distraught. Her regulars would be trying to contact her by now for she was almost two hours late. She decided that she would tell them that the police picked her up when she walked along the main street of town. They wouldn't be aware that she never did that. She had her regular meeting place in the motel on the outskirts of town, and she never walked, but always called a cab.

The cabbie knew her as Phyllis and was probably one of her best customers. She always called him from her cell phone when she completed the day's business. She called him now and told him she would meet him at the garage where she parked the car during the daylight hours. She made good money and planned to educate herself.

"I think it's time I found another place to live," she told Charlie the cabdriver.

"How come? I thought you liked living in the projects."

"I did, but now they want to see my bank records and I haven't claimed all the money I have in the bank. I'm not sure what to do. The Vice Principal at Sally's school wants to meet with us just as soon as Sally gets back."

"Well, that's not going to happen."

"I know. I've thought about hiring someone to pose as Sally, but I'd just be digging the hole deeper."

"I can look around for an apartment or a house if you'd like."

"I sure don't want a house in some neighborhood. They'd be sure to notice a bunch of cars coming by every day, and I don't want any of my customers to know where I live."

"You don't have to have them come to your apartment or house; they could come to the motel as usual. That's been working good for almost a year now. Besides Phylly you're not getting any younger."

"Thanks."

"Sorry, but it's a fact of life when you're in that business, you know that."

"I know. So what should I do?" She respected Charlie, but he was nosey and he found out about Sally right from the beginning.

"Well, if I wasn't married, I'd marry you."

"Oh, sure you would."

"No, I'm serious, I really like you, and it's not because of your line of work."

"It's because of my line of work that you would never marry me."

"Yeah, but you're at the top of the field. And you take care of me too, and I'm not just talking about the money. In a way I'm your pimp. I've thought about finding other girls and training them to do just what you do, but I don't want to press my luck."

Charlie drove into the back of the motel and stopped so Phyllis could get out of the cab without being seen. She opened the door to her rooms at the motel, and said a silent prayer for the girl that cleaned her rooms. She paid her extra to clean the room after every client, and it helped Phyllis and Bree too.

Phyllis dug out the cell that she used only for business and called four clients. She left a message apologizing for being late this morning. Her two afternoon clients cancelled.

Then Bree knocked on her door at the motel. "Phyllis I need to talk to you."

"Just a minute." She slipped on the flimsy robe and opened the door.

"The police stopped by the motel this morning. They were in an unmarked car and wore suits. I don't know what the manager told them, but I'm afraid they wanted to know about the guests that rented the rooms full time.

"I'm sure he told them about you and another couple. I heard the manager try to reach me, but I didn't answer my cell, I left it in one of the other rooms so I wouldn't be lying when they catch up with me."

"Thanks Bree." Phyllis grabbed most of her clothing and her extra cell and called Charlie. She then ran out of the door, locked it, paid Bree a good size tip, and ran to the back of the motel. Charlie returned to the motel within minutes.

"Get in, hurry, I think they're coming back, I've been listening to my scanner and when I heard them say they were coming here, I drove back. Where do you want to go?"

"Take me back to the garage. Then I'll go back to my apartment so I can pick up my stuff. You go back to work, and Charlie, find another girl to take my place. Tell her about Bree at that motel; tell her to pay Bree extra for helping her. She might want to find another motel on the outskirts of town; you can help her do that. Don't take all of her money, cut your fair share."

"Call me when you get settled."

"I will and thanks, you've been a good friend."

She knew she would never call him. By now she was street smart, and as she moved, it would be easier because she placed her money in safety deposit boxes at a local bank. When the bank started asking questions about the cash she deposited, she pulled out most of her money and put it into another bank's safety deposit box. That way she could add to it or retrieve it as long as she had the key and proper identification.

Phyllis packed her belongings into her car along with her computer. She removed her wig and contacts and packed them deep within her bag. It was time for Phyllis to take a break, so she took her new identity including her new driver's license, Social Security cards and even a new passport.

Her new identification stated that her name was P. Edna Stoddard and her age was twenty-one with the address at the housing projects. She definitely would contact Mrs. Powell and give her a new address, and this time it would be at one of those storage units that had private box rentals.

The descriptions on her license and passport stated she had green eyes and red hair. The contacts and wig confirmed those features. Before she drove out of town she mailed the postcard addressed to her mother. She also listed the address of the housing project, and knew that the police would hunt for her again. She grieved for her mother, but when she took the side of her stepfather she would never go back unless they handcuffed and forced her. She wanted her mother to know she was all right.

Long before the card reached her mother she had driven almost two hundred miles through small town after small town. She never took the freeways and tried to avoid popular areas where cameras picked up those passing.

She added Mrs. Powell's name to her list of people that she wanted to contact in the future. Charlie's name was on the list and Bree's at the motel. However they'd have to wait until she reached the age of eighteen, and that was four years away and she still had to make a living. She would tell each of them the truth, that her mother still lived, and there never had been a Sally.

She considered contacting Bree to come and live with her, and possibly she might, but she was not ready to make any life threatening choices until she settled into her new identity.

She learned at a young age that prostitution didn't have to be a life-long choice and before she could shed her past, she had to educate and train herself. She pulled into a parking lot of an apartment building that had an 'Apartment For Rent' sign stuck in a window. Underneath the sign it stated, 'Students Welcome.' She checked that her red wig was in place, picked up her identification papers, and knocked on the door marked 'Manager.'

She glanced at her car and was happy she'd changed the license plates. She even checked the DMV to make sure that the person's, car like hers, didn't have a record.

"Good afternoon, I saw the for rent sign in your window."

"Are you a student?"

"Yes I am. My name's Edna, but my friends call me Eddie."

"Hi Eddie, come on, I'll show you the apartment. We only have one left. My name's Connie Mark. I'm sure you'll like it."

"Yes, I'm sure I will." She followed the manager to a nice apartment with a garage right below. She glanced at a yellow cab that passed on the street and thought, *next, I'll find me a cabbie.*

REMEMBRANCE DAY

Anthony Spencer

Poppies poppies, oh so red,
From the men that now lie dead.
Poppies poppies all around,
Poppies poppies on the ground.
They look so tall, but oh so pretty,
What a shame they grew for pity.

Husbands and sons went to war,
And some got shot to the floor.
They were so brave, to war they went,
By politicians they were sent.
To the fields the trenches were dug,
Without food or water a kiss or a hug.

Peace and quiet it is today,
There is no war and children play.
In Flanders Field the crosses stand high,
As if they were trying to reach the sky.
Poppies poppies blow in the wind,
You almost hear the soldiers sing.

SUNSET CITY ESCAPADES

Mary Langer Thompson

Not everything that happens in Heaven's Waiting Room, or Sunset City, is heavenly. Take this morning. I'm fixing my hair at my dressing table, when the phone my kids make me keep by my side at all times, rings. It's one of those newfangled wireless phones, and so small I can barely see the "talk" button, so I fumble around to answer.

"Grandma?" asks my caller.

The voice sounds familiar. "Sid?"

Silence.

I realize it must be my other grandson who's not quite as articulate and who sounds far away. "Tony?"

"Yes," he says. "I have to tell you something, but you have to promise not to tell anybody, okay?"

"What's wrong, Tony?"

"I'm in trouble, Grandma. I need your help."

"What's happened?"

"My friend was getting married in Mexico and wanted me to be his best man. So we drove there, and after the reception we were driving to the hotel. They asked me to drive because I had only one beer. Everybody else was soused. The guy in front of me stopped too soon, and I hit him. It wasn't my fault, Grandma, but I'm in a Mexican jail. I want to come home."

"Oh, Tony. We have to tell your father."

"Oh, no, Grandma. You can't. Please. I have a lawyer, but he wants money. I need you to go to the Western Union next door to the K-Mart by your house. You remember where that is, right?"

"Yes."

"Write a check for $2,850, and have it wired to this address. Do you have a pen?"

"Wait a minute."

I went to get the pen. I knew something wasn't right, but I had this heavy feeling in my chest. I would need to do some checking. No harm in his thinking I was going along with his plan. But what if it really was Tony?

As soon as I hung up, I called my daughter, Mary Lou. "I need to talk to you and Brad right now. Both of you. It's important." I knew she'd think it was a medical emergency.

"What's going on?"

"Where's Brad?"

"He's at Home Depot buying light bulbs."

"Okay, I'll tell you. You have to call Tony and see if he's all right."

"Mom, what the heck…?" Good, I've taught her not to swear around me anymore.

I explained the call, but insisted she call my grandson.

"Mom, I'm sure Tony's okay. He'd tell us if he were going out of town, let alone out of the country. But I'll call him and get back to you. Did this guy leave a caller ID?"

I checked the phone. "No."

It took fifteen minutes to confirm that Tony was fine and at work as usual.

When Mary Lou called back, she told me not to answer my phone the rest of the day unless I knew who was calling.

"Tony" called back five times. I let it ring.

That night at Bunco, I told my friends about the call. Roz told me the same thing happened to her. She said she knew it wasn't legit, but also checked on her grandchild. Bob said he hung up because he had read about the scam in the latest AARP magazine.

That was when our Bunco host said we should do something about it.

Roz said she called the police. "All they offer is sympathy. There's no real way to catch them."

Some of the others became outraged at that. So we devised our scheme for the next time one of us got a call.

It didn't take long before our Bunco Host, Howard, got a call. He played along. He told his caller that he loved him and wanted to help. The only problem, he lied, was that he had fallen and was not ambulatory. But he had the money.

"If only you could find a lawyer from this area to come to my house, then we can get you home and be done with this mess."

"Well . . ."

"Or, I can call your dad and he can go over to Western Union."

"Oh, no, no, don't do that. I'll see what I can do."

"Have him here by 1:00 p.m. tomorrow afternoon because your mom is coming by with my pain prescription at 2:00. I'll give him the money and he can be gone before your mother gets here."

All of us were at Howard's house the next day by noon to firm up our plan. Or to play Bunco if no one showed up. Either way it seemed a win-win situation.

At 12:55, the doorbell rang. Howard and Bob, the two biggest men of the group, were in position outside. When I opened the door, they sneaked up behind our visitor and pushed him through it with a strong shove. A young man fell face first on the tiles at my feet, the heels of his athletic shoes twinkling with red lights.

"What the hell?" he gasped. What a trash mouth.

I grabbed his arm and helped him up. He was taller than I, and his dark hair was askew. I would have considered him handsome had he not looked dazed.

"Don't try to run," I said. "You're surrounded. We're not going to hurt you."

I was supposed to say, "Unless we have to," but I couldn't get that part out.

Then he focused on my old face. "What do you think you're doing, Granny?"

"Oh, there's more than a granny here," I warned. "The grandpas are out getting your license plate number and car make, and we've notified the front gate. So don't try to escape. Security is standing by. Come with me."

And with that, as planned, I led him into the living room where the other Bunco players were seated at tables.

Roz said, "We're just going to do a little intervention." She pointed to the couch. "Sit."

"Are you the one who called some of us pretending to be our grandson?"

"Um, um. I didn't call anyone. I'm just here to collect for the newspaper."

I said, "Don't give us that. We have you on our phone message machine. Nobody collects for the newspaper anymore. We all pay our bills online."

"Okay, okay. But I didn't mean to hurt nobody."

"Of course not," I said. "You just meant to steal our money."

Roz asked, "Do you have a grandmother or grandfather?"

"Um, yes."

"Would you try to steal from them?"

196

"It's not exactly stealing."

Howard, now back inside his house, said, "Just answer the question. I'm a retired cop. Do I need to get my lie detector out?"

"No, no. Don't do that." The pupils on the kid's eyes were huge.

"So would you?" Howard repeated.

"Would I what?" The kid had worse memory loss than any of us.

I repeated, "Would you try to steal from your own grandparents?"

"No."

"Thank you."

Howard added, "I can run your license plate and get a ton of information on you, but why don't you just give me your license and make it easy on me? In fact, give me your wallet."

As he reached into his baggy pants, I thought he could have produced a weapon, and maybe we should have thought of that, but he pulled out his billfold. Howard took it and studied his ID for a few minutes.

"You're only seventeen. You still in school?"

"Yes."

"From your address, you should be going to Sitting Bull High, right?"

"Yeah."

Having been a high school English teacher, I couldn't stand it. "Say 'yes,' young man."

"Yes."

I added, "I know the principal over there. Any of your friends there in on this with you?"

"No, no. Never."

"Never would they be in on this or never would you turn them in?" I pushed.

"I do this alone."

"Oh, the Lone Ranger in the Wild West, huh?" All my students knew I had a sarcastic side.

Howard interrupted. "Give me your cell phone."

"I don't have one."

"Give me a break. Do I have to frisk you?"

The phone was forthcoming.

"Do you have to be home by a certain time? Because if so, I'll call your mom and dad and tell them why you'll be here a couple more hours."

"No, please don't do that. Wh...why? Will I be here that long?"

I looked to my fellow Sunset City observers sitting in Howard's living room. "Please stand," I said to them.

Everybody stood, a couple behind their walkers.

"Now, at what table should our young friend sit first?"

"Huh?" he asked.

"You can start the Bunco round with us," said my neighbor. "You can be my partner."

"I don't know how to play," said our guest.

I took Johnnie's arm again and he stood. "You're a smart boy," I said, leading him to my friend's table. "You'll catch on fast. Howard, take a twenty out of his wallet for prize money. We start with one's. A bunco is three of a kind. Only the winners move."

THE WORK
OF HIS OWN HANDS

Dwight Norris

$\mathcal{T}$ad rose before daylight, sat at the rough-hewn eating table he made himself, and looked at his initials, *TG*, etched in the corner because it was the work of his own hands. By candlelight he penned a letter to his parents in Virginia City.

> *Dear Maw and Paw,*
> *Tough times. Rebekkah may be pregnant. Some days, hard to find enough to eat here in Dodge City. Crops destroyed by locusts, crows, and critters. No bullets for hunting. No jobs.*
> *I don't want you to worry. I'll figure out something.*
> *Tad*

"Tad, where are you?" his wife called from the bedroom.
"I'm out here, Sweetie."
Tad quickly folded the letter and jammed it in an envelope.
"It's pitch dark out. You come back to bed," Rebekkah called out.
"I'm comin', Sweetie."
Tad stood about six feet tall, thick brown hair, lean and muscular from working full days in the field, and at twenty-five, looked about as good as a man could. He dropped the letter into one of his boots by the front door and snuffed out the candle. When they were both under the multi-colored quilt made by

199

Tad's mother, Rebekkah started in. "What were you doin' out of bed?" she wanted to know.

"Oh, I was just gettin' a drink of water," Tad said.

"Well, you need to keep me warm, you know?"

"I know Sweetie." Tad moved into a cozy, even sensual, position.

"Not that way, you bastard. You know what that leads to, and you know how I feel about birthin'."

"But Sweetie, that's what married people do, and we ain't been together like that since we got married two years ago."

"Yeah, and what did I get out of it?" Rebekkah asked angrily.

"I think I could get better at it," Tad answered.

"Even if you did, you seen what happens to a woman's body after she's been on the birthin' table? Look at Florence in town. Her ass is wide as Buckthorn Canyon. And Hortense ain't much better. I ain't plannin' on nothin' like that happenin' to me."

"I know Sweetie. I understand."

Tad believed Rebekkah had the loveliest body no man ever saw.

"What you doin' today? You butcherin' some of those chickens and bringing vegetables in from the field?" she wanted to know.

"Well, I'm fixin' to go into town," Tad answered. "I got to pick up some things at the mercantile."

"And what about me?"

"Well, you can come in with me Sweetie, or you can stay here."

"You know I hate that bumpy dusty ride on the buckboard. It hurts my back, and I look a sight when I get there."

"I understand, Sweetie."

"I don't suppose you got enough money to order that new stove I wanted from the mercantile?"

"Well, not yet," Tad answered, "but I'm workin' on it."

Unlike Rebekkah, Tad enjoyed the buckboard and the six-mile ride into town. The countryside was beautiful, and the smell of spring was in the air, but mostly he enjoyed the peace and solitude.

"James, how you doin'?" Tad called out as he pulled up in front of the mercantile.

James was the storekeeper, a short, stout, strapping, old German immigrant, a friendly guy, but always ready to mix it up with contrary people. His white, broom-like mustache elevated as he broke into a wide grin.

"Tad, how *you* doin', my friend?" James responded warmly.

Tad enjoyed stopping at the mercantile. Being around James made him feel more alive, like he tapped into some of James' zest for life. And when he loaded flour, sugar, and dry goods onto the buckboard, he felt like he was doing something good for his wife.

Tad and Rebekkah were doing all right by most accounts, selling wheat and corn in the market, and eggs at the general store. Still, if only he had a little more money.

"James, you got any catalogs from them Eastern companies?" Tad asked.

"I got some in the back," James answered. "Let me go get one for you."

Tad looked around the store and, right there, behind the side counter, hung a string of pearls as beautiful as a field of golden wheat waving in the soft summer breeze.

Rebekkah would love those, Tad thought. He looked over his shoulder and, before he could stop himself, dashed behind the counter and snatched the pearls off the peg.

"Here's one of them catalogs," James called from the back room. He placed it in Tad's hand.

"Amazing some of the things they're comin' up with today, ain't it?" Tad asked.

"Yep, fifteen years from the start of the twentieth century. These sure ain't pre-Civil War days anymore," James added.

Tad got home an hour before dark and stopped at the barn to unload some tools before going into the house. Rebekkah walked outside. She approached and said nothing, but gave Tad a sharp look that pierced his heart. It was a look that convicted him for not being thoughtful and coming to the house first to greet her.

"Sweetie, look here. Look what I got you," Tad said as he held out the pearls.

"They're beautiful," Rebekkah responded. "At least you thought of me a little bit on your outing. I don't suppose they had matching earrings?"

Summer passed quickly with Tad working long hours in the field, battling the throbbing rays of the sun, rodents, varmints, critters, insects, crows and magpies, and the incessant pounding of a woman who would not be filled.

Despite his best efforts, it looked like the harvest would be less than good. If he could just get some more money, money to get some of those little extras a woman likes, maybe she would warm up and let him... well... let him be a husband.

The next morning, Tad saddled his riding horse and galloped to the other side of Dodge City. He holed up in a cavity in the oleanders behind a big boulder about four miles east of Dodge off the main road leading into town. He had a revolver on his belt, and a stout wooden club he had made for rats in the barn and around the grain bins. Tad knew that people passed this way heading into Dodge, and they carried money.

In about forty-five minutes, Tad's patience was rewarded. A small carriage wheeled along the road behind a single horse driven by an older man with a bushy white beard, dressed in fancy, Eastern clothes. Tad bolted from behind the boulder, startling the carriage horse and its driver. The horse veered to the left so sharply it caused the carriage to tip over to the right, throwing the driver to the side of the road onto the sharp rocks.

Tad was on the man in seconds and smashed his face with the heavy club, six, seven, eight times, reducing his head to a bloody pulp. He tossed the club aside and rifled through the man's pockets. Tad's heart was pounding so fast he could barely think. He found a heavy purse laden with coins, and was on his way.

A week later Tad took the buckboard into town. He had scored big in the robbery, and had ten twenty-dollar gold pieces in his pocket. He stopped first at the saloon, then at the general store, and then at the mercantile, flashing gold everywhere he went.

While he was stacking goods on the counter at the mercantile, Sheriff Tyler and a deputy walked into the store.

"You Tad Greenleaf?" the sheriff asked.

"Yeah, what of it?" Tad answered.

"You're coming down to the jail with us," the sheriff said. "You're under arrest for murder."

"What? What are you talkin' about?"

The next day, as Tad sat in a barren cell, Sheriff Tyler came in and told him why he was behind bars.

"About a week ago, a man was found dead on the side of the road 'bout four miles east of town. His head was bashed in," the sheriff said.

"We found this bloody club near the man's body, initials *TG* on the end of the handle. That's you," the sheriff continued. "Then you come to town spending twenty-dollar gold pieces like they're Indian Head pennies. The family of the dead man says that's what he was carrying, ten twenty-dollar gold pieces. You're in big trouble, boy." The sheriff left, shaking his head.

Just then Rebekkah Greenleaf marched through the door and flashed one of her hard looks at Tad.

"Now what's gonna happen to me?" Rebekkah snarled at Tad. "Who's gonna harvest the crops? Who's gonna do the chores? Who's gonna look out for *me*?"

She spun around on her heels and fumed out the door.

Sheriff Tyler walked back in.

"Telegram for you, boy. From Virginia City."

Dear Tad,

Sorry to bring you such bad news STOP Last week Grandpa was coming to see you STOP We told him not to make such a long trip alone STOP Too dangerous STOP He wouldn't listen STOP Insisted on bringing you money because of your letter STOP Ten twenty-dollar gold pieces STOP He cared so much about you STOP Some thug, some yellow-bellied river rat, robbed him and killed him STOP We are brokenhearted STOP Sorry for your hard times, too STOP Sometimes it just don't seem right, what life deals out STOP Coming to Dodge to pick up Grandpa's body STOP Can't wait to see you, son STOP

Love,

Maw and Paw

Crows and magpies snatched up the corn, and rats of the field scoured the ground for random kernels. The wheat got scorched in the sun and thrashed in the wind, and rooted out by varmints from the nearby wood. An old man was buried in the sod outside of Virginia City. A young woman took the stage to Boston to start anew. Parents cried, and a young man died, on the end of a rope just north of Dodge City, by the work of his own hands.

INTO THE VOID

Rica Gold

I lay motionless, on my back in the murky darkness as the faint, grey glow that seemed to permeate my closed eyelids signaled the break of day beginning. The day before had tired me beyond what I had realized. How many times had I felt daylight slip in and take me from the enchantment of dreams, and slide me ever so gently into a semi-conscious awareness that another day was about to begin? The soft cotton blankets were gathered around me and added to that deliciously lazy feeling, as I sensed the sounds of birds about to engage in bird chatter clatter and I allowed myself to linger in the floating stillness before I ventured to open my eyes.

Maybe I was wrong. Maybe it was still the middle of the night and I could check and then drift back to a deeper sleep. I almost smiled thinking of that. One could only hope, I thought wryly. I considered turning over to my left to glance at the neon lights on the clock. Ugh. I moved my foot to feel the smooth sheets. Oddly, I didn't feel anything at all. I shifted my body slightly toward the window. I didn't feel like I was even in bed. I felt a tinge of nervousness and my eyes flew open. It was dark, but not completely. A kind of purple haze surrounded me. I tried to slide both feet forcefully against the sheets I knew must be underneath me. Again… nothing.

I bolted upright into a sitting position and felt my body turning, easily, gently to my left, but without my will. I was not on the bed. I was not in my room. Nothing supported me. My whole body was suspended in air, or at least in the light purple substance around me.

Anxiety surged through me, but the mist around me was dissipating, becoming less dense, right in front of me. Hope flowed in for a minute that I'd be able to see what was going on.

I pointed my feet down to search for the floor. I couldn't feel anything. I was upright, in a standing position, but tentatively so.

"What happened to gravity?" I mumbled.

"Hello?" I called into space.

"Is anyone here?" I fervently hoped no voice answered me. I was scared, but somewhere inside knew that this felt a bit familiar.

It was silent. I had been alone at home, as usual, when I decided not to waste time watching any more bad TV and climbed into my big, wide, comfortable bed for the night. Nothing out of the ordinary had happened. I made sure the house was locked up, washed my face, brushed my teeth and threw on one of my favorite night shirts. I had grabbed the down filled pillow I liked to sleep on, and laid a blanket on the far side, foot of the bed for Antonio Banderas, my new Great Dane mix. I loved that name for him. The real Antonio Banderas was dashing, handsome and intriguing with wonderful, beautiful eyes. This camel-colored, big animal had run to me with his large tawny eyes beseeching me to welcome him and ran to me, wagging his tail. He let me pet him. He seemed especially loving with me. His eyes were rimmed with smudges of black hair that made them appear even larger and I thought he was incredibly gorgeous. His massive head was strong and square and the tough hombre moniker suited him dramatically. He became a family member that very moment.

Where was he? I looked around. "Antonio." I called him in my normal morning voice, as I peered through the dim light. I said it more forcefully, "Tony!" The silence continued. I stood still, suspended in air which I was breathing easily. My feet dangled, touching nothing. The air smelled faintly of sandalwood. I felt scared. This was the most lucid dream I could remember ever having. That was what it had to be…a lucid dream.

A flicker of light, colored golden against the now lavender shades, mixing with the receding shafts of purple light, beckoned me. I took a step. Well, not exactly a step, because I felt as though it was more of a slide. I was moving, moving through air. The sandalwood atmosphere seemed heavier than air I was used to. Whatever this was, my movement reminded me of watching suited astronauts from decades ago, bouncing awkwardly on their lunar forays. It was not a cumbersome slide, but it was ungainly.

Thank God I'm not wearing that claustrophobic, fishbowl headgear.

I peered toward the spreading gold light, now becoming more transparent. The colors were scintillatingly vibrant. They were unlike colors that I was used to. They seemed to be alive, bright and pulsating with sharp, intensity now. A slip of coral light appeared and faded within seconds. It tinged the circle of light as it expanded, pushing the lavender completely away. I was enthralled and for a moment did not think about being afraid.

"Antonio? Tony, come!" I whispered, looking to either side for him. I caught a glimpse of my hand. My fingers were slender, but my skin looked pale.

I need some sun.

A ring glinted on my finger in the slowly increasing light. It was made of three narrow bands of gold wire. In the center sat the clearest, bright, sun-yellow gem. I wondered if it was a topaz for a second. It wasn't my ring. I had never seen it before. It was beautiful, but what was it doing on my hand? Why did my own hand look different?

The sense of fear that had been suppressed ran through my body in the uncertain state I found myself in. I had studied and experimented with lucid dreaming, but this didn't feel like that. It felt more like the first time this had happened. *What do I mean, the first time? I don't remember a first time.* Still I looked around for some incongruous something that would jar me awake or into realizing that I was indeed dreaming. Summoning my courage, what there was of it, and letting curiosity take an upper hand, I drew in my breath.

"Ok—I'm smart and logical. I can figure this out."

Urging my body to slide uncertainly forward to where the transparent center of the surrounding colors was spreading, I saw a glimmer of light blue, a sliver of deep green. I took heart. I hoped it was sky and trees. I willed myself to move faster, and I did.

A crisscross pattern of what seemed like glass windows in French doors appeared and I cautiously reached out to touch them.

"Ahhh. These are real." Actual substance met my touch. The doors did not however, feel like glass and wood, but something softer, firm, but unknown. "I don't get this. This has gotta be some kind of a dream."

I tried to ignore my growing nervousness. Still hoping for the lucid dream explanation I looked for that tell-tale sign that would trigger an escape back to consciousness. The odd thing though, was that I felt completely conscious. What I was in was not a nightmare. I wasn't feeling terror. Those dreams, seldom as they were, did not resemble whatever this was. Still it would be a relief to wake up. I counseled myself that if this trip into dreamland got real scary I could find a way to wake myself up.

I pushed on the doors and they moved silently sideways as if they were pocket doors, gliding into invisible walls and disappearing. I stepped, floated, onto a broad stone balcony. At least it looked like stone.

A panorama of the most glorious blue sky, cloudless, hovered above a wide expanse of wonderful, apple-green fresh, new grass. The vision loomed before me. The darker green I had seen before belonged to tips of pine trees that surrounded the edges of the grass as far as I could see. A warm, friendly sun emerged from behind a deep violet mountain range and fringes of soft peach light spread eager fingers across the sky to the left.

It felt like Earth. It looked like Earth. There was nothing but the beauty and warmth within me of peaceful, secure contentment.

"Avria! Avria! a voice suddenly broke the stillness. I leaned forward to peer over the balcony wall. Down below and at a distance, a child called and waved in my direction.

"Avria!"

I looked over my shoulder. I wobbled a bit. No one else was there. *"Avria"*, the young girl called again, her smile easily visible as she ran closer, calling again and laughing.

I'm not Avria. Ok, I was about to wake up. I had never heard that name before.

I felt myself hovering unsteadily. It felt like I was only inches from a solid floor. I remained transfixed, watching the tow-headed girl running toward me.

A long, stone stairway descended from the balcony where I floated to a slick-looking road that bordered the grassy green expanse. The road shimmered a cobalt blue in the warming sun. The girl's hair streamed behind her as she ran faster than any young girl I had ever seen, taking the steps as if she were not even touching them. Her smile was wide as she bubbled over with the excitement of closing in on me.

What the heck?

"Avria, you're back! I'm so happy now," she gushed as she reached me and threw her arms around my waist. I felt a jolt, like electricity push me back and surge through my stomach.

In that instant, before I could process who the girl was, what to say or even what was happening, I felt myself being pulled backwards at warp speed, if there was such a thing. Colors merged and swirled and my sense of the young girl evaporated. My head whirred with imagery and the small circle of golden light that was all I could see, disappeared.

I was aware that my thoughts were racing and a familiar slightly light-headed, dizzy sensation began as though I was about to faint. I drifted, my thoughts gone. Something moist touched my nose and cheek. Images began to fade. My mind slid into inky darkness.

Awareness crept in slowly as I struggled to grab hold of wherever my mind was. I saw the grey on the other side of my eyelids that signaled light and thus the start of daylight and felt the wet tongue again. "Antonio? Antonio?" My eyes fluttered, my head cleared groggily. But I was not in my bed or even at home. I was sitting on white leather seats in the back of a car. All around me were the amazing tall trees of a forest. Sunlight sprinkled down through sky-high branches. Antonio wagged his tail happily and licked my face on the seat beside me.

"Where the heck are we?" I whispered, still dazed as I slung my arm around my giant friend.

"It happened again, Tony. It happened again."

THE JOURNAL (EL DIARIO)

Suzanne Holbrook-Brumbaugh

"*M*om!" Arlene shifted from foot to foot, her hands spread along the back of the sofa, trying to determine which way her little sister might run to avoid being caught and relieved of the book she held possessively against her chest. "*Mom!*"

Mrs. Ramirez rushed into the living room only to discover her daughters in an apparent stalemate, her younger daughter smug, as she stuck out her tongue and then grinned at her frustrated older sister. "What's going on here?" she asked. "What did she do this time?" She sighed, and gestured, with her head, toward her eight-year-old, Carlotta.

"She broke into my room and stole my journal. Make her give it back."

"Carlotta?"

"I didn't break in. The door was unlocked. I just looked to see if Arlene was in there. That's all." She quietly slipped the journal behind her back. "She wasn't there so I left. Honest."

"Mo-om."

Mrs. Ramirez held out her hand. "The book, Carlotta."

"What book?" Carlotta asked, feigning innocence.

Her mother sighed. "The one behind your back. Hand it over . . . now."

"But, Mama."

"No buts. Just hand it over."

Carlotta pulled out the journal, once again pressing it close to her chest, an impish grin on her face. "Do you want to know what's in it?" she asked, eager to tell. "Arlene's in love . . . with Miguel," she giggled. "She wants him to take her to the dance, and—"

"You . . . you . . . ooooo." Arlene flushed, dove over the sofa and wrested the journal from her sister's grip. "You had no right, you little—"

"Arlene!" Mrs. Ramirez stared at her normally docile daughter. "What's got into you? And you, young lady," she turned to scold Carlotta, "know better than to—"

"*Silencio!*" The screen door slammed. "Do we have a problem here? Do we need to share our difficulties with the entire neighborhood? Mama? Que pasa?"

Mrs. Ramirez was quick to fill in her husband. He turned toward his youngest daughter. "Carlotta, I'm disappointed in you, *mi corazon.*"

"But . . . but . . ." Carlotta burst into tears and fled to her room.

Crocodile tears, ran through Arlene's mind, as she hugged her journal and watched her sister disappear into the hallway. Her parents slowly shook their heads and sighed.

"Um . . . Mom?" Arlene turned toward her parents. "Miguel's coming over this afternoon to study for awhile. Can you please make sure Carlotta stays in her room and doesn't bother us? I'll just die if she says anything to him."

"I can try." Her mother breathed in deeply. "I will do my best to keep her busy while he's here. But you know how she is. She really does mean well, you know. Perhaps if you spent a little more time with her . . . no . . . I suppose not."

Mrs. Ramirez walked back into the kitchen to think about preparing dinner, while Mr. Ramirez went back to the garage for a little peace and quiet. Arlene stood alone in the empty living room for just a moment, before racing to her room to hide her journal. It would *not* happen again. She grabbed her books and spread them out on the dining room table. Miguel could be here at any minute, and she wanted to be ready . . . before he arrived. She glanced at the crucifix on the dining room wall. *Please don't let Carlotta ruin the day*, she silently prayed. *Please.*

Carlotta was on her best behavior. She opened the can of frijoles, dumped them into a microwave-safe bowl, and set it on the kitchen counter. She rinsed out the empty can of enchilada sauce, and threw it in the trash. Dinner was almost ready, and she was bored. Miguel and Arlene had been studying for almost an hour and she had not bothered them even once.

"All right, Carlotta, you may go get washed up for dinner. You've done a good job."

Carlotta grinned at her mother. "Can Miguel stay for dinner?" she asked innocently.

"I suppose, if he wants to. I'll call Margarita and ask if it's okay," she murmured absently.

"Can I ask him?"

"Sure, sure. Just don't bother them while they're studying."

Carlotta leaned her elbows on the dining room table, and rested her head in her hands. She stared at Miguel, a wistful smile on her face.

"What are you doing?" Arlene hissed, annoyed at her sister's obvious adoration of *her* best friend.

"I'm waiting until you guys get done to invite Miguel to stay for dinner. Mama said I could. Well?" She stared at Miguel.

"Well, what, little one?"

"Do you want to stay for dinner, or what?"

"Well . . . sure, if it's okay with your mom. I'd have to call home and—"

"No you don't. Mama already called. You can stay if you want to."

"Okay. That okay with you?" He turned to Arlene.

"Sure," she replied, giving her sister a 'what are you up to now' look.

"Okay then. I guess I'm staying."

"Miguel?"

"What, *hermanita*?"

Carlotta wasn't certain she liked to be called little sister, but under the circumstances—it would have to do.

"Are you gonna go to the Saint Patrick's Day dance next week?"

"Well . . . I haven't really thought about it that much. Why? Are you asking for a date, *pequena*?" He winked and tapped the tip of her nose. "I think I might be just a little too old for you, but thanks for asking."

"Oh, I wasn't asking for me. I was just wondering if you were going or not?" She ignored the panic spreading across her sister's face. "Would you go if you had somebody to go with?"

"Well, I don't know. Maybe. Got anybody in mind?"

"Do you?"

"I don't know. I—"

Carlotta breathed out a huge breath of exasperation. "How about Arlene? You could take her."

Arlene felt herself redden, and she sank deeper into her stiff-backed chair. She was going to die, but she would *not* die alone.

"Arlene? She wouldn't want to go out with me . . . . Would you?" he asked, turning to face her.

Arlene flushed but was unable to answer, her mind churning with discomfort.

"Good. Then it's all settled." Carlotta grinned at her sister. "I gotta go get washed up for dinner. Don't worry. I'll be right back."

***

Arlene stood by her sister's bedside and watched her as she slept. It had been the best night of her life, and she had her little sister to thank for it. The dance had been wonderful, and she had felt so beautiful in her shamrock-green dress and matching pumps. It was so much fun. Miguel had even asked her out for another date.

She lightly touched her bottom lip, still tingling from her first good-night kiss, and smiled. She sat down on the edge of her sister's bed and gently brushed the hair from her forehead with her fingertips. "Thanks, Carlotta," she whispered. "You're the best."

Carlotta snuggled deeper under her covers and smiled, a small book clutched tightly to her chest.

A SMALL MIRACLE

Winnie Reuff

here were three of us young ladies, each twenty five years old. We felt perfectly capable of a trip to "The Big Apple" from Chicago, Illinois. I had a brand new 1952 Chevrolet Bel Air hard top convertible, a new concept in the 50s. It was a light green color with dark green highlights and had a black top. I was so proud of my new car and the daring trip we were undertaking. Our plan was to go to New York City to see the sights and then on to as many states in New England that we had time for.

Jerrye was a good friend, who a year before had experienced a traumatic divorce. It had been an abusive marriage, and she had finally left him, but not before having a baby boy. I was with her when she delivered the baby. Her husband was nowhere around.

She had been living with her mother while trying to figure out what to do with her life.

Caroline worked at the same hospital I did. The Director of Nurses at our hospital thought travel was part of ones' education, so she happily gave us the time off we needed.

The trip through Indiana and Ohio was monotonous. The motels were interesting. Little houses at the side of the road with a one car garage on the side. They had different motifs. What would catch the eye of a weary traveler? Inside, they were all the same, a bed and a bath. Some had kitchen facilities. We weren't interested in those.

When we got to Pennsylvania the landscape became more interesting. There were hills! Very green hills! We had been driving through flat farm land, mile after mile of it, as far as the eye could see. This was a welcome change.

I was aware of the rarity of gas stations in places like this and didn't want to be stranded out in the "boonies" and out of gas. I decided we better "fill up" as soon as we could, and as long as it was near lunch time, have a bite to eat.

We drove on and on. Finally, up ahead we found one. I told them to go inside and use the restroom while I paid for the gas. We would meet in the lunchroom inside.

Caroline and I waited a long time and finally ate lunch without Jerrye. Where was she? She didn't come by the time we were through eating, so we went back to the car. She finally came out of the lunchroom *next door*. She was furious. Where had we been? *"I sat in that restaurant waiting for you and finally ate alone!"* Caroline and I turned around and there were two gas stations sitting side by side, both with small dining rooms. There was no other edifice that we could see for miles around. After all was explained, we had a good laugh. Poor Jerrye, her life was so unsettled at this time. She had no idea what the future held, and had a child to bring up by herself.

We continued on to New York City and drove around town looking at the sights. We found a hotel in the Bronx, across from Yankee Stadium and settled in for a two day stay in the city.

We thought it would be great fun to ride the subway. We studied the maps at the subway stations and found the connections to different parts of the city.

Caroline and I went to see the Statue of Liberty. Jerrye decided to spend the day visiting Bellevue Hospital.

After the two of us had looked at the pictures and read the history of Ellis Island, we decided to ride the subway back to the hotel. While traveling along underground I exclaimed, *"Let's go to an automat, I've always wanted to see one."* We watched and saw one ahead. Jumping up and rushing out the door, we made it into the restaurant.

We walked along the line of the cafeteria and chose a table. As we ate our lunch, Caroline said, *"Winnie, you won't believe this. Look in the line over there."* I looked where she pointed and there was Jerrye, oblivious to everything around, lost in her own thoughts and obviously happy, judging from the smile on her face. We called to her and she joined us. She didn't have to eat by herself this time.

We still laugh at the miracle of an unplanned meeting at the same time and place in a city of three million people.

MY ANGELS

Debbie Weltin

ne month and three days after I retired from Pacific Bell I had an incident that was so shocking and unsettling that I didn't think I could get through the hardship. It seemed that all was "dark and gloomy."

I had been stressed the past few days and hadn't been sleeping very well. I decided that warm summer night to take a tranquilizer to ensure a better night's sleep. I was in my bedroom with my slider open, wrapping a gift for the next day. I was planning to attend the retirement of a coworker. I used butcher paper to wrap the gift; then I used my acrylic paints and painted on the wrapping designs. As I was finishing, the lights started flickering. At first my heart leapt in my chest with the thought someone was messing with me. I quickly decided this wasn't the case. I went back to the gift wrapping. The lights began to flicker again. I went to my breaker box—the breakers were rather old—and checked them out. I turned them off and back on. I smelled smoke and thought *I better stop before I create a fire*. I closed the kitchen sliders and was ready for bed. I was quite drowsy by that time.

I proceeded to my T-shaped hallway and instead of turning toward my bedroom on the right, I went left to the garage door. To this day I don't know why I went that direction. I opened the door to the garage and found it fully engulfed in flames. My car was also on fire. I quickly closed the door, walked past my purse on the washer, and returned to the kitchen. I felt there might be an explosion at any moment. I tried to call 911, but the phone was dead. I ran out the back door in my nightshirt and panties around to the front and stood in the street yelling, "Help, help, help me someone. Call 911. Fire, fire, fire! Call 911. Help, help, help," for what seemed like twenty minutes before I was able to rouse anyone. Finally neighbors started coming out, calling 911, and then turning their hoses on my house. The roof was now engulfed with flames. God it seemed like an hour before the fire department arrived.

As I stood in the front yard, someone brought me some sweatpants, a jacket and a chair. I knew I was in shock. Two young red-haired girls came and asked if there was anything they could do for me. I said I would like a glass of water. I never saw those two young women before or after. I thought about that quite a bit in the days that followed. A neighbor across the street offered me a place to rest in her house. By this time it was near midnight. During the confusion I called my son and told him I needed him. He arrived with his sleeping kids and they too were offered a place to rest in my neighbor's house.

The next morning, at about six a.m., there were cars all over the place and photographers and people rushing to my attention. Each one wanted a word before the others. They were the various adjustor leeches. The firefighters were still around and rescued me from the hordes. They asked if I would like to see the house. I said I would and followed them. The place was such a mess. It was rather interesting to find everything I had on walls or tabletops or desks that were of spiritual nature were not touched. A cross on one wall was not touched. Fire, I know, has a mind of its own; but all spiritual matter, and anything that mattered to me in the way of photos and important papers, including my PC, was not damaged. I couldn't get over that.

I knew at that time my angels were with me. I knew I was protected. Remember, I was under the influence of a tranquilizer. My slider in my bedroom was open and so was the slider off the kitchen. Once the door had been opened in the garage the fire

220

was sucked through the rest of the roof. I should have gone back in the direction of my bedroom; instead, I went to the garage. I believe my angels were with me then. If I had once laid my head on the pillow, I'm sure I would have died. I would have been so out of it that I never would have felt anything.

Yes, I believe the young girls that brought me water were angels. I also believe I was guided by those same angels to go the opposite direction down the hall. I believe all my spiritual items and valued items were protected by my angels. That is why I truly believe that no matter how bad things are there is always something good that comes out of it. The good that came from the fire itself was a brand new home.

EXPECTATIONS

Patrick Wallace

I expect the rain in the middle of the desert.
I expect the sun to shine on a cloudy day.
I expect strength in my moments of weakness.
I expect tomorrow to be a better day.

My expectations are high, even at my lowest point,
enabling me to feel young again,
as if the fountains of youth were in my reach.

I don't expect you to understand,
or see what I see.
I don't expect you to challenge yourself,
I don't expect you to be free.
What do you expect?

THE DOLL TRAP

Anthony J Enriquez

S he was the one; he knew it when he saw her. She was standing by a car with a bag of groceries in her hands as she kicked the tire in frustration.

"Hi! Having problems?"

She looked up at him and said, "Would you believe my car won't start?"

Looking at her, he saw a trim young woman with brown hair and the biggest brown eyes. She smiled at him and said, "Can you help me?"

He started to speak when he felt something poking his back. "Don't yell and don't move or your dead."

Looking down, the Good Samaritan saw a short muscular man holding a gun on him. "I'll give you my . . ."

"Shut up. Trixie, you drive. As for you, get in the back." Once inside her car, The Good Samaritan handed over his wallet and timidly said, "I don't want any problems. Just let me go."

Taking his wallet, the muscular man said, "Let's see, your driver's license sez you're Mr. Peabody and you live at 11231 Oakhurst Ave. We know where that is; let's go Trixie."

"Don't get us mad. Trixie is even tougher than me." Trixie winked at him in the mirror. Soon after, she was looking at the road again. As they drove to Mr. Peabody's house, the muscular man said; "You can call me Homeboy. We're just going to your place to get your money and valuables. Is there going to be anyone there?"

"No," Mr. Peabody said, "I don't even own a dog."

"Good. This should be simple," said Homeboy.

Once they got to the house, they all got out of the car and gathered together. Homeboy put the gun into his pants and then placed his hand on the gun butt. "Remember, No problems."

Mr. Peabody put his hands in his pockets and with one hand pulled out his keys. He opened the door and they stepped in. Homeboy gently pushed Mr. Peabody in as Trixie locked the door. On the floors were blue plastic tarps.

Homeboy said, "Are you going to paint?"

Mr. Peabody turned and pulled out a closed stiletto with his other hand. He flicked it open and plunged it into Homeboy. Twisting the blade, he pulled it out and then stabbed Homeboy three more times. Homeboy was in shock. He tried to pull out his gun but was too weak; he fell to his knees and curled over.

Turning, Trixie gave a stilted scream and turned to unlock the door. Mr. Peabody was against her immediately, pressing her to the door. "I don't usually kill men. That was quite an experience." He continued, "You and I are going to be partners. You are going to help me get what I want."

Trixie shuddered when she saw Homeboy. She pressed her body to Mr. Peabody and pled, "Don't hurt me." As she said this, she gently put her hand in her side dress pocket and pulled out a .22 derringer. She palmed it and wrapped her arm around Mr. Peabody.

"You can trust me," he said as he placed the knife softly by her side.

Trixie placed the gun near the back of his head and said, "I know I can trust you."

As he thrust the knife under her ribs, she pulled the trigger. They held each other tightly as they felt a rush of pain and pleasure. A moment later, they parted and fell to the ground.

THE SUN CONURE

Diane Neil

Sun Conure: Small, brilliantly colored tropical bird. Intelligent, personable (requires daily interaction of at least one hour). Mimics sounds/words. Can be messy and loud.

Two weeks after Barbara's fifty-sixth birthday in late May, she made the second most important decision of her life. The first, after a disastrous youthful love affair, had been to remain single.

Cleaning up her classroom after the departure of her fourth grade students, she wondered why a faculty meeting had been called for a Friday afternoon.

Fifteen minutes into the meeting, the District Superintendent announced a twenty percent staff reduction effective at the end of the semester. Amid the gasps and protests of her colleagues, Barbara, as stunned as anyone at the news, strained to hear the announcement. The Superintendent handed the microphone to the Director of Personnel, who outlined transfer procedures and substitute mandates.

The Director uttered the words that led to Barbara's second most important decision. "Teachers who have served at least twenty-five years in our district will qualify for retirement at ninety percent of present salary."

Barbara restrained herself from leaping up, waving her hand and shouting "Take me! I've got thirty-two years in!"

All weekend Barbara basked in the glow of her good fortune.

225

Saturday, when she saw her neighbor Millie two aisles over in the grocery store, she nearly knocked down a gum display to tell her the news. Millie was a bit brash and loud, not necessarily Barbara's favorite person, but she was bursting to share her news.

"That's wonderful!" Millie's orange curls bobbed. "Now you can plan a cruise to meet Mr. Right!" Thrice married—once divorced and twice widowed—Millie was always on the lookout for a man.

"I haven't made any plans yet," Barbara said. "It's nice to know I won't be a slave to clocks and schedules anymore."

"I just got a brochure for some fall and winter cruises," Millie said. "I'll drop it by." It had been eight years since Millie had lovingly laid her last husband to rest, but Barbara had to admit she wore her widow's weeds well. Today, that garb featured a bright purple pantsuit and a pink paisley scarf. Millie believed in magic colors, good luck charms, and who knows what else.

"Cat food's on sale." Millie added toilet tissue to her cart, piled high with pet food. "It's double coupon day. I'm only buying sale items today."

"I didn't know you had a cat," Barbara said.

"Oh, yes. And she just had kittens."

Barbara shuddered. She couldn't stand cats.

Barbara spent June in a happy daze, bidding farewell to students and staff, doling out her finely honed lesson plans and the secrets of her successful teaching career. On the final clean-out work day, she asked the janitor to carry three boxes of plaques, awards and testimonials out to her car. She stashed them in her garage and forgot about them.

One morning in early July, she lingered over her morning coffee, gazing at Millie's cruise brochure for the umpteenth time, when she got a phone call from her brother Leo that sent her euphoria crashing.

"Hi, Leo. How's Dad?" Barbara asked. Their father had finally consented to accept Leo's invitation to stay with him after languishing in their family home since their mother had suffered a fatal stroke the year before.

"Same old buzzard." They shared a mirthless chuckle. "He's doing better. I tried to introduce him to some single ladies, but nothing doing. All he does is sit around talking about Mom. It's getting on my nerves."

"I can imagine the barflies you introduced to Dad!" Barbara huffed.

"Oh, give me a break. I took him to the Senior Citizen's Center, but he refused to join."

"What happened?"

"Men were so scarce; all those biddies flocked around Dad and scared him off. I even had one old gal flirting with me!"

Barbara smiled. "Mom was his life. He never looked at another woman."

A few beats of silence followed. Barbara knew Leo must be wondering, as she was, why they couldn't have inherited their parents' perfect marriage genes.

Leo cleared his throat. "I wondered if you could take him for a while. Just enough time to give me a break."

Barbara knew her brother was a master manipulator. You could believe about half of what he said.

"For how long?" She needed to pin him down.

"I've got a business trip coming up, and I hate to leave him alone."

"How long, Leo?"

"Maybe until Christmas."

There goes my cruise. "How about Halloween?"

"How about Thanksgiving? Good chance for us to gather as

a family."

"Okay, he can stay until Thanksgiving." Hopefully, she could still book a winter cruise. "I'll drive up to get him next Tuesday."

"No, no," Leo said. "I'll bring him over next weekend. Is Saturday good?"

"Sure, that's fine. I'll invite Aunt May and Uncle Ned. It would be good for Dad to see them. The last time was at Mom's funeral."

They discussed a few more details and Barbara hung up, turned around and looked at her peaceful living room. *There goes my privacy.* She felt her bubble had burst.

She spent the next few days preparing the guest room for her dad. She emptied the closet and drawers and bought a new plaid bedspread to replace the flowered chintz. She moved in her small bookcase stacked with the Zane Greys she knew he liked.

The following Saturday, Aunt May and Uncle Ned's sleek old Buick pulled up in front of the house forty minutes earlier than Barbara had told them to arrive. Barbara chucked the vacuum cleaner in the closet, opened the door and was enveloped in Aunt May's perfumed hug and a wolf whistle from Uncle Ned.

"How's my girl?" he boomed. "Looking better than ever. The men in this town must be crazy to leave you single!"

Chuckling, Barbara ushered them in. *They'd be good medicine for Dad.*

They were still chatting when Leo roared up in his Tahoe SUV an hour later and parked in the driveway. Both doors opened, and Leo and Dad got out. They all went out to greet them, Uncle Ned helping Leo bring Dad's luggage in.

Barbara gasped. *What was that bulky crate Dad was cradling—a cat carrier?* She glimpsed a scruffy gray thing inside. Leo hadn't mentioned a word about Dad having a cat.

228

Now she knew why he had insisted on bringing Dad down instead of her driving up to get him.

Leo and Uncle Ned took the luggage to the guest room.

"This is Tigger," Dad said, following them. The three of them returned sans luggage and cat.

In the effusive hugs and chatter from her uncle and aunt, Barbara stifled her protests about the cat. Surely the day would develop as she had envisioned, and Dad would cheer up.

Well, *that* didn't happen. Dad and Aunt May spent hours reminiscing over old times, and Uncle Ned sniffled and kept them supplied with Kleenex. Leo, the sneak, didn't even stay for dessert.

Somehow the sad, subdued reunion ended and her aunt and uncle departed. Except for Dad's brief introduction, Tigger remained out of sight in the guest room. All during dinner, Barbara mulled over what she'd say about the cat when their company left. But seeing her dad's crestfallen face, she decided to wait until morning to confront him.

Barbara learned it would take more than all the skills of persuasion honed during her teaching career to reason with her father. He would NOT part with his beloved Tigger. True, he did keep the cat in his room and tended to his feeding and litter box. From all his fussing over Tigger's poor appetite, Barbara surmised that the cat had gone through most of its nine lives.

Each morning Barbara attempted to deliver the get-rid-of-the-cat speech she'd rehearsed during the night, and each morning the words stuck in her throat. How could she deprive her father of his only source of comfort?

She had more serious concerns. Dad must have lost thirty pounds since Mom died. She'd been a great cook, and they had always been rather portly. Alarmed at his weight loss, she scheduled a full physical. All the tests came back normal. "For a man pushing eighty, you are in excellent condition," the doctor said. "You should get a hearing aid, though, and you could work on your muscle tone. Get some exercise; maybe take up golf."

That evening, Barbara felt self-satisfied smugness emanating from her father, and she decided she would renew her Tigger attack. There was more than one way to skin a cat! She decided to use psychology.

"Now we know you're in good health, we should get a checkup for Tigger," she said. It came as no surprise that Dad agreed more readily to that than he had to his own checkup. That scruffy old cat was his life.

The morning of Tigger's appointment, Barbara rinsed her breakfast dishes, put them in the dishwasher, dumped coffee grounds and fruit peelings into the sink and turned on the garbage disposal. Its whirring and grinding drowned out the blaring TV news her father watched at full volume.

Grabbing a towel, Barbara walked back to the table where her father still dawdled over his breakfast. "Dad," she shouted, "you need to hurry. The vet appointment is at nine. We have to get going."

"I'm done. This is for Tigger." He mashed up his egg yolk. "Maybe he'll eat some."

"We'll see what the vet says," Barbara answered, hoping he'd recommend euthanasia.

Her father scraped the egg into Tigger's bowl atop the untouched cat food. Tenderly, he propped the inert cat next to his bowl.

Rinsing her father's dishes, Barbara glanced at him, rumpled and unkempt as usual. "Dad, you need to change your shirt before we go. You spilled coffee on it."

He shuffled out of the room, mumbling under his breath.

"I'm getting the car out," Barbara called after him. "You get

Tigger into his carrier."

Barbara sat in the van with the motor running for ten minutes before her father emerged down the front steps toting the cat carrier. He still wore the coffee-stained shirt. She sighed. Had she really expected him to change?

The appointment at the animal hospital was far different than Barbara's hoped for outcome. Instead of euthanasia, the vet prescribed pills, a cortisone shot, and outrageously expensive cat food available only by prescription.

"That should perk up the old boy's appetite," he said, patting her father's shoulder. "I also recommend a down-filled kitty bed. It'll be easier on the poor fellow's hip. You can get one at Pampered Pets."

That was the most expensive pet store! Where celebrities shopped! She'd seen the commercial with a simpering starlet leading her oh so itty bitty twin Chihuahuas through the store on their little pink leashes.

The veterinarian's assistant ushered Barbara and her father to chairs in the waiting room while Tigger had his treatment. A rack of pet related books and magazines caught her dad's attention. Barbara never knew so much pet information existed.

Nearby, an old couple sat huddled, the woman sniffling into a hanky as she cuddled a limp poodle in a baby blanket. The man, as rumpled as Dad, kept patting her shoulder. Barbara shuddered.

"Mr. Taylor?" The veterinarian's assistant emerged from a side door with Tigger in his carrier. "He's a bit woozy from his shot," she told Dad. "Just let him sleep. He should perk up by this evening, and he might be hungry. This is a two week supply of his senior diet food." She placed a paws-printed bag on the cashier's counter.

As her father approached the counter, the cashier beamed at him. She punched data into a computer and announced, "Tigger's visit, with the exam, cortisone shot and Lov'm Bits diet food, comes to two hundred and twenty dollars." She paused and brightened up her smile. "But with your senior citizen discount, your total is only one ninety-seven ninety-five. Would you like to pay by cash, check, or credit card?"

Dad offered the credit card he'd already fished out of his wallet, and the girl took it, finished her computer magic, and returned the card and receipt for his signature. Barbara could swear the girl winked at her father as she handed him the bag of cat food.   "Thank you, Mr. Taylor," she purred. "You take care of Tigger, now. We'll call tomorrow to see how he's doing."

Barbara noticed her father walked more vigorously as they returned to the car. She opened the hatchback and he put the carrier in, giving it a tender caress.

"You're going to be fine, Tigger!" he said.

She didn't have to remind him to fasten his seat belt. As she started the engine, he turned to her.

"Would you mind stopping by Pampered Pets? I'd like to get that kitty bed right away."

"Okay." The store was twenty miles out of their way and commuter traffic was increasing, but she wasn't about to break the good mood the cheery vet and the flirtatious young woman had induced in her father.

When they pulled into the parking lot at Pampered Pets, Dad fairly leapt out of the car. He grabbed a shopping cart, put Tigger's carrier into it and led the way into the store, where more beaming young people greeted them like visiting royalty. Barbara, marching to the Beds section, noticed her father lagging behind, distracted in an aisle of exotic birds. There, among the screeching parrots and parakeets, she found him staring at a lone bird in a cage labeled "Sun Conure." The brilliantly colored tropical bird seemed to be staring right back at him.

She glared at her father. Was he losing his mind? "You're not thinking of buying a bird, are you?" She couldn't stand caged birds.

"No," he shook his head. "Not with Tigger." He tapped the window, communing with the bird again. "I just think he's lonely and needs someone to talk to him."

The commute traffic was heavy by the time Barbara hustled her father through the store to buy Tigger's bed and left all the beaming clerks.

To Barbara's surprise and her father's delight, Tigger made a full recovery. She began to notice subtle changes about him as well. He finally agreed to get a hearing aid, stopped escaping into mindless television, and helped with household and gardening tasks. He took more care with his appearance and shaved and showered more often. Every evening he took Tigger out for a walk on his new green leash. Oh, yes! He found many occasions to 'stop by' Pampered Pets, and he never failed to visit his buddy, the Sun Conure.

One day, the Sun Conure's cage was gone. In alarm, Dad approached a young man in a blue vest and asked, his voice trembling, "Did he die of loneliness?"

"Oh, no!" the clerk answered. "A young couple came in and bought him."

"That's good, that's good." Dad murmured.

The next day Dad returned from one of his frequent walks sporting a green felt Fedora.

"Where did you get the hat?" She'd only seen him in baseball caps before.

"From a buddy down the street." He carried Tigger up the steps.

Barbara was glad her father had found a friend. Several elderly couples lived in the neighborhood, and at least one fellow was a retired teamster like Dad. It was a good sign he was becoming sociable again. His walks became more frequent and of longer duration, and she imagined him playing checkers with his new buddy.

One morning Dad announced he was having dinner at his buddy's house. At four o'clock he emerged from his room showered, shaved and positively reeking of Old Spice. He hooked up Tigger's green leash and they sauntered down the sidewalk.

"Where in the dickens is he going?" she wondered. As she ate her sparse dinner in front of the now seldom used TV, she tried to 'mind her own beeswax,' as Mom used to say.

She fussed and fumed until she couldn't stand it any longer. Tossing a sweater over her shoulders, she stood on her porch, shielding her eyes against the setting sun, peering up and down the street. There was no sign of him.

Walking to the corner and around the block, she looked everywhere. She turned another corner and was nearly back home when she heard music blaring from Millie's house. The living room was alight, the drapes were open, and there was movement inside. Was that her father? She couldn't believe it. He and Millie were dancing!

Barbara had no idea what to think. As red-faced as if she'd been caught in the act of spying, she skittered home and was in bed long before Dad came in, chuckling to himself.

What are vows and promises? For people like Leo, they may be expedient tools of persuasion. For some people, like Dad and Millie, there might be no promises at all, but just the chance to live each day as fully and happily as they can. Yes, Dad did move in with Millie, and they clipped their grocery and restaurant coupons and lived cozily with their cats. Not forever, but long enough.

Perhaps the promises we make to ourselves are the strongest

fetters. The vow of a bitter twenty-year-old does not fit an older, wiser woman. It didn't happen overnight, but Barbara felt her old opinions and judgments fall away.

Three months later, in Cabo San Lucas, she danced with a man who held her close and firm, and for the first time in her life she felt the tug of possibilities, romance and fun. Perhaps it was only a dance, but she thought of Millie's 'magic' scarf encircling her waist and dared to hope for more.

ALL ROADS LEAD TO WATSONVILLE

Rusty LaGrange

We drove down endless highways lined with blurs
Of vineyard rows and graying harrow bales.
Only a little ways to go
And the signs all declared: "This way to Watsonville."

The beach disappeared beyond the fog bank hues,
Misty, clinging dew and the air so thick with garlic and smut
And new mushrooms. Steinbeck's Land: he knew the strong
Swells of Moss Landing and Carmel. I wonder if he knew
Watsonville?

We parked our tired car and crumpled on the cliff together,
Snuggled in damp cotton. Behind us
Tractors droned like crickets, and diesel fumes
Hung on heavy clouds of fish oil.

This historic ground grew rich along its coast.
Seagulls hovered over lovers on the strand,
Yet just beyond the sandy dunes, Mexican pickers bent
Toward cabbages and artichokes.

Without the sun, we packed our wet towels and suits.
We packed our baskets of strawberries
Like school children, dripping
In summer sweetened smiles.

Through only verse and prose;
No Chesapeake Bay on a sunny day,
Only gray seascapes drawn on canvasbacks,
Ever the foghorn—silence-torn.

Our slick tires stirred mustiness in our trackless minds.
We flew by fields. The farmhouses century-old and leaning
On strong shoulders glowed white in foggy moonlight.
The signs we followed faithfully recalled the towns we knew.

We pointed to highway off-ramps shrouded in fog,
Yet always the signs to Watsonville peeked through.
In dreamy thoughts, I hooked an arm over the seat back;
Watched the sparkle headlights dance on wet pavement.

'It ain't no Martha's Vineyard,' you said.
I threw a wet towel at your head and laughed.
We found a good laugh, and we're laughing still
When we remember all roads lead to Watsonville.

HOMES OF THE BRAVE

June Langer

The Search

$\mathcal{J}$t was difficult coming out of a deep sleep. But the insistent banging on the front door required it, especially in the early 1900s, and especially in Poland. When Joseph opened the door, he encountered a group of Cossacks, rifles at the ready, bayonets fixed.

"This is the Chrystofovich home?" the Captain asked.

"Yes."

"You have a son, Walter?"

"Yes."

"He reached his twenty-first birthday last week and did not report for military duty. We are here to escort him to his post."

"Walter no longer lives here. We are waiting for him."

"You and your family will stand quietly against that wall. Do not move or speak. We are going to search the premises."

No one disobeyed the Cossacks. They were the fiercest and most ruthless of all the Russian troops.

The soldiers poked their bayonets into every nook, cranny, and closet. If Walter had been there, he would have been bloodied.

"Return to your beds and finish your sleep," said one soldier. "If Walter returns, inform him we are waiting for him."

The soldiers left.

Walter did not return to the Chrystofovich household. At that moment, he was stationed in Fort Sheridan on Lake Michigan in

Chicago, Illinois, proudly serving in the army of the United States of America.

The frightening search convinced the Chrystofovich family that they could not wait much longer. They would follow Walter to the United States. They had another son, Ignatz, age fifteen. The soldiers would be back.

The Escape

The family waited until the night was very dark, and they would not be seen. The wagon was greased and oiled so that it would not creak and packed with only necessary belongings. The horse's hooves and trappings were treated to move quietly.

Joseph warned the children, "Do not speak or play. Breathe quietly. Do not even sneeze."

The family was ready to leave—all but Joseph. He decided to remain at home. He had a good job as a supervisor in a silk factory. He would come later.

Josepha and their five children, Ignatz, Valeria, age twelve, Helena, age eight, Pelagia, age three, and baby Joseph, one year old, would make the journey to America. The plan was to cross the border into Germany and then proceed to the ship, the *Bremen*. That ship would take them to Ellis Island.

All went well, until they came close to the border. Someone spotted them and yelled, "Halt!"

The wagon picked up speed, and the family rode for their lives. A shot was fired, but they kept going. Finally, they crossed the border unscathed. They were safe, and could continue unchallenged to the ship where two staterooms awaited them.

The Crossing

The remainder of the journey was not without misfortune. As soon as the ship left port, eight-year-old Helena became seasick.

She remained sick for the entire voyage. Little Joseph contracted pneumonia, so mother and baby were confined to sickbay. Valeria was put in charge of her younger siblings, Helena and Pelagia.

It wasn't unusual for a twelve-year-old to be in that position in the early 1900s. Often girls of that age had the responsibility for entire households when their mothers had babies. Ignatz was free to roam and even to court young women on the ship. Valeria did her duty, and never complained.

When the ship docked at Ellis Island, mother and baby were taken immediately to the hospital. The rest of the family was looked after by people in charge of such things.

After a few days, Helena got the measles. She was placed in a hospital ward where there were no other patients. She was lonely and the nights were long. Unable to sleep, she longed for her mother and wondered what was happening to the others and where they were. She even missed the bossy Valeria.

Eventually, Helena recovered from the measles, and the family was reunited, except for Baby Joseph. He died in the hospital.

Before they left, a few alterations were made to their names. The ovich was cut off the end of Chrystofovich. They were now the Chrystof family. Valeria became Viola. Helena became Helen. Pelagia became Pauline. Josepha was now Josephine. Only Ignatz kept his original name.

The family continued their journey to Chicago where they reunited with Walter. They were ready to begin their new life as Americans.

NIGHT

J.P. Newcomer

*"Within the caves of Ansillar
the children play from dawn to dusk
and the walls weep sunny tears of light and
the day is bright, and there is no fright—until the night."*
                                          Anon.

Trapped within the holofield, the figure leans forward on his florcush, and speaks slowly with effort. His eyes dart back and forth in a quick, nervous motion. He is a study in contrasts—this man—attired in the insignia of everlasting power, speaking in the frail voice of a child. I listen intently.

"I was designed to guard the light," he intones, "to keep it bright, to shepherd the flock, to lead them safely through the labyrinth. It was my destiny—my only purpose for being. Can you understand this? I was genetically engineered to overcome any obstacle in my path—to succeed—to persevere. How did I fail? How?"

Once again, perhaps for the thousandth time, I watch the scene play out: my father's anguished words, the fever-racked gleam in his eyes, his painful grimace. "Ahh, Vasha, we are lost in this underworld. I cannot go on. Forgive me, child." The recording ends, and the image vanishes.

I no longer weep in despair at seeing this. I no longer fling myself to the floor in hopeless rage. Rather, I sit in meditative stance, cross-legged, arms folded, eyes closed, searching for the path.

Before the sickness took him, my father knew the way through the silken streams of light. He knew the route to the surface where rain falls and twin suns hug the heavens. Is he not my biological father? Do I not share some of his genetic determinants? Enough, perhaps, to find the way? Tomas insists it must be so. I wait for the path to beckon.

***

"Vasha, Vasha, where you go? Vasha, Vasha, what you know?" The younger children chant in unison, marching up and down the narrow boundaries of their lair.

"Children, children, let me in. Then I'll tell you where I've been."

"That's not what we want to know! Vasha, Vasha, where you go?"

The words chill me. Tomas has been talking with them, I see. Promising them magic—telling them I can lead them home. He strides toward me from their midst. "Forgive their impudence," he says, waving a hand at them. The children giggle and jostle each other as they scatter.

"It's you who are impudent," I snap at him.

"No, Vasha. You're gifted. I—we have faith in you."

"I don't want your faith."

"It is your legacy."

"Damn you, Tomas."

"You mustn't be frightened. I'll be your Lieutenant. I'll lay down my life for you, if need be. You'll lead and we'll follow."

"Lead where?"

"Be patient. You'll find the path."

"I want my father," I blurt out. "I want my mother. I want them back."

"Me, too." He takes me in his arms. "We all want that. But they're gone, and we're the oldest. We have to be strong." We hug for a long time—so long the children return to ogle us. I promise to keep on searching.

***

Always the path eludes me. Tomas and I mate. The younger children grow, and eventually pair off. Some leave us, determined to seek their fortune elsewhere in this labyrinth. Most return. A few vanish, and we grieve for them.

We build our lives in rock-strewn caverns lit by incandescent glow holes and our eyes adjust to the gradual dimming light within our subterranean recess. Tomas says the light may eventually die out—that it is generated by a weakening electromagnetic force field. Most of us refuse to accept such a prediction.

Our son is graced with luminous eyes, such as none of us have ever before seen. "Glow Hole," the children call him. They are children no longer, but I still think of them as such. "Son of Vasha, Traveler of the True Path. Leader of our People. Pioneer. Healer. Rescuer. Lead us home."

The infant coos, and gurgles in my arms. "He will lead you home," Tomas promises. "He and his mother will lead you home."

***

"I can never leave the caves," Tomaro announces on his seventh birthday, "but I can lead those who wish to depart to the surface." Our entire clan, including Tomas and myself, stands before him. "I leave in the dawn-glow. Who wishes to follow?"

We are all stunned. Not a single hand shoots up. Not a single voice responds.

"Mother?" He turns to us. "Father?"

Tomas is silent.

"We shall go," say Vanca and Ariel, two of the youngest of the original party, now in their early twenties.

"Fine!" Tomaro sounds pleased. "Who else?"

"Will we go blind on the surface?"

"Not if you take precautions."

"And what of you, son?" Tomas asks.

"Those born of the darkness may never enter the light. There are several of us now. The rest of you are free to leave."

"Then, we'll go," I say.

"Vasha!" Tomas twitches, and his face hardens. "We can't"

"We can. We will. We were his age when we came here, remember? He'll carry on. He's his grandfather's heir. He belongs here. Can't you see that? We don't!"

Tomas falls silent, his smooth-stone features resembling the texture of the cave wall before which he stands.

Tomaro runs to us. "Oh, father, please. Don't be angry." The boy clings to my knees. "No one has to stay. I know the path."

Tomas lifts the boy in his arms. "We're not going anywhere without you," he says, catching my gaze. "Isn't that right, Vasha?" As I watch them, I imagine a pale sick thrill of hope racing toward the surface. I imagine my father's smile.

"The path waits," I tell him.

THE RIDE

Linda Bowden

W̲e were on the road again, the long road that seemed to never to end. It was not enough that the car was hot, and the wind blew in like something from the devil. But my mother looked at the countryside as if she were in a place of pure bliss. The first words out of her mouth as I propped one eye open were, "Isn't it beautiful?"

Beautiful, I thought. *What's beautiful about sand, scrub brush and a lot of nothing? What's beautiful about relentless heat, no air conditioning and an annoying sister, who's always getting car sick and throwing up on my side of the floor boards?*

I couldn't wait to get to Missouri.

There was something about visiting Grandma and Grandpa, something magical, full of surprises. New experiences, my mom would call them, because we were city girls and going to my grandparents' house was a vacation from the city. They lived on a rural farm in Missouri, no inside plumbing, not even running water. We had to draw water from the cistern and baths were a weekly, not daily, adventure. If you got there on a Tuesday, you might have to wait until Saturday to get a bath. After all, people bathed before church on Sunday. Yeah, we washed up every day in a basin, but that's comparable to a hospital bath. Not a very clean feeling.

"Where are we?" I asked Mom.

"New Mexico," Mom answered. "We're still a long way away." I hated when she said that. It was her way of saying, "Stop asking." No matter how many times she said it and in how many different ways she said it, one of us would ask again.

Later, on trips with my own children, I would think back to the numerous times I bugged her and "Yes." You get paid back for your childhood annoyances.

Hours went by. As the car lulled me into sleepiness, I wondered if we'd ever stop again for the bathroom or maybe something to eat.

"We'll stop when we need gas," said Dad, answering another question from my sister. I wondered how many times we would ask before we got there and how many times our parents would answer that question. One more time, two more times, a thousand times? Who knew? It just depended on how many more hours would pass before we reached our destination. I could tell that my father's matter-of-fact tone would be ignored if my mother, who was driving, decided to stop. She was all about enjoying the ride. He was all about getting there, single focused, a one-track mind.

Oh yeah, she had spied the Indian Reservation Store sign. We were stopping, even if we didn't need gas. My dad sighed, but he knew it wouldn't do any good because my mom had already pulled in. Somehow, I knew I was about to get that ice cream.

"Where are we?" I asked Mom.

"New Mexico," Mom answered. "We're still a long way away."

I hated when she said that but that was her answer.

SHAPE OF MY WORDS

J. McAllister

What comes around goes around,
Like the echoing voice of a mother to her unknowing child.
Lost in a cloud of doubt,
We stand on the cliffs of right and wrong,
Unable to lick the wounds of our choices.
Full circle in a world full of squares,
I form a triangle that can never be broken by the dissonant tones
of a life,
Well spent looking for change.

THE BRIDGE

Michael Raff

*L*eaving a dark alleyway, the young woman stepped over the debris from a fallen trash barrel. Although she was bundled in a heavy, woolen jacket, the night's dampness managed to seep through. Her long dark hair, moist from the never-ending fog, dangled behind her. The hurried pace of her boots disrupted the stillness of the night.

On the other side of the street, she noticed two young lovers leaning against a building. With their arms locked around each other, they gazed at her in fleeting wonder. As the girl hurried by, she could hear their laughter echoing through the night. Wiping away a tear, she quickened her pace.

Still drenched from the fallen rain, the concrete sidewalks glistened with an array of frightening and distorted images. Suddenly, the scent and sounds of the ocean forewarned her; she had reached her destination. Somewhere just beyond her depth of vision lay the bridge.

Her journey concluded as the steel structure gradually revealed itself. Stretched boldly within the fog, it resembled the skeletal remains of a towering behemoth, an untold, barren, and lifeless entity. She crept forward, as if to not disturb the slumbering giant. There were no passing headlights, no strolling bystanders. The deafening quiet unnerved her as she inched toward her objective.

The girl leaned against the railing and gazed at the waters below. The calmness of the canal seemed to transform itself into a monstrous snake . . . a cold, heartless viper, so deceptively subtle as it meandered its way toward the harbor.

She shuddered and stumbled back. It didn't seem possible, but the waters were now beckoning her. Like the voice of an anxious lover in a vivid dream, it shred away her will and drew her toward its loving embrace.

Trembling, she returned to the railing. The canal no longer appeared cold and heartless. Incredibly, it had evolved into a world where heartaches and betrayals ceased to exist, a chance for her to thrive and revel in fulfillment, where gentle waters would welcome her into their eternal domain.

Her eyes flashed with bitter resentment. She took a breath and clutched the railing.

"Hello," murmured a cryptic voice.

Startled, the young woman whirled around. Barely visible, a dark outline stood motionless within the fog.

"W-what are you d-doing here?" the murky silhouette asked. It was a male's voice, and he sounded both peculiar and indistinct.

The girl moved away from the railing. "Nothing . . . just looking."

The figure stepped forward. He was young, short, and limped as he approached. His bulging eyes blinked continually from behind a pair of thick bifocals. A hesitant smile revealed crooked teeth and clumsy lips. His dark hair hung from a tattered baseball cap.

The girl shook her head and turned away.

"M-my name is Gerald, what's yours?" He sounded child-like, extremely naive.

She turned and glared at him. He stood stationary with his hands behind his back, waiting for an answer. She had to force herself. "Lisa," she lied.

"It's way past my bedtime!" He snickered while gaping inquisitively over the railing. "How come you're out here s-so late?"

She found herself staring at his pallid face. His protruding ears reminded her of a toy monkey she had once owned as a child. "I was just taking a walk . . ." then lowering her voice, she murmured," . . . like if that's any of your business."

"M-me, too!" He seemed to be having a problem maintaining eye contact. "Yep, I couldn't sleep, not a w-wink! So now I'm here with you! Mrs. Laughlin, m-my caretaker, would have a cow if she found out!"

He limped toward her and cringing, she inched away.

"G-gee, you shouldn't be out here so late. Something *bad* could happen!"

"I can take care of myself," she scoffed.

Gerald nodded. "Yep, m-me, too." He straightened his shoulders and placed his hands on his hips. The gesture seemed to cause him to sway precariously from side to side. "W-why, if somebody tried to bother me, I'd punch them right in the old snot locker!" He raised his right fist to emphasize the point.

The girl nodded, and to her profound amazement, found herself smiling.

"Well, I b-better be going. Mrs. Laughlin will give me what for if she catches me."

She watched Gerald as he turned and limped away. He raised an arm to wave goodbye and then tripped over something unseen in the fog. He hit the concrete with a sickening thud. She winced and was about help him, when he maneuvered himself nimbly about and leaped to his feet.

Embarrassed, Gerald smiled at her, and even through the murkiness, she could see his reddened face. As he brushed off his pants, he blurted, "Stupid cracks! You have to get over those nasty things!" He swiveled on his heels, and with renewed vigor, disappeared into the fog.

The girl suddenly felt an immense solitude sweep through her. She swallowed, stepped up to the railing, and gazed at the canal below. She could no longer hear the enchanting voice pleading for her to join it, nor feel the magical allure of the waters. She could only perceive the coldness and treacherousness of its depth.

She sighed, folded her arms across her chest, and realized how late it was. Wiping the moisture from her eyes, she whispered, "Yep, you have to get over those nasty things." She took a breath, turned and hurried home.

GRANDMA-TYPE LADY AND SAFETY PIN FACE

Jenny Margotta

$\mathcal{G}$ met Marcus in a web design class at the local community college. His first words to me, on the initial day of class, raised my social barriers. As I waited by the locked door to the classroom—ten minutes early for the scheduled start time—I heard a young male voice behind me say, "Hey, Grandma-type lady? You takin' this class?"

I turned around to see a very thin, very oddly dressed young man standing behind me. He had shoulder-length dreadlock curls, partially covered by one of the scruffiest knit hats I'd ever seen. His T-shirt was emblazoned with a skull and crossbones and text of some kind in an extremely intricate font that I couldn't begin to read. His jeans were threadbare and torn in multiple places and on his feet were glaringly bright, orange high-top tennies, no ties.

It was his face that put me off the most. He had the most alarming array of safety pins decorating every possible place on his face. There were several through each eyebrow, three through one nostril, two through the other, and one at each corner of his mouth. Knowing all too well the habits of current teenagers, I felt fairly certain the safety pin accessorizing continued on to his ears, although the abundance of hair precluded my actually confirming that suspicion.

"Yes, I'm taking Mr. Wallace's Flash class." Turning back around, I hoped my cool tone of voice, and obvious reluctance to continue the conversation, would send him on his way. Not so.

"Cool, Grandma-type lady. How come you're back in college?"

Would this offensive person ever leave me alone? If this was the caliber of students at the college, I was beginning to be sorry I'd signed up for the class. But I'd long ago been taught it was rude to ignore a direct question, so I turned once again to speak with my tormentor. I wasn't about to tell him the real reason, but I thought quickly and gave him what I hoped would be a believable answer. "I've grown bored with my life, and just want to expand my knowledge, that's all."

"More power to ya', then. That's rad." The silver stud through the middle of his tongue flashed in the overhead lights.

What was this kid? Some kind of hippy throwback wannabe? Did young people really still talk like that? My personal musings were cut short by the arrival of a well-dressed, older gentleman. He was impeccably garbed in crisp, pressed sports pants, a tweed sports coat with leather patches on the elbows, and a pipe sticking out of his breast pocket. Not a strand of his pure white hair was out of place. He was the epitome of a college professor—and the exact opposite of my odious companion. There was no doubt in my mind that this latest arrival was none other than our instructor, Mr. Wallace. He proceeded to open the classroom door, turn on the lights, and move to the front of the room. *Good*, I thought, *here's the instructor. I can now get away from this deplorable young man.*

It was not to be. For some reason, Safety Pin Face had decided I was his long lost grandparent, or newest best friend. As I took my seat, he slid into the seat next to me. Cracking his chewing gum and ceaselessly jiggling his foot up and down, his jittery, never-still antics soon began to annoy me even more than his inability to shut up. For the next five minutes, I was treated to a non-stop monolog of his life's history, not that I bothered to listen.

Finally, Mr. Wallace called the class to order, and began taking role. About halfway through the approximately thirty people in the room, he called out "Marcus Symes?"

"Yo," my seating companion replied.

You can imagine my surprise when Mr. Wallace paused in his role call. "Marcus, I'm so glad to see you're taking one of my classes again. I've missed you the last few semesters."

Marcus, my safety-pin-faced shadow, laughed, and replied, "Missed you, too, teach. You up to date on all your material, or you gonna want my input again?"

Oh, nice, I thought to myself. *It's bad enough he's latched on to me in a totally unacceptable manner. I'm just another student. But to lack the manners to treat the teacher respectfully, well . . . it's just not acceptable.* I shot a look of reproach at Marcus. He either failed to see it, or chose to ignore it.

Once roll call ended and class began, an unbelievable change came over the twitching, jiggling, irreverent young man. He immediately stopped talking, took out a laptop computer from his backpack, and for the next ninety minutes he hung on every word the instructor uttered. He asked several very intelligent questions, I might add. By the end of that first session, I realized there was much more to this unattractive teenager than I first gave him credit for.

At the end of the class, he turned to me once again. "Hey, Grandma-type lady. You got a name? Mine's Marcus. See ya on Thursday." Not waiting for my reply, he jumped up and skipped—yes, actually skipped—out of the room.

Over the course of the next six weeks, my initial opinion of Marcus did a complete 180. I was in awe of his grasp of computers, software, internet technology, electronics . . . there didn't seem to be anything about those areas Marcus didn't know. He could have taught the class we were taking, so extensive was his knowledge. I even asked him at one point why he was taking the class. He just smiled and said, "Gotta have the creds for that sheepskin, ya know."

One evening, Marcus asked me, "Grandma-type lady, you interested in gettin' a cuppa coffee with me after class? A coke or somethin', maybe?" I'd long since told Marcus to call me Tabitha, but he insisted on his own form of formality. "Oh, I could never call an older woman by her first name," was his reply. "Guy's gotta have some manners."

Unknown to Marcus, I was eager to meet with him away from class. A plan had been forming in my mind for some time, and I had a sneaking suspicion that Marcus was just the person to help me with it.

Perhaps this is the time for a little background on me. I was indeed old enough to be a grandmother—having just turned sixty a few months prior—although I was not, in fact, a grandmother. I had no children. I did have a brother and a sister, but had been estranged from them for nearly thirty years. It's a long story, much too long and too complicated to go into here. Besides, those relationships were not germane to my immediate problem. My immediate problem was my husband, Dale Henry Mahoney. Dale Henry, you see, was addicted to gambling.

At the time of this writing, Dale Henry owed, as near as I knew, a little over ninety-two thousand dollars in gambling debts. Our credit cards had all been maxed out, and we were three months behind on the mortgage. He'd pawned everything of value he could get his hands on, and tapped every friend and acquaintance he could think of for loans. The constant phone calls for collection attempts were growing increasingly threatening. Add to that the fact that Dale Henry had decided the best way to alleviate his stress was to use me as his personal punching bag, and you can begin to understand my problems.

Over the past few months, a daring plan had come to me. I decided I was going to run away from home. Literally disappear into the world where no one could find me. *How* I was going to disappear was the problem. I had liquidated my one remaining asset that I'd carefully hidden from Dale Henry—a one-hundred-thousand-dollar life insurance policy, face value twelve thousand, one hundred, fifty-three dollars and forty-seven cents. Not much to start a new life on, but it would have to do. But just how does a person go about disappearing? Without creditors tracking them down?

Just the evening before, I'd happened to see a program on television about computer hackers and all the databases they could hack into. The program went into some detail about how, in this electronics-based world, it was possible, with the right knowledge, to totally erase your computerized existence. I had a hunch Marcus just might be able to help me with that.

"Yes, Marcus." I finally recalled where I was, and realized I'd taken a long time to answer his question. "I'd like that very much." So, the two of us—one of the strangest couples you've probably ever seen together—walked off to find an empty table at the nearest Starbucks.

Once seated, me with a plain black coffee and Marcus with some $5 triple-latte-double-espresso-nonfat-soy-creamer-with-caramel-sauce-type concoction, I grabbed the conversation ball and explained my problem. After ten minutes of steady explaining, I took a deep breath and asked the important question. "Is that something you can do for me, Marcus? I can pay you, not much, but something."

"Grandma-type lady, don't insult me with an offer to pay. Playtime ain't pay time. And hackin's definitely my idea of playtime. 'Course I can help. Come to my place Thursday after class and we'll get you squared away." He paused, "Oh, is Thursday too soon?"

"Thursday will be fine, Marcus. Give me your address, and I'll drive straight there after class."

He laughed. "Don't have to drive. I live in the apartments above the store here. Great location. I grab their wi-fi signal, and nobody can trace me past the shop."

Tossing the last of my coffee into the trash, I walked back to my car and made my way home. My nightly slap-around by Dale Henry didn't even faze me that night. I was going to disappear. Nothing could stop me now.

Wednesday passed in a blur. I packed and moved my bags into my neighbor's empty trash cans while Dale Henry was out of the house. My neighbors were on a month-long cruise and the trash wasn't scheduled for pickup until the following Monday, so I knew my two small bags would go undetected until Thursday night. Thursday I cleaned house and even made three casseroles that I wrapped in foil, neatly labeled, and stuck in the freezer. All right, so Dale Henry was an abusive sleazebag; I was still his wife and I felt duty-bound to leave him with at least a few meals.

I arrived a full half hour early at the college, and the ninety-minute class seemed to last nine hours, but finally it was over. Marcus and I walked to the Starbucks, and took the stairs up to his second floor apartment. Expecting the apartment to reflect Marcus' lack of cleanliness and ragged appearance, I was stunned when he opened the door. The place was absolutely immaculate and crammed with racks of high tech electronics gear. I counted a total of five laptop computers and three desktop computers, all obviously state-of-the-art. There were enough colored lights flashing on enough pieces of equipment that I fleetingly thought the room must look like the internal workings of a pinball machine gone wild when the lights were off.

"Okay, Grandma-type lady," Marcus said. "Let's get started." He sat down at the largest of the laptops, cracked his knuckles several times, and started typing, his fingers flying faster than my eye could follow.

"Full name?" he snapped. "Birth date? Place of birth? Mother's full name, including maiden? Father's full name? Social security number?" One question followed the next faster than I could answer them. Each time I answered a question, I noticed a red point of light appear on the digitized map of the world displayed on the laptop's screen. "Library card number? Checking? Savings? Credit card numbers? Mortgage?"

I dutifully answered. More questions. More lights. The screen was now crowded with them.

Finally the questions stopped. Marcus sat silently for a time, again cracking his knuckles. His left leg jiggled faster than ever, and I could barely restrain myself from laying a gentle, please-stop hand on his pumping kneecap. Finally, he turned towards me. "You sure you wanna do this, Grandma-type lady? Once I make you disappear, you can't change your mind, ya know?"

Without hesitation, I answered, "Yes, Marcus, I'm sure."

He briefly explained that each of the little lights on the screen represented my electronic presence somewhere in cyber-world. I appreciated his attempt to share his knowledge, but having come this far, I was eager to get on with it.

"Okay, then," he said, when I expressed my impatience. "Watch." His fingers flew across the keyboard as he hummed a tuneless melody. His left foot once again pumped his knee up and down non-stop. I watched the screen, fascinated, as one by one the lights began to disappear. At last only one little light blinked in a corner of the screen. "Last chance," he said.

"Do it, Marcus." I replied.

With a final, single keystroke, the last light winked out. The weirdest thing happened as I watched that last light go out. It was as if twenty years of unbearable life were suddenly lifted from my shoulders. I felt young again and somehow, inexplicably, free. "That's it?" I asked.

"That's it. You have now officially ceased to exist. No mortgage. No bills. No ID of any type. No husband. No family. No birth certificate. No *life*." He grinned up at me. "Now, who would you *like* to be?"

I smiled. "I've always liked the name Sarah James," I whispered. Marcus grinned, his fingers renewed their intimate dance with the keyboard, and one by one, new little lights began to appear on his screen.

THE END . . . OR BETTER YET, THE NEXT BEGINNING

THE LETTERS

Suzanne Holbrook-Brumbaugh

I took my little brother
to the mailbox down the lane,
to mail some special letters,
and see if any came.

We always hope for something,
but nothing ever comes.
We sit and wait forever,
just twiddling our thumbs.

It seems like everybody else
gets lots and lots of things,
Such pretty cards and letters,
whatever each day brings.

They place them on the mantle
so everyone can see,
they haven't been forgotten
like little Tim and me.

So I'll take this special letter,
and mail it to myself,
so I can get a letter,
and place it on the shelf.

And won't my little brother
be surprised as he can be,
when he gets a special letter
from his favorite sister, ME!

LIGHTS, CAMERA, DARKNESS
An Original Screenplay

Robert Isbill

The following two scenes are excerpted from an original feature-length screenplay. The actions take place in different cities in Southern California, and in very disparate locations. The first scene involves the main character, Nick, a successful (but frustrated by the system) screenwriter observing his devious studio boss stealing intellectual property. The second scene shows the subplot character, Nakeesha, dealing with her own set of problems. A short glossary is provided for those readers who don't normally read scripts...

Glossary:
INT = Interior
EXT = Exterior
OS = Heard from off-screen but not seen

EXT. STUDIO CITY, CALIFORNIA - DAY

A once-prosperous section of the city, its structures and streets now going seedy.

Atop one of the buildings is a large billboard sign: LAWSON STUDIOS

261

INT. LAWSON STUDIO EXECUTIVE OFFICES - DAY

HENRY LAWSON, gruff 50 year old mogul, takes a pitch session with two writers.

As they talk, Lawson presses a button under his desktop. He flips a switch.

INT. LAWSON'S SECRETARY'S OFFICE - DAY

Nick sits and waits in Lydia's office with Steve Cameron, an effeminate 40-year old writer.

A light flashes at the computer, accompanied by a soft CHIME. Nick nudges Steve's shoulder and nods towards Lydia.

LYDIA, the typist, puts a Bluetooth on her ear, sits at the computer.

She keyboards the content of the conversation. The words appear on the computer monitor screen.

Something is different, though. The words that the two writers are saying are not exact. Names change. Places called by names change.

> WRITER #1 (O.S.)
> So by now... Jeff just thinks he's a vampire. He doesn't know it for sure.

The computer monitor screen shows "Harold thinks he is a monster, but cannot name it."

                    WRITER #2 (O.S.)
          But his fiancee knows he's a
          vampire and loves him even more
          for it.

The typing on the monitor continues,
delayed action, "His lover is certain he is
a monster; however, it's attractive to
her."

INT. LAWSON'S EXECUTIVE OFFICE - DAY

Lawson continues to listen, scrutinizing
the writers. He is thoughtful, pondering.

The writers continue, inaudible, describing
their script.

INT. LAWSON STUDIO, SECRETARY'S OFFICE

Lydia continues to type, revise, type.

                    LAWSON (O.S. OVER THE
               INTERCOM)
               Lydia, what's the name of that
               thing that Jack gave us the other
               day? That horror idea?

Lydia types a label that is inserted in her
typewriter: "THE MONSTER WHO LOVED ME" by
Jack Swanson.

                    LYDIA
               Horror? The monster... Just a
               minute. I think it was "THE
               MONSTER WHO LOVED ME".

Lydia types in the space above her page on the computer monitor screen, "THE MONSTER WHO LOVED ME".

> LAWSON (O.S.)
> That's it! I knew I'd heard this one before! Would you please bring in that file, Lydia?

Nick and Steve watch. They exchange knowing looks.

Lydia pushes the print key. The pages glide out of the printer and, just as gracefully, Lydia back-date stamps the titled sheet and sweeps the small stack into the labeled folder.

As though in one swift action, she's through the door and into...

INT. LAWSON'S EXECUTIVE OFFICE - DAY

Suddenly the folder is on Lawson's desk. He slides it over to the writers.

It's his apology at its finest.

They look at one another quizzically, then open the folder.

LATER

Lawson ushers the writers out.

> LAWSON
> Listen, guys, it's not the end of
> the world. That's the hazard of
> doing spec scripts. That's why
> they're called "speculation,"
> right?

EXT. SOUTH CENTRAL LOS ANGELES NEIGHBORHOOD
STREET - NIGHT

A dark Lexus is parked at the curb.

INT./EXT. TYRONE'S CAR

NAKEESHA, 25, African-American living,
breathing poster-girl of "Black Is
Beautiful," dressed in something new, sexy
and attractive, gets into the car.

She carries a little party whistle and hat.

TYRONE, a black keg of dynamite with legs,
is in the driver's seat.

> TYRONE
> Where you think you goin'?

> NAKEESHA
> With you, I guess.

Tyrone gives her a suspicious glare.
He pulls the car into the street.

                    TYRONE
          One funny look from anyone and
          you goin' home!

Nakeesha says nothing, arranges her outfit
and relaxes in anticipation of a fun
evening. Tyrone heads off and merges into
the busy highway.

A car pulls next to them as they stop for a
traffic signal. The driver, a good-looking
African American man, notices Nakeesha and
gives her a smile and an appreciative look.

Tyrone notices.

Suddenly, the light still red, Tyrone
leaves rubber and SCREECHES across the
intersection, does a U-turn in front of
cross-traffic, skids all over the place and
shoots off in the opposite direction.

Nakeesha hangs on, looking with amazement
at Tyrone.

Tyrone bitch-slaps her. Hard.

Nakeesha holds her face in both hands.

Tyrone takes it up to 95 in seconds.

He weaves in and out of the city traffic,
barely missing parked vehicles, oncoming
cars, pedestrians, curbs.

From full speed to zero, Tyrone brakes to a
halt. He reaches across Nakeesha and flings
open her door.

                    TYRONE
                    (continuing)
          Out!

Nakeesha is unresponsive. Horrified.

                    TYRONE
                    (continuing)
          Get the hell out!

Desolate, unfamiliar streets.

Nakeesha looks around. Hesitates.

Tyrone unlatches her seat belt. Pushes her
hard.

Nakeesha puts one spiked heel on the street
and moves to get out.

The car pitches forward, tires SQUEAL.

Nakeesha, half-in, half-out, grabs the
door, the back of the seat, holds on as
best she can.

The Lexus zigs and zags at 30,40,50 miles
per hour.

Her left foot is braced against the
interior corner of the floorboard while her
right leg, beaten by the door, dangles
outside, and her foot scrapes the street.

Nakeesha's shoe flies off into the night.

REFLECTIONS

Winnie Reuff

I look at your picture little girl
And you smile back
Are you me—or am I really you?
Bangs, long black wrinkled cotton hose
Scuffed, untied shoes and bashful smile
A secret in your eyes.
My eyes hold no secrets now
And my lips are set
Jewels draped on loose and wrinkled flesh
The smoothness and their firmness gone.
Both of us an equal distance, dear
From eternity and Home.

A GAME OF CHANCE

Michael Raff

$\mathcal{M}$y great-granddaddy, Billy "Tex" Stockwell, was a whopping ninety-two years old when he passed on. He was wearing his boots at the time, not to mention a contented smile across his face. He lived to see John F. Kennedy become president and the dawn of the space program. For him to live to such a ripe old age is especially amazing considering he smoked cheap cigars and hand rolled cigarettes, chewed tobacco, drank whiskey, ate red meat, gambled obsessively, and even when he had to get around with a walker, chased after the ladies. I don't know why he was nicknamed "Tex," because he was born and raised in Colorado. But I consider myself lucky to have known him, even if he was a shifty old rascal.

Tex was born in June of 1870, and from that day on he collected a lifetime of the most outrageous, tallest tales a great-grandfather could ever conceive. As a matter of fact, I must have heard the majority of his stories six or seven times. They aged like fine wine, becoming even more grandiose as the years rolled by. According to Tex, he saved this wonderful country at least three times, swam the length of the Mississippi, and rubbed elbows with everyone from the likes of the Dalton gang to Teddy Roosevelt. Of course, no one in our family ever believed him, except for me, that is.

His most convincing yarn remained distinctly consistent over the years, which was indeed a rarity. It was about a poker game, and thanks to the Internet, I've done a little research and can't find anything to disprove it.

The year was 1884 and Tex was fourteen years old, living with his folks in the mining town of Leadville, Colorado, which oddly enough was a silver mining community. My great-granddaddy was never keen on education, and unsurprisingly, spent his formative years hanging around all types of taverns and bars. "Red" Conway, the owner of the Watering Hole Saloon, took a shining to Tex and hired him to clean out the spittoons, scrub the floors, and a bunch of other, less glamorous activities.

According to great-granddaddy, this particular saloon saw more than its share of seedy characters, including bushwhackers, rustlers, train robbers, and even, by golly, tax collectors. But there was a trio of no-goods that Red, for some reason, put up with. Bud "Swindler" Jones, who couldn't read or write, was their leader, if you can imagine that. The other two were Lewis "Ace" Gunnison, who never could appreciate the value of a hot bath, and another fellow who was simply known as "the Swede," because his last name was about thirty letters too long.

Well, these three so-called desperados fancied themselves as card sharks. In all actuality, they were rank amateurs, hopelessly incompetent, and the biggest buffoons that ever fell off a horse. As Tex used to say, "It was a wonder they never got a load of buckshot for their trouble."

This down-on-their-luck gang hung out at the Watering Hole Saloon, hoping that some poor slob who knew nothing about poker would drop all kinds of money into their laps. One rainy day the trio found their pot of gold, or as they would often refer to it, their "little fish."

I'm not sure how Swindler found the gent, but he looked to be an easy enough mark. He was of average height, but scrawny, and judging by the way he dressed, was from somewhere back east. He said he didn't really know much about poker, but was willing to try. Believing they'd finally hit the big time, the trio darn-near had conniption fits right then and there. Over some cheap whiskey they sat the stranger down, and "learned" him five card stud. They even let him win the first few hands, at a measly two bucks a throw.

Incredibly, the stranger never took his eyes off his cards. Even my great-granddaddy couldn't believe it. Ace would wink to the Swede and he would fold, or Swindler would tug his earlobe and Ace would ante up. The stranger never seemed to notice a thing. So the Swede would win one hand, then either Ace or Swindler would win the next. The stakes kept growing, and pretty soon the three sharks had a hefty pile of chips amongst them.

Swindler kept the conversation going, which was just another ploy to distract the stranger. They talked about the local silver mines, the ever-expanding railroads, and naturally, the finest brothels in the glorious state of Colorado. The stranger didn't say much. He just mostly nodded and answered their questions when he had to. In fact, sometimes he barely looked like he was awake. Tex watched the game the entire time. He would walk by their table on the pretense of sweeping the floor. He even stood behind the stranger for a full minute and the man never seemed to notice. Swindler, Ace, and the Swede were all struggling not to burst out laughing.

After a while, Swindler noticed that the stranger spoke with a Southern accent. Just out of curiosity, he inquired where he might be from.

Still keeping his eyes fixed on his cards, the gent replied, "I was born and raised in Georgia."

With the pot rising to an obscene amount, Swindler kept trying to distract the stranger even further by asking him his name. Silently, the man reached down to his holster, pulled out a shiny Colt .45 and placed it smack down on the table. Then, finally, he looked away from his cards and gazed at each one of them.

"John Henry's my name, but people call me Doc, Doc Holliday."

Well, Tex claimed that it got so darn quiet, you could hear a mouse fart from all the way across the street. The looks on the trio's faces were the makings of yet another fable. Swindler's jaw dropped open, the Swede nearly fainted, and Ace had something dripping out from the bottom of his dungarees. Needless to say, the remainder of the winnings went to the stranger. Whenever one of the three tried to quit, all Doc had to do was to look at him, and the poor chump sat back down. Before long the trio had lost everything. Swindler even had to wager up his boots, pocket watch, and gold tooth as collateral. Considering the stranger was a dentist, it was a lucky thing he came up with the cash. Tex estimated that the gang lost over three hundred dollars, mere pocket change for the notorious Doc Holliday. I guess you could say that the "little fish" had the three card sharks for lunch that day. Afterwards, he didn't even offer to buy them a drink.

Of course, I would like to think that this little saga was authentic right down to the mouse fart, but considering the source, I can't really say. Like I mentioned, I conducted my own research by means of the Internet, and Doc Holliday was indeed living in and around Leadville during that time. To his dying day, great-granddaddy swore that his "game of chance" story was completely factual. He even pledged it on a bible, which I have to admit, meant no more than a lick to him. Then again, he also swore that he once dated Annie Oakley.

After Tex's funeral, I was rummaging through his belongings and found an old, rusted spittoon. On its bottom was the faded inscription, "Property of the Watering Hole Saloon." I'm sorry to say that my great-granddaddy's request to be buried at Boot Hill was emphatically denied, and now he resides at Forest Lawn. His tombstone reads, "William "Tex" Stockwell, 1870-1962, The End of an Era."

THE LEDGE

Dwight Norris

On this ordinary Monday morning, Harold Zimmerman and his wife Stella sat at their little wooden table in the kitchen of their corner fourteenth floor Flatbush Avenue apartment, in Brooklyn, New York. As they had for years, they shared a breakfast of oatmeal, poached eggs, English muffins, an open jar of peach jam, and sundry cups of boiling, black coffee.

Only today was different. Today they were free. Harold, a slightly built man, turned sixty-eight years old last winter, and after forty-two years of taking the subway down to Wall Street five days a week, his career as a stock broker was over. He even put in a couple of extra years to make sure their retirement was comfortable. Stella worked almost as long as the head librarian for the Kings County Unified School District. Friday was her last day of work as well. Their future was secure, and retirement would be sweet.

Breakfast was consumed in relative silence as was their custom, but with a happy undercurrent of anticipation. They always said, "April showers bring May flowers," and so it happened this year as well. Summer was just around the corner.

"When do you want to pick up the motor home?" Stella asked.

"Well, we gotta stock it with food, and drink, and the cameras, and clothes," Harold said. "But mostly I want to sit down with the folks at AAA and go over our itinerary."

"They give you maps, too," Stella said.

"Yeah, we gotta get all the maps."

273

"But we're gonna take our time, right?" Stella said. "I mean, we don't have to be in a hurry, right?"

"Yeah, we don't have to be in a hurry," Harold smiled as he looked at Stella. "We can go anywhere we want, and take all the time we want."

Stella smiled back and was glad she married Harold all those many years ago. They reached with their hands and held on for a precious moment of sunshine.

Just then the couple heard the animated cry of a baby alarmingly close by. How could this be? With a fourteenth floor, corner apartment, no neighbors were that near. Harold walked to the double-hung window that was partially open, and shoved the bottom casement fully upward. He rarely operated the window because he was terrified of heights, but he stuck his head into the opening to investigate the sounds. Stella rushed to his side.

"Oh my God!" he shouted.

Off to the left, lying on her back on the twelve-inch ledge, was a nursling little babe, wearing only a diaper and scanty pink shirt. She continued to cry in an agitated manner, and kicked with her short pudgy legs.

"Aah!" Stella exclaimed, placing a hand over her heart. "What are we gonna do?"

"Call 911!" Harold yelled.

"But they could take twenty minutes to get here!"

"I know, but we still have to call," said Harold. "I'll go out and get her."

"But you'll freeze up!" Stella said.

"Well, I gotta do something. I can't just watch her roll off that ledge!"

Harold crept out onto the meager slab. Swirling winds buffeted his face, and the narrow rim creaked beneath him. He inched forward on his hands and knees, staying as close to the ancient brick wall as he could, forcing himself to not look down.

Stella made the call to emergency services and leaned out the window to watch. The baby lay with its feet toward Harold, very close to the corner of the ledge, about fifteen feet from the Zimmermans' window. Harold wondered how did the baby get there? How mobile was this child? Could she flip herself over and roll off the side? He knew that when people hurried they most often made mistakes. He tried not to hurry, but with each crawl, tried to conserve time and be as efficient as possible.

He was two feet away now. One foot, yet still not within reach. How shall he secure this child? Cradling the baby in his arms would be ideal, but not possible on this ledge. Such an action would throw him off balance, plunging both of them to their deaths. The only sure way to save the baby was to grasp her left calf with his right hand, firmly and decisively, and inch his way backwards. He hoped his action would not hurt the baby, but if it was the only way to get her off this death-dealing shelf, so be it.

He was upon her and it was time. He wrapped his hand around the lower portion of her leg, above the ankle and below the knee. Her flesh was cold to the touch, and looking into her face he could see the child was not well. He began his backward retreat and pulled the babe with him. Her crying intensified, but he maintained his firm grip and continued his backward motion.

Just then, a crazed, wide-eyed, spiky-haired woman popped her head around the corner and screamed, "What are you doing?"

Harold almost lost his balance with the staggering jolt, but accelerated his retreat, dragging the child with him. The maniacal woman leapt to her hands and knees with startling alacrity as if she'd lived on the ledges all of her life. Harold scooted quickly to the rear, but to no advantage. The woman was on the child in a second, yanking on her arm.

The baby's cries were wild and tameless. Harold didn't know what to do, but he knew he couldn't let go. The woman pulled vigorously on the little arm, hurting the baby. Harold moved toward the child and covered her with his entire arm, trying to gain control. He lay flat on his stomach, struggling to keep his legs on the ledge, which diminished his leverage. He grabbed the woman's wrist with his other hand, but she wouldn't relinquish her hold. He dug his fingernails deep into her flesh, and finally she released.

Harold grabbed the child's calf again and retreated as rapidly as he could, dragging the baby in foot-long swoops. His window was near, but the woman would not surrender, and lunged forward in a desperate effort to obtain a controlling grip on any part of the child's body.

The force of her action knocked the babe off the ledge, and the space just occupied by the infant's body left a flagrant, hollow void. Harold, however, did not loosen his grip on her leg, and though she dangled upside down in the air at the end of his fully extended arm, she fell no farther, and was quickly yanked through the open window.

Stella took the shaken baby from Harold and cradled her in her arms. Harold's heart was racing and he gasped for breath. Stella was so upset she quickly sat down with the baby, rocking and comforting as much as she could. Harold stretched out on the floor, trying to slow his breathing.

"Help me! Help me!" the cries from outside were heard.

Stella ran to the window and saw the woman's hands clinging to the outer part of the ledge. She hung six feet from the Zimmermans' window.

"Help me!" she cried out. "Help me!"

A siren sounded in the morning air.

Harold sat up and started toward the open window. Stella turned and blocked his way.

"No, you can't," she said. "You've got nothing left. You'll *both* fall to your deaths!"

Harold looked into Stella's eyes.

"But . . ."

The fire trucks got closer, and the sirens louder.

"Aah!" the scream from outside diminished as the woman fell to the unyielding concrete below.

The next morning, two newspapers published an account of the tragedy. One called Harold a hero; the other called him a bum. People across the city spoke of what happened on a narrow ledge a hundred and forty feet above a sea of ultimate finality, and they spoke of what they did not know—of a humble little man from Brooklyn, and the wife who loved him.

MY FATHER

Robert Foster

I wait outside the intensive care unit wondering what I will see. I was told that dad looked horrible. What does that mean? The ping pong ball bounces back and forth in my head. Is this his time to die or will his historically inner tenaciousness help him bounce back?

He is eighty-six years old and has lived a hard life. Part of his leg was blown off in the Korean War. Not an athlete, he has lacked muscle strength for decades. A heart bypass surgery lengthened his life and revealed that thirty years of Pall Malls caused serious lung issues.

His greatest fear is to lie in bed like a vegetable until he dies, or is his greatest fear really death itself?

I finally walk into his room, but only for a few minutes. He is on his way to several procedures to find out why he is slowly bleeding to death. His veins aren't good. A pick line will be surgically inserted to allow for quick IVs and medication delivery. His hands are bruised and puffy from multiple needle insertion attempts that only reveal how weak his veins really are.

He is gaunt, pale, and unable to move in the bed. He recognizes me with a one word exclamation, "Bob." All his answers are one word responses. It takes all of his energy to get the one word out.

I look into his eyes. I have a multitude of thoughts. Does he remember the cool watermelon on a hot Iowa summer evening? No, it isn't there. Maybe deeper. I see his father in his eyes and probably his grandfather. There is look of a solid stance in life from years of farming. His Marine Corps machismo is still there.

278

Yet, there is a warmth right behind his strength, barely a flicker.

Don't get me wrong. I love my dad, but most of the time he has been unlikeable. His stern voice often demanded the impossible, much like a drill sergeant. I don't remember sitting on his lap or being told he loved me. I am sure he did, but it was so long ago that the memory is gone.

I have learned to like him more in his later years, as he mellowed and listened instead of demanding. He shared instead of telling.

The ping pong still bounces back and forth. I hope he passes away peacefully as a man and not a vegetable. Caring for him is now beyond my mother and his day-care provider's capabilities. He has been a severe stress on my already frail mother, hastening her demise I am sure.

A visit to the nursing home would kill him faster than any disease. Then again, I see the marine fighting the valiant fight. His legendary stubbornness might prevail again. Back and forth goes the ping pong ball. This is tiring, really tiring.

Life has a way of coming and going without my control. It is obviously not up to me, which I am thankful for every minute of my visit.

I can do what I am able. I talk to him. Tell him I love him. Hold his hand. I say good bye for now as he is rolled to his next procedure.

I think I will stop the ping pong ball and let God decide what is best.

CURIOUS TALES

Thomas Kier

I stood looking up at the imposing brownstone, undoubtedly a common sight to any New Yorker. But I wasn't one anymore, and it had always troubled me—that tall house with dark window-eyes, and its closed mouth, hiding maybe nothing at all, at the top of the steps. The "Curious Tales Publishing" plaque next to the door was unchanged.

I knew by now there would be a soft chime sounding at someone's reception desk; maybe the position belonged once again to my wife. Well, my ex-wife, if you want to get technical. I had never accepted the fact that she was gone. A disappearance is very different from a death, and I couldn't believe she had gone anywhere except deeper within the company. She always was one of its most enthusiastic proponents. It was her incredible zest for life and for her work that drew me to her and eventually here, where I was offered a make-work job sorting mail.

At first, I didn't care about secrets behind closed doors, until Diana got sketchy about going home with me after work. I just couldn't believe in an affair, not from her, and I never did find one. What I found was a wall, protected jealously by Mr. Curious, and a warning that the business ethics of employees did not concern me. That was the day he stopped being a kindly, self-effacing old man to me. That was the day I stopped having the occasional drink with him after work, and started thinking about where else I could find a job.

Coming here again had seemed like inescapable fate after all these years. Not now. Before, I could simply walk back the way I had come. The door opened and there he stood on the stoop. I suddenly realized it was Thursday again, story night. The night everyone got paid overtime to hear the latest tale.

"You look like a man with some questions, Mr. Crass," he said softly. "Why don't you come inside?" His voice carried clearly over the New York background noise.

"Are questions allowed?" I asked, mounting the steps uncertainly.

"I will allow your questions now, sir." Mr. Curious's eyes were impassive. "But what is done with the answers is your responsibility. I have seen men come and go. Some find that too intimate a knowledge of what we do here is not to their taste."

"What exactly do you do here, besides the obvious?" My voice sounded hollow to my own ears.

"Why, we let men tell their tales, each in his turn."

"So how do you know whose turn it is?" My fear drained away, overcome by my curiosity about the next tale, and the next. At times, I had been sure there were things waiting in the shadows of the reading room—hungry things.

"If a man doesn't know when to tell his tale, usually the tale itself will know." I was standing in front of him now. "They are much wiser than the mouth they are given to, you know—the tales are." He paused. "It's as if they come from outside."

"Outside of what?" I blurted out. I saw in Mr. Curious's eyes that he would answer all my questions. I was no longer sure I wanted that.

The fear I had left in the street returned, and again I wished I hadn't come. Every man has skeletons in his closet, but I didn't want to know anymore what had become of my wife and her fast car, and her impatience with speed limits and the frightening, wild beauty that I glimpsed every time she tried to explain to me why she did it—the shortcuts, always the thrice-damned shortcuts. I could gladly push that brittle collection of finger bones back through the bars forever now, rather than face this demon from my past. The sweat was cold on my spine as shadows clinging to this narrow roofless stoop deepened. Maybe the darkness oozed out through the door, not between the planks, but from the very fiber of the wood, as though it had held back the gloom for so long, it was saturated. A finger pressed against its bloated surface would naturally allow the escape of it. I shuddered.

Mr. Curious had his hand on the door, not quite caressing it. "Wouldn't you feel more comfortable inside, Mr. Crass? There we wouldn't be interrupted by the rush and bustle of the disenchanted." He winked. "I can get you a drink to set you more at ease." He always was the perfect gentleman's gentleman.

I let myself be led inside.

The reading room was just as I remembered, with the shifting shadows of the eternal hearth fire. The chill here was pronounced after the noon heat in the street, and the flames didn't seem warm and inviting as they always had at story time. Whispers seemed to crowd in from every corner.

"The bar is this way, Sir." Now he led me toward the alcove in which I had passed pleasant hours with him. I saw the bookshelves lining the big room's walls, the antique chairs all facing the fire, the small door leading ostensibly to a game room, or maybe, sometimes, somewhere else. This place now held no warmth for me.

"Scotch, neat. Sir." Mr. Curious pressed the drink into my hand. He went back around the counter, and motioned for me to sit on the only stool there.

"You're looking for Diana, and you think I might know where she is."

"Uh, well, yes." He acted as if our falling out had never happened.

"I understand you've remarried, Mr. Crass." Mr. Curious settled the bottle carefully back in its place. "Why this wish to find someone who no longer interests you?"

"We were high school sweethearts, and she reminds me of my glory days of football jocks and short-skirted cheerleaders." It seemed easier to lie to him when I was only looking at his back.

Now he turned. "Is that the truth, Mr. Crass, or is it what you've told yourself so often you almost believe it?"

I looked down at my glass. "I married her, and she's mine. If she's still alive, she belongs to me." I was sullen, and didn't care.

"I was under the impression slavery was illegal in the here and now." Mr. Curious's voice was icy. His argument didn't change my mind.

"You saw it, didn't you?" he asked me. "How young do you think she was the last time?"

"I knew it!" I looked up at him with hatred, but it died against his blank expression. "She's still out there, isn't she?" My question faded into a whisper. My heart ached.

"Sometimes people find new life when they have left an old one. It isn't easy for most, but the rewards can be great." What I saw in Mr. Curious's gaze might have been understanding, but there was no forgiveness there.

"I just need to know." Another sip of my drink steadied me. I couldn't remember when I'd last tasted anything this grand.

"Knowledge isn't always satisfaction."

"Who are you, my mother or my judge?" I growled up at him.

"I am host to the tales, and keeper of the men telling them. I do what I must to smooth the way, but sometimes things, or people, present a problem. I solve problems." There was a shadow on the man's face from which eyes must have been looking at me. I was no longer sure those eyes were human. The one thing I *did* know was that I had come too far to walk away.

"You need to see, don't you? You need to see it all." There was a touch of sorrow in his voice.

"If you've got something to show me, I need to see it." The whiskey was making me bolder, too bold for my own good, but I wouldn't have to deal with that until later.

"Very good, sir. I suppose I knew that today would be your day." He reached into a pocket and produced a small, black envelope.

"I thought story time came in the evenings?" I was suddenly disoriented. "There's no one else here."

"The tales are all in white," Mr. Curious confided in me. "What you will do now lies beyond the vision of most of my people. This is the path you have chosen to follow." He motioned toward the fireplace.

I moved as if in a dream, approaching the hearth. If not for the hand on my shoulder, I might have walked straight into the fire, and perished without a thought. I watched my hand toss the packet into the flames, and darkness swallowed the light. In the gloom, it was all too easy to see the terrible red glow that flashed behind the small door, and faded away. Guttering flames bloomed again.

"This way, Sir." Mr. Curious led, and I followed, through the door just over half my height. I didn't remember seeing him stoop down, but there he was before me when I straightened up again. "The steps can be a little slippery."

We descended a stone stairway in the blackness. The railing to which I clung possessed a thin coat of warm slime. The excellent drink I had welcomed earlier now sat in my stomach like a slug of slow poison, mocking me.

"Allow me to turn on the lights, Sir."

I stood still as the barely visible white collar of Mr. Curious's shirt danced away from me as the rest of his suit remained as black as our surroundings. Wooden boards creaked under me as I swayed slightly. That was the only noise.

A faint green light bloomed to my right, and I could see Mr. Curious caressing a bulb at the top of an iron post. His lips moved, but I couldn't hear any sound. The glow brightened slowly. Mr. Curious moved on, lighting each lamp in the same careful way; five of them now marked the edge of an old wooden platform like a train station. He turned back to me, a soft green glow fading from his eyes.

"It is almost time for the arrival of tonight's tale. Do not agitate the characters for some of them do not take kindly to surprises."

I sat on a wooden bench to wait. I could see a gulf past the platform that seemed to have no bottom. Beyond it was a bank of purple mud, shifting and oozing, but holding its shape. Sprouting from it were tall grasses, restlessly waving in a wind I couldn't feel. Trees reared up, weeping willows which nodded and dipped gracefully. Birds with long feathers that iridesced through all the colors of the rainbow, bright, translucent, transparent, then starting over again, slithered through the grass to drink from a stream of orange water. Frogs hopped from the top of stems where there were flowers growing only a moment before. Fish flew from branch to branch among the trees, passing through the leaves, and taking on a greenish hue before returning to yellow.

I felt ill, and closed my eyes, trying to return to the world I knew.

A faint humming sound brought me out of my daze, and I looked left. A monstrous bus moved toward the platform as if it were floating in water. Ice covered its surface, but was steaming and melting rapidly. The driver stopped it skillfully, just touching the dock. Through foggy windows along the side, I saw a man moving back through a center aisle between the seats. He wore a low-slung gun belt with two huge revolvers, and carried what must have been a full-on assault rifle.

"Last stop! Up 'n' git!" I could hear his shout from where I was. The door opened, and a couple of ordinary-looking guys filed out, followed by a big hairy troll that was almost wider than it was tall. When it reached the platform, I saw it was female. I gasped.

"Rest easy, Mr. Crass," Mr. Curious warned, from behind the bench. "It would be less than pleasant if tonight's story was unsatisfied."

The guard lifted something carefully from a seat, then an amorphous cloud of dimness floated out into the open air. At its center was a small, green shape with a single white eye, which quickly settled on me. It lunged, a crackle of electricity flaring through the air, and the guard whipped a small butterfly net from his coveralls, and reigned the thing in.

"Not yet, my precious. Not quite time," he crooned to it softly. The eye turned toward him, and closed slowly. "Sleep for now." The man's voice was soothing. He released it, and it hovered close to the other refugees.

The driver had exited the bus, and now talked with Mr. Curious, but I couldn't take my eyes from this motley crew.

"This is all for this trip," a woman's voice said. "They are almost tame, not at all like last week."

"Yes, I imagine it was a very easy crossing," came Mr. Curious's cultured baritone. His voice was almost longing when talking to the woman. I turned to see.

"Hello, Jim. I've been waiting for you to get over this way." She was watching me, and she was the most beautiful thing I had ever seen. I could faintly recognize the wife I used to know, buried somewhere there, but she was more—*complete* somehow. My heart beat hard. I couldn't stop staring.

"Close your mouth, Jim," she giggled. "One of these could do some real damage if it ever got inside you." She held up a jar. In it were three or four small blobs floating in clear liquid. I watched while one grew to several times its size while most of the liquid disappeared. Another one came at it with tiny fangs bared, and bit it almost in half. The first creature blew the liquid back out, and finished separating. I shivered. She gave the jar to the guard.

I stared at the woman's face again. Now I recognized nothing about her. "What. . .who are you?" I gasped out, breathlessly.

She raised her arms imperiously, and a yellow-silver light filled the area. Across from the platform, deep in the pseudo-woods, I heard the creaking and croaking of all the night creatures I could imagine, and many more that I couldn't. The howl of wolves started sporadically from several locations and then joined as one melodious song that slowly faded into silence. I wished for it to go on.

"I am Diana," she proclaimed. "I am the goddess of the hunt and I am midwife to these tales, bringing them into this world to satisfy their hunger. I am that which you knew, and that which no man can understand. I am the incarnation of renegade imaginations and unslakable lusts. I am the ruler of the night." She lowered her arms and the glow faded except from her eyes.

Then she was human again. She was my ex-wife again, but younger and fiercer than I had ever seen. My blood raced. My face flushed. Adrenaline and desire roared through my body. I could not let her walk away.

Mr. Curious suddenly stood before me with his hand up in warning. I moved to go around him, but he was much quicker than I, and so much stronger. His eyes were kind, but resolute.

"Please wait here," he said softly, motioning me back to the bench. I was seated again, though I hadn't remembered moving at all. His hand on my shoulder made me faint. Nausea washed over me. My eyes followed the lady I had once thought I knew, but I could no more approach her than I could understand her now.

I watched the guard help Mr. Curious usher the story's characters through a door in the stone wall labeled "Cast." They exchanged a few remarks—small talk, uninteresting. The girl before me watched me. She was nowhere near old enough to be a woman.

"It was nice to pass some time with you, Jim, before I found out who I truly am. But I belong to no one now, not even to myself. I have a purpose here, and to deny it would be to discount worlds of vision and wonder. Some of the tales I bring are dark, and some are bright. But they are all fascinating, and I complete their purpose." Her eyes were wild and lonely. "Fare thee well." She blew me a kiss, and my heart fell again at her feet.

Diana turned to Mr. Curious. "They must be fed before tonight's tale."

"Very good, Miss. This is the path he has chosen." And nodded toward me.

Diana walked back toward the edge of the platform, and climbed into her Mercedes go-devil where the bus had stood a second earlier. She slid into the driver's seat, and called, "Come, Homer. There's work to be done."

Homer glanced at me, and grinned. "She's a bit rough 'round the edges, but got a heart of gold, as I expect you know." He winked, shook Mr. Curious's hand, and ran for the car. If he was the silent, aging custodian I had once known, he had grown younger as well.

The car was gone with its driver and its passenger in a flash and a roar.

"She knows a shortcut back," murmured Mr. Curious. He turned toward me. "This way, Sir." I was standing next to him, though I hadn't stood. He led me toward another door. The sign on this one read "Dining Hall." I followed him through, fighting it with all my strength and unable to deviate from our straight path. He never laid a hand on me.

"Wait here, Sir."

I stood in the dark as he exited through a far door, and it closed. Soon it opened again, and I heard shuffling footsteps in the dark, and the soft crackle of electricity.

I closed my eyes, and prayed for it to be merciful.

IN JOHNNY'S SHOES

Bernadine Joyce

(in sing song)
Weirdo, weirdo, Johnny
Looks just like a zombie
Walks like one
Talks like one
Weirdo, weirdo, Johnny

I think I wrote a great jingle! And so does *Johnny*. He grins and jumps around when I sing it. He likes it, for crying out loud! But my teacher doesn't. She said it was a mean thing to do. She said Johnny can't help the way he is . . . and how would *I* like it if I was *Johnny* and people made fun of me . . . just because *I* was different.

So now I have to play with him. What's wrong with playing with him, you ask? Well, duh! He doesn't know how to play. He is a regular *goofball*.

My whole recess is ruined. None of the other kids will come near me as long as I'm with Johnny. When I throw him the big basketball, he puts his arms up and wiggles them like a jellyfish. Then the ball hits him in the chest and drops to the ground. He waddles like a duck when he chases the ball, but he doesn't quack. He keeps saying, "Oh no, oh no, oh no." Over and over until I yell at him, "Stop saying that, Johnny!" He picks up the ball and holds it tight . . . he won't throw it. Then he stares at me with those weirdo eyes of his, and scowls. His mouth hangs open, and his big teeth hang out.

He just stares like that for a gazillion minutes and then says, "You fine . . . Johnny fine . . . You fine? Johnny fine . . . You fine? Johnny fine."

Until I scream, "No! I'm not fine. And I won't be fine until you stop saying that!"

"Okay . . . okay . . . okay!" He looks at the ground as he bobs his head up and down.

"Go for walk?"

"Okay, then . . . *Okay?*" I'm starting to talk like him. This has got to stop! He has got to stop talking before I go *bonkers!*

"How about we go for a run instead of a walk, Johnny?" If he runs, maybe he'll stop talking.

"Yeah, yeah!" He bobs his head and claps his hands in a funny way.

"I'm a duck." I said. "And you want to pet me. Catch me if you can!"

We ran. Not really. We waddled fast. Johnny started quacking so loud that the other kids started laughing at him.

Johnny laughed louder. Then he quacked louder. Then he waddled faster and didn't stop until the bell rang. It rang just in time. I couldn't run or waddle one more step.

When we came into the coat room, I helped Johnny take off his shoes like he always does when it's winter and he wears his boots. But he doesn't know that it's not winter. You can say to him a gazillion times, "Johnny, you don't have to take your shoes off, it's not winter anymore! You don't wear snow boots now!"

But he still takes his shoes off. Now he runs, or waddles fast, into the classroom, leaving me holding his shoes.

He has big feet for a little guy whose head comes only to my shoulder. His shoes have those sticky-tape closers. I wonder how big his shoes are. Would they fit me? I'll just slip off my shoes and try on Johnny's. There! They feel kind of funny. No, *I* feel

kind of funny. I feel so tired . . . I think I'll stretch out on this
bench for a few minutes . . .

* * *

*What is that music? My teacher doesn't play her guitar until
the end of class. It must be near 2:30. I must have fallen asleep. I
better hurry into class before I get in trouble for being late!*

*Why is it so hard for me to get up from this bench? My feet
feel like they have lead weights holding them down. Oh! I still
have Johnny's shoes on! I'll just take them off.*

*Hey! What's going on? My fingers don't work right! It's hard
to get these shoes off. Well, forget that for now, I have to get to
class. My legs are wobbly; they won't move the way I want them
to.*

*Here comes Sally down the hall. She's asking me something.
What is it? She talks too fast and she's taking me by the hand
and taking me with her.*

She called me Johnny!

"Ahh . . . hah . . . hah . . ." *Why can't I say I'm not Johnny?*

"I'll take you back to our class, Johnny. How come you're
out here by yourself? Where's your aide, Miss Brook?"

"Uh Oh! Not Miz Book . . . Uh oh! No Miz Book . . . Uh oh!
No Miz Book."

"It's okay Johnny, I'll take you to her."

"Johnny okay . . . Johnny okay . . . Johnny okay."

"Hey, Sally? What are you doing walking with *him*?"

It's my friend, Buddy. He doesn't know this is Me. *I'll tell*
him.

"Johnny say *Hi*?" *Why did I say that? I'm not Johnny! Why
do I keep talking like him?*

"I wasn't talking to you, *weirdo!*"

Buddy just pushed me away from Sally.

292

"Don't you say anything to me! You got my best friend in trouble. He had to stay with you the whole recess time!"

Buddy pushed me down again.

Hey, Buddy, it's me, Stop it. "I cry . . . I cry . . . I cry."

"Go ahead and cry . . . I ought to punch you one good, for my friend."

Buddy pushed me down again!

"Stop it, you bully! Stop pushing Johnny down . . . and stop calling him names!"

Sally is mad! She pushed Buddy away from me.

"How can you stand to be near him? He looks weird . . . he walks weird . . . he acts weird . . . He talks weird and says the same thing over and over and over again. He'll drive you crazy. Oh, and did I forget to tell you? Johnny even smells weird!"

"He can't help it! His brain doesn't work very well. But yours does . . . and you can help it! You don't have to be mean to him!" Sally scolded.

"I don't have to let him drive me crazy, either. If you want to let him drive *you* crazy, that's your problem! But he better stay away from me."

Buddy is walking away . . . he still doesn't know this is me. *I'll call him back.*

"Buddy, Buddy! Please wait!"

What? I'm now on the bench in the coat room. I must have gone to sleep. What a nightmare! I've got to get Johnny's shoes off. My fingers are working again. Yes. Yes. Yes! My feet and legs aren't wobbly . . . Yes! I can talk again . . . Yes! But what a nightmare! Why did I have a nightmare in the daytime? The shoes! It must have been Johnny's shoes. Now, I remember.

My teacher read us a story about Indians. An Indian brave told his friend, "You can't really know someone or why a person is like he is, until you walk in his moccasins. That's it! But it wasn't moccasins . . . it was shoes.

Here comes Johnny with that silly grin. Class must be out.
"Johnny, I've got your shoes! Come here and I'll help you put them on. And if you want me to . . . I'll play with you for a few minutes at recess tomorrow."

Johnny is jumping up and down. He understands what I said.

"Hey, are you nuts?"

Buddy just came out of the classroom. He's yelling at me.

"That weirdo has cost you your whole recess! And now you're going to let him ruin tomorrow's recess, too? I stood up for you! I almost knocked his block off for you. He drives me crazy just being around him."

"No, if I spent the whole recess everyday with him, he'd drive me crazy too."

"Then why are you going to be around him at all?"

"Because . . . I've walked in *Johnny's Shoes.*"

CHANG FENG'S LITTLE FINGER

Diane Neil

Serendipity seems to rule my life. I have no other explanation, and anyway it's the excuse I always give my family for the crazy things I do. They're used to it, and I don't mind that my weird doings come up in my daughters' conversations. At least they know I'm alive and kicking.

Let me introduce myself. I'm Lottie Lily Dillingham, but Lottie will do. I'm not much to look at, just a skinny old broad with frizzy orange hair. The frizz is all mine and the orange comes out of a bottle. I've never been one to fudge on my age, but the thing is when I admit to eighty, you might picture a frail old lady.

I'm none of the above. Old, maybe, but not frail and certainly no lady. I grew up smack dab in the middle of a family of seven kids. My three older sisters were always shooing us little kids out of the house, and I never learned to knit or crochet or do fancy work.

My father was a furniture dealer. He used to go around buying old broken-down tables and chairs and cabinets for next to nothing—sometimes for free just for hauling them away. Then he'd work his refinishing magic and produce beautiful, gleaming objects that people were proud to own.

My two younger brothers and baby sister and I were recruited to help in Daddy's workshop. We learned to fetch and haul his paint and varnishes, clean brushes, and sweep up shavings. The other kids resented such drudgery, but I took to it like I was born with a paintbrush in my hand.

I learned to sand and scrape and caulk and fill and strip off old finishes. The smell of turpentine was like perfume to me. Long after the boys had escaped into the Army and my younger sister got married, I was still working right alongside Daddy. People had a hard time distinguishing my work from his.

But a couple of things happened that put a big kibosh on our business.

Along came World War II, and nobody was buying furniture, new or used. Also Mama took sick, and I had to take over the household chores. Daddy closed up his shop and got a job in town.

During those lean war years there was so much to do I didn't think about furniture. When Mama recuperated, I found a factory job. When the war was over and the servicemen returned, I married one.

Walter and I set up housekeeping in a little flat while he studied engineering on the G.I. Bill, and by the time he graduated, we and our two toddlers were able to move into a new tract home.

Five years and two more children later, we bought a two-story house and were living the American dream.

Fifty years ago. How it all zoomed by!

Now widowed, with nine lively grandchildren and a couple of greats, I was out with my daughter Sarah and granddaughter Emily one Saturday. Emily just loves yard sales. She and her new husband are slowly furnishing their house on a strict budget. I remember how it was. But I must say, Walter made a very good living and I am left with my big house and much more than I need.

Sarah and I were strolling around looking at books and CDs when we heard Emily squeal.

"Mom! Gram! Look at this!"

She was standing by a big black sideboard with carved panels flaring out like a pair of wings. There were three small drawers across the top and a cabinet beneath with a round brass circle embellished with leaves and an intricate, engraved key. I'd never seen anything quite like it before, but I could tell it was completely handmade and of old Chinese origin.

I felt an odd stirring thrumming within me as I opened one of the drawers.

Just as I thought, someone had painted over the original finish. The shiny black paint was slathered on by an amateur's hand. Scratches and gouges revealed streaks like a red sunset in a dark sky.

Emily was already off seeking the homeowner. She came back to the jumble of furniture with a portly woman in tow. She wore a green eyeshade and a change belt on her waist.

The woman peered at the three of us and took a drag on her cigarette. "That's a fine piece. You won't find another one like it. It's been in my family for three generations."

Right! You old con artist. Anyone could see it had been left out in the rain. It was warped, the drawer handles were rusty, and one of the cabinet doors was cracked.

But I held my tongue. This was Emily's business.

"Look at this!" The skinny one began fiddling with the drawers. "Wouldn't it make a great TV stand?"

The shorter boy opened the cabinet. "Yeah! We could put all our movies in here."

Emily looked nervous, but I smelled a rat. The kids looked like shills to me.

The tall boy approached the woman. "How much for the cabinet?"

She shifted her cigarette. "I could let it go for two hundred."

"We'll take it. I just have to go home for the money."

Emily looked crestfallen.

I had my eye on the teenagers. Instead of heading off to the makeshift parking lot, they were still wandering around. *Definitely shills. Probably the old lady's grandsons.*

"Two hundred is a steal," the woman told Emily. "Of course, if you have cash I might let it go for less. No telling if those kids will be back."

I inserted myself between them. "How much do you have?" I asked Emily.

She pulled bills from her pocket. "Three twenties," she said. "But I could go home for more."

"Nothing doing." Pulling myself up to my full five feet, two inches, I craned my neck and looked the woman in the eye. "This old broken-down piece of junk has been sitting outside for years." I nudged the cracked door with my sneaker. "It's falling apart. You'd be lucky to get fifty bucks for it."

The woman didn't flinch. "Sixty," she said, eyeing Emily's three twenties, "and we'll deliver it." Scanning the yard, she called to the teenagers. "Kenny! Bring the pickup. We have a delivery."

Long after the boys had followed us home and unloaded the sideboard onto Emily's front porch, Sarah and I were chuckling over my chutzpah.

"I have to hand it to you, Mom. You're really a wheeler-dealer."

"I learned from the best. You should have seen your grandfather in his younger days."

Emily went in to make tuna sandwiches while Sarah and I stayed out on the porch with the sideboard. We walked around it opening and closing drawers and running our hands over the scarred, uneven top.

"It's in sad shape, isn't it?" Sarah stooped to inspect the unique apparatus that kept the cabinet doors closed. A round brass circle about ten inches in diameter spanned the center, neatly split between the doors. Each half held a heavy grommet with a long narrow key pushed through. Small copper leaves dangled underneath, matching the leaf designs carved into the side 'wings.'

"I've never seen anything like this." She pulled out the key and opened the doors. The whole inside was black.

I felt a cold chill as I looked in.

"What do you think of it?" Emily came out with a tray of sandwiches and lemonade and a satchel. She set the tray on a table and plopped the satchel on top of the sideboard. She pulled out a stack of decorating magazines sprouting yellow Post Its between the pages. "This is my dream furniture file," she told us. "I've been collecting ideas ever since Jack and I got engaged."

While we ate lunch, Emily fanned out pages of glossy painted furniture in amazing room makeovers. *Turn Flea Market Finds into Your Taj Mahal! Update Your Tired Old Headboard!* A small Before picture featured an elaborate carved mahogany antique. AFTER! showed the transformed headboard painted an eye-popping red and hung with pink and orange gingham heart pillows.

Sarah oohed and aahed politely, but I held my tongue. I knew my father would turn over in his grave to see such a travesty.

"This is my favorite!" Emily held out a double page spread featuring an activity room/message center transformed from 'Granny's seldom-used dining set.' A lovely old breakfront had been decimated to create this monstrosity. Its glass doors had been removed and the shelves repositioned to allow for a flat screen TV. The table had been sawed in half for twin computer/study centers. The whole room was decorated in Life Saver colors of lime green, yellow and orange, from the glossy paint to the wallpaper, pillows and carpeting.

I shuddered. Then I took another look at the original

breakfront. It was just like mine!

I pointed to the 'before' picture. "Did you notice that breakfront is exactly like mine?" It was a Drexel Heritage. Walter's parents had given it to us.

Emily's eyes went all innocent. "Oh, no. I didn't notice." She was a terrible liar.

"Anyway, I thought we'd start with this sideboard, maybe saw off those ugly side pieces."

"Emily!" I croaked, determined to save the broken-down thing. "I'll tell you what. If you want my dining room set, I'll trade you. I'd love a refinishing project."

"Mom!" Sarah looked like she was about to feel my forehead. "Your lovely furniture!"

"What good is it doing me? It's only collecting dust since your father died." It was true. The big holiday gatherings had switched to informal buffets at the kids' places, served on countertops, TV trays, people sitting everywhere, half the children on the floor.

So began my latest bout of serendipity. Sarah and Emily came the next day and packed up the good china and all the other tripe I'd stuffed in the breakfront over the years. Jack and two buddies carried out the furniture.

It did me good to see it hauled away. I eyed the poor sideboard they'd left on my porch, my blood stirring and my fingers itching to get to work.

On Monday, Sarah took me to Home Depot for my refinishing supplies.

They had some potent gel stripper my father would have appreciated. Each day as I put on an old sweatshirt, jeans, eye goggles, face mask and rubber gloves, I felt like a deep sea diver taking a plunge into murky waters, even if the ocean was only my newspaper-covered porch.

And like a diver, I couldn't stay down for long. I'd daub thick brush-loads of gel on sections, scrape off the caustic goo with steel wool, rotating from side to side, top to bottom, front to back, and then inside. The garbage can was filling up with blackened papers and goop.

My poor strained muscles were screaming at me to quit. "You old fool!" they told me. "What are you trying to prove? You'll kill yourself!"

Well, there are worse ways to die, I thought.

Each afternoon as I cleaned up and dragged myself in to soak in an Epsom salts bath, I thought of how proud my father would be of the job I was doing.

One day I was reaching way back into the corner of the cabinet, and my scraper pinged on something. I wedged it out. It looked like a twig.

But wait! Was that a fingernail on the end? I held it closer. It *was* a little finger.

I rocked back on my heels. The whole cabinet was crudely made, and I'd found pieces of wood wedged in, even a flat rock in one place. But this!

I knocked off early that day. As I eased my aching body into the Epsom salts bath, I puzzled over my grisly find. Such a tiny finger. Even with the desiccation of three hundred years, it was obviously from a child's hand.

How could a child be involved in such a dangerous situation? Even if the furniture was family-made and an accident occurred, wouldn't a loving parent have retrieved the finger?

I didn't have the heart to eat dinner. I sat in my kitchen and drank some chamomile tea and went to bed early.

Around midnight I bolted upright. In eerie light I saw a specter at the foot of my bed, a small Asian boy dressed in rags and holding up his hand, the little finger missing. He was crying plaintively in a language unknown to my brain but clear to my heart.

"Give me my finger!"

Then he gestured to a tableau behind him, and I saw children laboring over wooden boxes, trays, tables and chairs as they struggled to keep up with the demands of overseers with whips.

"Who are you?" I asked.

"Chang Feng. And I'll be back for my finger."

My first thought in the morning was to call Sarah and tell her what happened. But I cancelled that. She would think I'd flipped for sure.

I made myself a hearty breakfast of bacon and eggs and fried potatoes. I needed to stoke my furnace to finish my project.

Before I resumed work on the sideboard, I rummaged through all the gifts and trinkets my family had given me over the years. I found a lovely old redwood puzzle box my father had carved for me when I graduated from high school. It still had his note inside.

Choose carefully what you put in here. Once you seal the latch, it can never be opened again.

I wrapped Chang Feng's finger in a blue velvet ribbon and placed it in Daddy's box. It fit perfectly, like a tiny corpse in a casket.

With renewed energy I finished the sideboard and had Jack and his friends bring it into my newly painted sitting room/activity center. (Oh, yes! Sarah and Emily had offered to redecorate it for me.)

Chang Feng never visited me again, but I knew he would approve of his handsomely ensconced little finger taking pride of place atop the sideboard.

And I decided that my father would approve of Jack and Emily's new activity room/message center. Even if he didn't care for the neon Life Savers color scheme, he would admit that they did a terrific job.

IT'S A BIRD ...
IT'S A PLANE ...
IT'S A RECLINER

David Winkler

*H*ello, I'm Herb, the pilot of a wingless, brown Naugahyde recliner. I'm the result of an inquiring mind seeking adventure and an aging body that could care less. As my mind sits enraptured atop high mountain peaks, my body is seeking rest after walking all the way from the recliner to the refrigerator for a beer. The walk back to the recliner carrying a full can is tiring. My body sighs pleasantly as the recliner warmly welcomes us to its comfortable cushion.

My old recliner and I are much traveled, as one can tell by the stickers I have pasted on the exterior of the chair. I subscribe to several travel magazines, and before dozing off after lunch, I browse the pages for places I would like to visit. After returning from a good trip, I cut and tape a picture from the article to the side of the chair. My recliner and I have logged thousands of accident-free miles together, even in the early afternoon when the skies are filled with recliners carrying their dozing adventure seekers.

I once spent a wonderful afternoon with Ernest Hemingway watching the running of the bulls in Pamplona, Spain. We had a great time dodging about, evading the horns of the irritated bulls. That was one time I was glad my lazy body hadn't been along. It would have been totally worn out.

We are propelled, my old recliner and I, by two of the most

potent fuels in the world, imagination and curiosity. These fuels have formed mighty nations and set man on the moon. They are mankind's greatest friends. I know I'm not using them to their fullest potential, but it's enough for me. They let my tired old body stay home and rest while my active mind seeks new places to explore. If I happen upon a place of interest, my body can follow later.

This afternoon my recliner and I are scheduled for a trip to the Grand Canyon. I'm so excited. I'll have lunch, take all my pills, settle back after adjusting my back cushion, and comfortably await our departure.

WONDERMENT

Mary Langer Thompson

The headline reads
"Elderly Man Wonders off,
Dies in Desert."
How did reporters know
he was wondering?
Was there still brain activity
from some wonder drug
when they found him?

Did he have something
in his hand, like a female
Pronuba moth,
the only living organism
to pollinate the Joshua Tree?
Were his arms outstretched
in admiration or awe with
his face toward Heaven?

I live in the desert, too, and marvel.
It might not be awful
to leave this earth
wonderstricken.

BIOGRAPHIES OF THE AUTHORS

Jennifer Bayless—I am a South African residing in Victorville, California, with my husband and two miniature schnauzers. It gives me joy to volunteer at my church in the nursery, and wherever they need help with young babies to infants. Furthermore, my experience led me to volunteer with foster teens who were in the Independent Living Skills Program. Dogs are definitely my passion, and I feel that they deserve to be treated with respect, just like human children ought to be. Charter Oaks State College in Connecticut afforded me the opportunity to finalize my Bachelor's degree in Psychology/General Studies. The ocean's purpose is twofold: firstly, it always calms my busy mind, and secondly, its magical powers somehow inspire my outlook on life.

Janis Brams—I have been an educator for over twenty-five years at the elementary, middle school, and community college levels. Writing and literature are my favorite areas to teach, and I have spent a good part of my professional life trying hard to encourage a similar passion in my students. Teaching writing, especially to ten and eleven year-olds, has been an incredibly enriching experience for me, but last year, I retired from teaching and now am focused on honing my own writing skills.
I have Masters Degrees in both Education and Writing Composition and have had two pieces of short fiction published in separate Plymouth Writers Group Anthologies.

My husband, Michael, has been a pediatrician in the High Desert for the last thirty-five years, and our two grown daughters, a writer and a nurse midwife, have graciously provided us with our own boy tribe, three wonderful grandchildren.

Gregory Caruth—To all the curious readers out there, I'm Gregory Caruth, an aspiring author born and raised in Clinton, North Carolina, a small town filled with good old country folks.

At the tender age of thirteen, my family and I moved to Goldsboro, North Carolina, a slightly larger town with a twinge of urban attitude. At the age of nineteen, I was incarcerated and sentenced to 9-1/2 years of imprisonment. But everyone knows that the sun still shines after it rains and that's how this short story came about.

Bonnie Darlene—The youngest of the five daughters of Phil and Helen Pacina, I lived in the desert in Barstow, California from infancy until I was eight years old. Life took me many places before finally landing me in Vermont, although I remain a Californian at heart.

Quick Stop is about one of my Dad's many encounters at his service station in the 1950s. This story, I hope, will be one of many I plan on including in a future book: *Stories and Memories of an American Family.* The book will be a collaboration with my sisters, Bernadine Joyce and Bobi Sullivan.

I enjoy historical fiction and have published three books in that genre: *Plimoth: A Life Changing Odyssey, Plimoth Revisited* and *Plimoth: A Remembrance, historical fiction with a little time travel fantasy included.*

Linda Bowden has been writing poetry and short stories since the age of nine. At nine years old she was stricken with an illness that put her in bed for a year and she began writing poetry and short stories. She also tried to teach herself different languages such as Spanish and German. She read, read, and read some more.

Today Linda resides in her home in Adelanto, CA and continues to write on a daily basis. She holds a BA in accounting, an MBA, and is currently working on a doctorate in Organizational Leadership. She finds writing both rewarding and an escape from the hustle and bustle of everyday life. Maybe you will find yourself in one of her stories.

Jim Elstad was born on Staten Island, NY, and was raised in Southern California. He started writing stories while in junior high, but it wasn't until he joined the High Desert Branch of the California Writers Club that he really started to focus on his work.

Jim recently retired from active duty with the California Army National Guard which completed a twenty-eight year career, which included a three-year enlistment in the U.S. Marines.

Currently Jim is working on a sequel to his first novel, *Comes The Southern Revolution*. He's hoping to publish *Comes The Retribution* sometime in the summer of 2013. He also plans on writing a series of four mystery novels, and has written several short stories.

Robert Evan Foster has worked in education for twenty-five years as a parent, teacher, and administrator. He was raised in the land of frozen lakes, Minnesota, and lives in smoggy Southern California which has given him a different perspective on education and life. Robert is a writer who teaches.

Rica Gold, Ph.D., formally practiced as a licensed Marriage Family Therapist for more than twenty years and hosted her own live radio and television shows. She is currently the President of the High Desert Branch of the California Writers Club. An online college instructor in Communication Studies, she published her first non-fiction book recently and is currently hoping to finish her first fiction book, *DIMENSION NORRÆNA* in early 2013. Professional tele-seminars, and public speaking are additional engaging activities.

Madeline (M. M.) Gornell has four published mystery novels—PSWA awarding winning *Uncle Si's Secret* (2008); *Death of a Perfect Man* (2009); Eric Hoffer Fiction finalist and Honorary Mention winner, the da Vinci Eye finalist, and Montaigne Medalist finalist *Reticence of Ravens* (2011); and PSWA award winner and Hollywood Book Festival Honorary Mention *Lies of Convenience* (2012). Both *Reticence of Ravens* and *Lies of Convenience* are Route 66 mysteries.

Madeline is also a potter with a fondness for stoneware and reduction firing. She lives with her husband and assorted canines in the Mojave Desert in a town on internationally revered Route 66.

George Gracyk relates to an extremely happy childhood in suburban Chicago. Marriage and family prospered for twenty-six years, but then found him widowed. Marriage to Marj in 1985 has given them twenty-seven happy years. Employment consisted of thirty years with the Pacific Gas & Electric Co. Retirement from a mid-level management position was in 1987.

Being well known at the Marysville-Yuba City Appeal Democrat as an inveterate writer of "Letters to the Editor," he signed on as a feature correspondent and later had a column. An Apple Valley resident and club member since 2001, his short stories have appeared in our *Inkslinger*. He has held various elected club offices and was privileged to serve as editor of the 2010 Anthology.

Virginia Hall is a retired high school mathematics and science teacher. A native Californian, she now enjoys traveling and writing. This story is an excerpt from *It's MY Life*, a novel in progress.

Michael Hawley is from Longview, Texas. He has a B.S. degree from the University of Texas. He has two children, one girl and one boy, Sydney and Cross. He currently works as a teacher at the federal prison. He enjoys writing in his spare time. He enjoys reading books of all types. He writes mostly poetry and draws his material from life and its experiences.

Ann Miner Heimback has been a contributing writer for commercial newsletters with various companies. She was Senior Editor at University of Nevada, Las Vegas for a Circus Circus project. As a workshop leader, she devised and led Divorce Recovery Workshops in California and Nevada. She has been keynote speaker for numerous conferences and was Woman of the Year for the Business and Professional Women's Club in Apple Valley, California.

Ann attended San Diego State University, University of Redlands, and University of Nevada. She is a member of San Diego Christian Writers Guild and High Desert Branch of the California Writers Club.

She writes *Parkinson's Postings*, a bi-weekly column for the Daily Press on Parkinson's disease, and is the facilitator for the local Parkinson's Support Group.

She teaches piano and voice, and is a substitute teacher at the Lewis Center for Educational Research in Apple Valley, California

Suzanne C. Holbrook-Brumbaugh wears a lot of hats. She is a writer, primarily of children's literature, a musician, an artist, and a crafter. She is also a guest teacher in Southern California. Her personal anthology–*Pen Pearls*–has been released. She has been a member of the California Writers Club for many years, and is a critique leader for the children's critique group.

She is married to Willard, her husband of three years, and between them they share seven children, nine grandchildren, two cats, two parakeets, two toads, a paddle tail newt, and numerous fish. Suzanne enjoys gardening, baking, and entering the County Fair in various capacities. She and her husband live in Victorville, California.

Bob Isbill lives in Apple Valley, California, with Judi, his wife of forty years. For a long time, his passion has been to study the craft of writing, and especially to learn what helps to make a story good and what causes it to go badly. He loves spending time with his family—especially the part about being a grandfather—and with his fellow writers. Bob has been a member of the High Desert Branch of the California Writers Club since 2009.

Bernadine Joyce—In my two historical fiction novels, *Davy* and *For the Love of Davy*, obtainable through Amazon.com, I drew upon my nostalgic California roots, telling the story of a family saga set in the Sierra Nevada Mountains of Northern California during the Civil War period.

The short story *In Johnny's Shoes* draws upon my years of experience as a teacher of children and adults with special needs. A storyteller at heart, I enjoy both history and literature and draw upon memories that evolve from living on both the west and east coasts of the U.S. It is my hope that my readers will gain insights and compassion for persons with physical and mental handicaps who are often misunderstood and devalued. I'm also planning on coauthoring, with my sisters, Bonnie Darlene, and Bobi Sullivan, a book titled *Memories and Stories of an American Family*.

Marilyn King (pen name of Marilyn Ramirez), former full-time mom and business owner, has been studying the art and technique of writing for forty years. Marilyn took a correspondence course in 1982, *Writing To Sell Fiction*. She is a member of the ACFW. She worked with Mary DeMuth's

Writing Spa, and attended her second year at Mount Hermon's Christian Writers Conference. A first-time author, her book *The Winds of Grace* came out May 2012.

A member of the High Desert Branch of the California Writers Club, Marilyn is the historian. She spear-headed the first of five critique groups for the club and in September 2012 gave her second presentation on *Organization for Writing Great Fiction*.

Marilyn and her husband Bob, parents of nine grown children, live in Apple Valley, California. When Marilyn is not writing, she enjoys sewing, crafts and gardening. She is involved in weekly Bible studies and is a board member of the Orchard Christian Church Women's Ministry.

Thomas Kier was born and is still living in California. Some of his written works deal with very dark subjects, and not all have happy endings—much the same as real life. He tries to shield his family from the worst of what comes from the dark corners of his mind, but he has found that not giving release to those demons can affect his own outlook on the world. If any of what you read frightens you, you're not alone. The author was frightened first.

Rusty LaGrange is an avid writer, proofreader, freelance marketing consultant, ghostwriter, and a blogger. After thirty years in the Mojave Desert, she finds daily events to be entertaining or intriguing at her Rusty Bucket Ranch in Lucerne Valley. Her love of journalism and graphic arts, coupled with her creative style, give readers a refreshing read. She was first published as a ghostwriter for Anthony Pasqualetti's life story, *Born to Survive–Will to Live*. Her second book, coming soon, is tips and techniques for interviewing, *A Microphone is Not the Muzzle of a Gun*. She is currently the HDCWC *Inkslinger*'s editor-in-chief.

Find out more about Rusty at www.aFlairForWords.com and numerous blogging sites as well as the new blogging community at www.HighDesertBlogging.com

June Langer considers herself a late bloomer. She was due to be born on June 1st, but waited until June 21st. She started her teaching career at age forty, began painting at age eighty, and began her memoirs at age eighty-eight. She usually starts figuring her taxes on the 13th of April. She is a life-long learner, and can't wait to discover something new to learn.

J. McAllister is an aspiring author and poet. He divides his spare time between being an educational instructor and art director in Adelanto, CA. He currently resides in Las Vegas, NV.

Rocky McAlister shed his reporter's corduroy coat and bow tie and then retired after four decades in Southern California newsrooms to move eighty miles east of Pasadena and 7,000 feet up to Big Bear City where he now observes the human condition beneath smogless skies.

He published his first novel *Legacy Encounter* in 2011 and *Earth's Last Warrior* in 2012. He is currently working on his third novel, *Welcome to Mars!* and enjoying the research process. Publication is planned for spring 2013.

Jenny Margotta—Some time ago I found myself out of work— not by choice. With two degrees, a long career as an administrator, and forty plus years experience writing, I knew I had several options. I quickly realized that writing, editing, proofreading—all the facets of building words into readable formats—was the work I most enjoyed. So I decided to turn my unemployment into a personal opportunity. I am now a freelance writer and editor providing a full range of services.

313

As time permits, I write for pleasure, too, drawing from a wide range of life experiences, real life and, of course, my imagination. I read voraciously and I also do a bit of photography, mosaics, crochet and cross-stitch. I found the love of my life late in life and together we built a home full of art, books, good food and, above all, love and laughter.

John Margotta (pen name of John Ferrara)—At his recent art show, John was asked to describe himself in a single sentence. His reply? "I am a collector of experiences."

Unfortunately, those experiences stopped when John passed in 2012.

John experienced life as a truck driver, soda jerk, roofer, deep sea diver, bartender, photographer (for over sixty years), cook, model, teacher, artist, and of course, writer. He was a combat veteran, having served in the U.S. Navy Seabees, and in the Battle of Okinawa in World War II.

"Don't try to pin me down to writing in one genre," John would tell you. "Don't put me in a box."
He published work in fantasy, adventure, technical publications and poetry. This anthology's submission, *My Brother*, is dedicated to his brother-in-law, a three-times-decorated Vietnam veteran, as well as all the veterans who have served our country.

Diane Neil has scribbled stories since childhood. She enjoys snooping in closets and under beds to learn what makes her characters tick. She hopes you'll share her journeys with a wink and a nod. Her previous (self-published) books are *Egg Noodles and Sunflowers* (a family memoir); *A Bucket to Carry My Tunes* (poems); and *The Sunny Side of Seventy* (a humorous look at aging).

314

J. P. Newcomer is a Licensed Clinical Social Worker with a private practice in psychotherapy and clinical supervision. A long time California resident, originally from Boston, she enjoys writing short stories with psychological themes, often in the science fiction or fantasy genre.

She is currently working on a science fiction novel, based in part upon characters from her short story *Night* which appears in this anthology. She has been a member of the California Writers Club (CWC) since 2009 and was both pleased and honored to have one of her short stories selected for publication in the inaugural issue of the CWC Literary Review.

Dwight Norris is a teacher, writer, and speaker. His first novel, *The Gentleman Host*, is about a serial killer who throws middle-aged women off cruise ships at midnight. It is available on Amazon.com and has some worthy reviews. His second novel, *My Name is Inferno*, is about a cruise ship in the Caribbean that is overtaken by pirates. It will soon be self-published and available on Amazon. Dwight's plan is to complete a third novel in the series by the end of this year, and then move on and see if he can write about anything else.

Dwight likes many forms of writing and has two screenplays to his credit, as well as a dozen or so short stories, sundry poems and quotations. He is the father of two adult children who live in Southern California.

Michael Raff was born and raised in Chicago, Illinois. He discovered his love for writing at the age of thirteen while still in grammar school. He moved to California in 1968, and attended creative writing courses at Cypress College. He became a psychiatric technician in 1974, and worked for the state of California until he retired in 2007. He discovered he had a flair for writing horror in 1983 when he wrote *The Door*, the first of his many short stories. Currently, he is a member of the High Desert Branch of the California Writers Club. His nonfictional, romantic, coming-of-age book, *Special,* was self-published in 2011. Additionally, he has written three horror anthologies entitled: *Seven: Tales of Terror, Stalkers,* and *Scare Tactics.* He and his wife Joyce live in Hesperia, California along with their amazing assortment of horses, dogs, cats and a pigmy goat.

Winnie Rueff has been writing all her life. Her first writing was done for the newspaper in Cicero, Illinois in the early 1940s, and she has had poems and articles published in magazines and newspapers over the years.

In 1950 Winnie wrote a study book for nurses in eye surgery at Wesley Memorial Hospital, now Northwestern University Medical Center, while she was in charge of eye surgery there. She was raised in Chicago and went into nurses training at age eighteen. Her book is about her student activities and about her life as a nurse during the 40s through the 70s.

The reader gets to go along with her on her trips all over the country during this time, as she describes what she sees and feels. Her book, *Calling Nurse Mearns, a Nurse's Story* can be bought at Amazon.com and at your local book store. It is also on ebooks. Winnie had licenses as a professional model, a travel agent, and real estate agent, but she always went back to nursing, her real "calling." *Calling Nurse Mearns* is a memoir. It is Winnie's first book.

Frances Smith Savage is an accomplished copywriter and has written well over three-hundred articles in the past year and a half. She also completed her fourth book. *The Journey Continues* will complete the trilogy of her first two books: *Julie, A Time to Live* and *The Serial Killer My Son.* Although the trilogy includes the subject of serial killers, they are not the usual gore.

Also to her credit is her book *Inspiring Moments* that includes uplifting short stories. Her books and short stories all have the subtle theme of her Christian faith.

She lives with her husband in the High Desert of Southern California where her books and short stories take place.

A. J. Scott was born and raised in Southern California. He is the author of *Lord, I Can't Keep Livin' Like This!* He is presently working towards his Master's Degree in Theology through Channel Island Bible College & Seminary. He has earned his Credentials of Ministry and his credentials as a Christian Counselor from Channel Island Bible College & Seminary. He has earned his diploma as a Paralegal and Legal Assistant from Blackstone Career Institute, and is presently certified through the Foundation for A Drug-Free World as a Drug Prevention Specialist.

In his spare time, Mr. Scott teaches legal writing and is a Suicide Companion to fellow inmates experiencing the difficulties that come with incarceration. His next project is to become a mentor to at-risk-youth. He is a lover of life and believes that God has a divine purpose for each and every one of our lives.

Anthony Spencer is a native of New Zealand (Maori) and now resides in Park City, Utah, and is still battling his case and the constitutionality of our judicial system and the drug laws. An avid writer with a passion to share thoughts, experiences and stories through poetry and short stories, he is an advocate for Human Rights and strongly believes in what our forefathers set forth in the original constitution. A proud father of three beautiful daughters, his goal is to always succeed and be the best by working hard and playing hard.

Roberta Smith is a native of Southern California and a graduate of the University of Redlands. As she puts it, she likes serendipity, synchronicity, and things that are strange. She's been known to stay in haunted hotels in hopes of experiencing just that. She writes mostly paranormal novels with a splash of romance.

Roberta has studied screenwriting, story structure, character development, and writing dialogue. In the past she has served as co-critique chair and membership chair for the HDCWC. Currently she is the club's Vice President and co-editor of this anthology. For four years she was editor of the newsletter for the Victor Valley Vettes (Corvette club). She and her husband are members.

Roberta has written two children's plays, both of which were produced and received high acclaim. She has published three novels that are a part of the Mickey McCoy Paranormal Mystery Series: *The Secret of Lucianne Dove*, *Chapel Playhouse*, and *The Accordo*. She has also published a book of short stories titled: *Distorted – five imaginative tales on the dark side*.

Roberta has completed a fourth novel titled *Bouquet of Lies*. It falls in the contemporary romance genre and is also a murder mystery. Currently she is developing a fifth book, a prequel to the Mickey McCoy paranormal series.

Denny Stanz was born and raised in Pennsylvania, graduated from Penn State University, and spent three years in the Army, including a one year tour in Vietnam as a young Lieutenant. He developed an interest in writing in grammar school. However, it took him fifty years to publish his first work, *Food Stories*, a short biography of his adventures as a single dad who learned how to cook on the fly.

He is currently working on a series of short stories tentatively titled *Dinner with Dead People*.

Hazel Stearns—In my younger years, the heroes who shaped my life were Huck Finn and Amelia Earhart, who represented freedom and independence, the Unsinkable Molly Brown

318

because she never gave up, and Auntie Mame because she wasn't afraid to try something new.

Writing fiction is *my* something new—something I've always wanted to do.

Most of all, I hope my writing makes people laugh. The biggest thrill I can imagine is to walk into a waiting room and hear someone laughing at something they're reading from a book I've written.

I was self-employed most of my life. I retired in 2006 from two careers, the first in weekly and promotional newspaper publishing, and the second in real estate brokerage. I have four children and three grandchildren, and live in Hesperia, California. My debut novel, *Shaping Kate*, was released in April 2012.

Bobi (B.V. Lee) Sullivan—Although born in Barstow, California, I lived most of my adult life in many diverse cultures and climates before retiring. After years of writing texts, training manuals, and speeches, it's thrilling to finally have the time to write what I want—fiction and 'faction.'

My current book-in-progress revolves around young Marines adapting to the little town of Barstow and its people just prior to the Korean War. As is the case with many books, mine is really a series of short stories highlighting many of the high desert's colorful locales and places of interest.

When not working on my book or spending days doing research, I also write fun little pieces such as I've submitted for this anthology. People tell me "at your age, you should be slowing down." My reply? "Not on your life! I don't have time to get it all done as it is."

319

Mary Langer Thompson's writing appears in various journals and anthologies, most recently the new *CWC Literary Review*. Born on the south side of Chicago, she traveled Route 66 to live in Glendale, California when she was just ten. She and husband Dave moved to Apple Valley, California in 2005 so that Mary could open a new public school as principal. She now writes full time, and just recently left her position as Member at Large on the board of our High Desert Branch after serving for three years.

David Tisdale was born and raised in Baltimore, MD., the place he still calls home. Early on in life he fell in love with words and the art of storytelling. He has turned that love into a passion for writing. From music lyrics, poems to screenwriting, Mr. Tisdale has written many well-received projects and has dedicated his life to perfecting his craft. A proud father of two daughters and a stepson, the poem in this anthology was written for his wife, doll baby.

Patrick Wallace is an author and the co-founder of King-Wallace enterprises and "WEE," The Wallace Empowerment Experience. He is a businessman from Dallas, Texas and is married with four children. He is a lover of life and believes there's a miracle waiting to happen to anyone that is willing to discover themselves.

N.C. Ward is a native of Idaho, educated in California with an AA in Journalism from Chaffey College. Naomi worked as a Special Feature Writer for the *Pomona Progress Bulletin* immediately after graduation. After family started arriving, she moved to the High Desert to raise two boys and a girl. During that time, she edited a church newspaper for fifteen years and did extensive publicity for USO and Future Farmers of America as community education in support of those entities. After eighteen years of state service in Barstow, Ward retired and moved to Sacramento and went to work for the state, again, for another eight years, living in a large RV during that time. She then retired and started traveling for the next fifteen years, both here and abroad, experiencing the broad range of places and people only read about in prior years. Alone, again, she returned to the High Desert to be near family and to continue exploring avenues of growth, as well as her beloved desert.

Deborah Weltin is a native Californian living in the High Desert since 2007. An aspiring writer, Debbie is currently working on her memoirs. She lives with her rescue Lhasa Apso, Buckley. She retired from telecommunications in 1996 and has a Bachelor's degree from the University of San Francisco. Deborah has a vast interest in many disciplines from metaphysics to massage therapy.

David Winkler—I am a happily retired plumber and pipefitter. Gaynell, my wife of the past fifty-three years and I have lived enjoyably in Spring Valley Lake for twenty-four of those past years. We have three wonderful daughters and six beautiful and handsome grand children.

I am a Korean War vet but luckily never saw any combat nor did I go to Korea. I was in the army for three years: a year-and-a-half at Fort Sill, Oklahoma and a year-and-a-half in Verona, Italy. It was a wonderful adventure for a seventeen-year-old boy and helped me build a solid foundation on which to begin my adult life.

I have always wanted to write but have never had the discipline needed to sit still long enough to complete a topic of interest. At seventy-four years of age though, I find that sitting is becoming more of a pleasure as I gaze out the window at chores that need to be done.

I am glad to be a member of the club. It seems well organized and a good source of inspiration to us beginners. Looking forward to our association.

Curtis Yarbrough was born and raised in Los Angeles, California. He is currently writing a novel titled *Glory to Glory*, which is the story of a man in God's redeeming fire who doesn't even know it. He is presently teaching and tutoring Microsoft Classes (four per day) and Beginners Typing to as many as are willing to learn. A former All American Football Player, Curtis appreciates hard work and a finisher's attitude.

In his time away from teaching, Curtis facilitates NA and AA meetings, leads a fellowship of men looking to appreciate life lessons from the Bible, and is an avid sports fan, basketball and football (college and pro) being his two favorite games. Curtis is a believer in fitness (mind and body) and diligently does Pilates and yoga routines five days a week.

His vision is to turn *Glory to Glory* into a series that will include a nonfiction newsletter and web-page as well.